HOUSTON NOIR

EDITED BY GWENDOLYN ZEPEDA

BROOKLYN, NEW YORK, USA
BALLYDEHOB, CO. CORK, IRELAND

This collection consists of works of fiction. All names, characters, places, and incidents are the product of the authors' imaginations. Any resemblance to real events or persons, living or dead, is entirely coincidental.

Published by Akashic Books
©2019 Akashic Books

Series concept by Tim McLoughlin and Johnny Temple
Houston map by Sohrab Habibion

ISBN: 978-1-61775-706-8
Library of Congress Control Number: 2018960607

Akashic Books
Brooklyn, New York, USA
Ballydehob, Co. Cork, Ireland
Twitter: @AkashicBooks
Facebook: AkashicBooks
E-mail: info@akashicbooks.com
Website: www.akashicbooks.com

ALSO IN THE AKASHIC NOIR SERIES

MOSCOW NOIR (RUSSIA),
  edited by NATALIA SMIRNOVA & JULIA GOUMEN

MUMBAI NOIR (INDIA), edited by ALTAF TYREWALA

NEW HAVEN NOIR, edited by AMY BLOOM

NEW JERSEY NOIR, edited by JOYCE CAROL OATES

NEW ORLEANS NOIR, edited by JULIE SMITH

NEW ORLEANS NOIR: THE CLASSICS,
  edited by JULIE SMITH

OAKLAND NOIR, edited by JERRY THOMPSON
  & EDDIE MULLER

ORANGE COUNTY NOIR, edited by GARY PHILLIPS

PARIS NOIR (FRANCE), edited by AURÉLIEN MASSON

PHILADELPHIA NOIR, edited by CARLIN ROMANO

PHOENIX NOIR, edited by PATRICK MILLIKIN

PITTSBURGH NOIR, edited by KATHLEEN GEORGE

PORTLAND NOIR, edited by KEVIN SAMPSELL

PRAGUE NOIR (CZECH REPUBLIC),
  edited by PAVEL MANDYS

PRISON NOIR, edited by JOYCE CAROL OATES

PROVIDENCE NOIR, edited by ANN HOOD

QUEENS NOIR, edited by ROBERT KNIGHTLY

RICHMOND NOIR, edited by ANDREW BLOSSOM,
  BRIAN CASTLEBERRY & TOM DE HAVEN

RIO NOIR (BRAZIL), edited by TONY BELLOTTO

ROME NOIR (ITALY), edited by CHIARA STANGALINO
  & MAXIM JAKUBOWSKI

SAN DIEGO NOIR, edited by MARYELIZABETH HART

SAN FRANCISCO NOIR, edited by PETER MARAVELIS

SAN FRANCISCO NOIR 2: THE CLASSICS,
  edited by PETER MARAVELIS

SAN JUAN NOIR (PUERTO RICO),
  edited by MAYRA SANTOS-FEBRES

SANTA CRUZ NOIR, edited by SUSIE BRIGHT

SÃO PAULO NOIR (BRAZIL),
  edited by TONY BELLOTTO

SEATTLE NOIR, edited by CURT COLBERT

SINGAPORE NOIR, edited by CHERYL LU-LIEN TAN

STATEN ISLAND NOIR, edited by PATRICIA SMITH

ST. LOUIS NOIR, edited by SCOTT PHILLIPS

STOCKHOLM NOIR (SWEDEN), edited by
  NATHAN LARSON & CARL-MICHAEL EDENBORG

ST. PETERSBURG NOIR (RUSSIA), edited by
  NATALIA SMIRNOVA & JULIA GOUMEN

SYDNEY NOIR (AUSTRALIA), edited by JOHN DALE

TEHRAN NOIR (IRAN), edited by SALAR ABDOH

TEL AVIV NOIR (ISRAEL), edited by ETGAR KERET
  & ASSAF GAVRON

TORONTO NOIR (CANADA), edited by JANINE ARMIN
  & NATHANIEL G. MOORE

TRINIDAD NOIR (TRINIDAD & TOBAGO), edited by
  LISA ALLEN-AGOSTINI & JEANNE MASON

TRINIDAD NOIR: THE CLASSICS
  (TRINIDAD & TOBAGO), edited by EARL LOVELACE
  & ROBERT ANTONI

TWIN CITIES NOIR, edited by JULIE SCHAPER
  & STEVEN HORWITZ

USA NOIR, edited by JOHNNY TEMPLE

VANCOUVER NOIR (CANADA), edited by SAM WIEBE

VENICE NOIR (ITALY), edited by MAXIM JAKUBOWSKI

WALL STREET NOIR, edited by PETER SPIEGELMAN

ZAGREB NOIR (CROATIA), edited by IVAN SRŠEN

FORTHCOMING

ACCRA NOIR (GHANA),
  edited by NANA-AMA DANQUAH

ADDIS ABABA NOIR (ETHIOPIA),
  edited by MAAZA MENGISTE

ALABAMA NOIR, edited by DON NOBLE

BERKELEY NOIR, edited by JERRY THOMPSON
  & OWEN HILL

BELGRADE NOIR (SERBIA),
  edited by MILORAD IVANOVIC

BOGOTÁ NOIR (COLOMBIA),
  edited by ANDREA MONTEJO

COLUMBUS NOIR,
  edited by ANDREW WELSH-HUGGINS

JERUSALEM NOIR, edited by DROR MISHANI

NAIROBI NOIR (KENYA), edited by PETER KIMANI

PARIS NOIR: THE SUBURBS (FRANCE),
  edited by HERVÉ DELOUCHE

SANTA FE NOIR, edited by ARIEL GORE

TAMPA BAY NOIR, edited by COLETTE BANCROFT

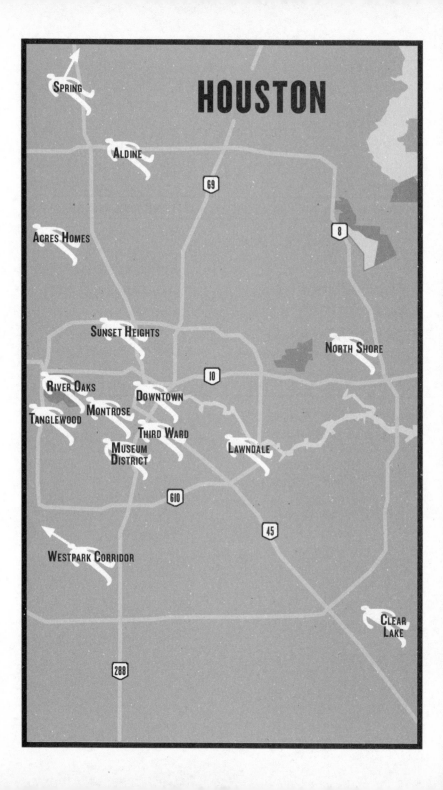

TABLE OF CONTENTS

PART III: MINUTES FROM DOWNTOWN AND NIGHTLIFE

PART IV: UP-AND-COMING AREAS, NEWLY REVITALIZED

INTRODUCTION
A CRUEL, CRAZY TOWN

I t's a rare publisher who'll let you write something really
dark.

"What about the book clubs?" I've heard editors say.
"Book clubs want something light to read while drinking
wine, Gwen. Can you lighten it up?"

I can lighten it up, yes. I can even *lighten up* in general.
But it hurts a little to do so, and a little more every time. It
feels like lying, and until a writer sells film rights, lying feels
like selling out.

That's why it gave me immense pleasure to be charged
with (and to charge for!) editing this book. It was pleasur-
able from the very beginning, when I contacted writers I knew
and writers I wanted to know and invited them to write me
something noir-ish. Several were already practiced in the dark
(literary) arts and agreed off the bat. Others were unsure.
"I've never written noir," they told me. For those, I put on a
pair of horns, picked up a pitchfork, and said, "But you *could,*
couldn't you? Don't you have a story you've been wanting to
tell—something tragic? Something full of anger? Something
totally fucked up?"

I saw the glints in their eyes, right through the e-mails on
my monitor. Oh yes—they had ideas.

Then I received more e-mails, texts, and confessions over
frozen mojitos: "My god . . . Writing this stuff is so much fun. I

like it." And I reveled in my newfound power to warp talented minds.

Then I received the stories. Oh man, the stories. They *hurt* me. They *burned*. Some made me cringe, some made me cry. One made me push away my laptop and hoot very loudly, like a barn owl overcome with shock and revulsion. Others made me laugh . . . then hate myself for laughing.

It turned out I had no power, after all—only the means to extend invitations to people with true power. Their writing toyed with my emotions, overwhelmed me, and left me weak.

I thought of you, then.

You, who like to read alone. And you who binge tear-jerking movies on Thanksgiving. You, the ones who laugh inappropriately at serious moments and draw disgusted glares. Who watch the latest awful news and roll your eyes, thinking, *This is probably just what we deserve.*

If you also live in this city I love, then you definitely know the effort required to *lighten up* and the futility thereof. You can't ignore the mentally ill people shouting between our beautiful towers of glass. You've tasted the sugarcoating of words like *Generously sponsored by Enron* and *Hundred-year floodplain*, and you spit it out. You've heard the promises that things will get better, and yet you're stocked up on canned goods, bottled water, and ammo. You know happy endings don't come easy, and a World Series win doesn't ease the pain of decades of football heartbreak.

And yet you stay.

I know what you're looking for: someone to lay it on the line. Something to make you feel less alone, less misunderstood. A fucked-up story to indulge in, and not (for *once*) because you had no choice.

* * *

The stories in this book are sectioned by neighborhood type, using euphemisms and clichés local realtors employ to sell our socioeconomic topography. Their settings range wide across the three near-concentric circles of cement that define our city. There's the Inner Loop, or Interstate 610, that encircles our Downtown, our trendiest enclaves, and our oldest neighborhoods that, as of this writing, represent every phase of the gentrification cycle and all the seething resentment that engenders.

Our second ring of ~~hell~~ humidity, between the Loop and Beltway 8, is the middle ground for Houstonians who can't afford the Inner Loop but don't want to spend more than an hour on the freeway per commute. Then comes FM 1960 (or State Highway 6) and the first layer of our true suburbs. Beyond that is an expanse of land being chewed up, bit by bit, by the city's maw.

In a 2004 essay, Hunter S. Thompson described Houston as a "cruel, crazy town on a filthy river in East Texas with no zoning laws and a culture of sex, money and violence. It's a shabby, sprawling metropolis ruled by brazen women, crooked cops and super-rich pansexual cowboys who live by the code of the West—which can mean just about anything you need it to mean, in a pinch." For what it's worth, that quote is now posted on a banner somewhere downtown and regularly, gleefully repeated by our local feature writers.

Houston is a port city on top of a swamp and, yes, it has no zoning laws. And that means it's culturally diverse, internally incongruous, and ever-changing. At any intersection here, I might look out my car window and see a horse idly munching St. Augustine grass. And, within spitting distance of that horse, I might see a "spa" that's an obvious brothel, a house turned drug den, or a swiftly rising bayou that might overtake a car if the rain doesn't let up. Because I've lived here so long, there's no story in this book I can't easily imagine taking place. Some of the plots might seem outrageous, but not compared with real-life crimes that have taken place here in the last fifty years, which have inspired books, TV movies, and Wikipedia-readers' nightmares.

River Oaks, one of the wealthiest neighborhoods in the state, has been home to politicians, Texan and Saudi oil barons, pastor Joel Osteen, and Jeff Skilling of Enron infamy. From 1969 to 1973, the neighborhood was rocked by the mysterious death of socialite horsewoman Joan Robinson Hill, the subsequent murder of her husband Dr. John Hill, and the murder of *his* murderer after that. This story is immortalized in *Blood and Money* by Thomas Thompson.

Between 1970 and 1973, serial killer and Heights resident Dean Corll, nicknamed the Candy Man, murdered at least twenty-eight people. The Halloween after that, optician Ronald Clark O'Bryan became Houston's *second* Candy Man— killing his son Timothy for the insurance money, by feeding him poisoned Pixy Stix. O'Bryan tried to cover up his crime by giving the poisoned candy to his daughter and three other children as well, spawning a generation of trick-or-treat fears.

Throughout the 1980s and 1990s, orthopedic surgeon and Museum District resident Eric Heston Scheffey came under fire for performing unnecessary surgeries that disabled and sometimes killed his patients. In 2005, his license to practice medicine was finally revoked.

In 2002, Friendswood dentist Clara Harris was convicted of manslaughter for running over her cheating husband with a Mercedes-Benz in the parking lot of a Hilton hotel, with his daughter in the car, while filmed by the private investigator she'd hired.

In 2007, astronaut Lisa Marie Nowak drove from Houston to the airport in Orlando, Florida, where she attacked and failed to kidnap US Air Force Captain Colleen Shipman, the new girlfriend of Nowak's former boyfriend, astronaut William Oefelein.

Several of the stories in this book discuss human trafficking. According to a study by the University of Texas at Austin's School of Social Work, there were an estimated 313,000 victims of human trafficking in the state in 2016. Houston is widely considered a hub for such activity due to its port, its proximity to Mexico, and its many conventions and sporting events.

Right now, Houston is one of the most ethnically diverse cities in America. That creates opportunities for clashes and crimes in a wide variety of cultural combinations, throughout the city. This, too, is poignantly reflected in these stories.

Overall, this collection represents the very worst our city has to offer, for residents and visitors alike. But it also presents some of our best voices, veteran and emerging, to any reader lucky enough to pick up this book.

Congratulations!

Gwendolyn Zepeda
Houston, Texas
February 2019

PART I

DESIRABLE LOCATIONS WITH PRIVATE SECURITY

TANGLED

BY ANTON DISCLAFANI
Tanglewood

T*angled in Tanglewood,* Lisa thought as she glanced at her watch and stepped out onto her back porch.

The heat overwhelmed, because it was July in Houston and everyone who could go was gone, out to Galveston or Clear Lake or even farther. The Blue Ridge Mountains. The Great Lakes. The Olsens would leave first. Then the Ramirezes. Then the Maclains.

Lisa had not left not because she didn't want to leave—she did, very badly—but because she had a few things to set in order, first. And then she would leave for good. Or, if not for good, for a very long time.

She stood on her porch, protected from the mosquitoes and no-see-ums by a thin layer of screen. She glanced at her watch again. It had been her grandmother's, was what she told people. A slim Cartier with a face encircled by diamonds. No one wore watches anymore.

Lisa did.

In short order, Lisa's history: Born to a father who worked the oil rigs in Midland, a godforsaken place. A mother who, when Lisa was young, tried to keep the dust out of their house without the aid of a vacuum cleaner. Only the rich people had them.

Even now, or especially now, Lisa closes her eyes and can

so easily see her mother with her broom. The *sweep, sweep* that will haunt Lisa until she dies.

Lisa married a boy who lived in a two-story dustless house. At the time, the house had seemed a sign of great wealth. They were both sixteen. A shotgun wedding, nobody happy but Lisa and her new husband. Moved to La Porte so Gary could do something related to the ships. Then Pasadena. Got closer and closer to Houston, inch by inexorable inch.

Victoria was born in La Porte. Lisa thought her daughter's name sounded regal. Like old money. Or old enough for Texas, anyway.

By the time they moved to Houston, Lisa had shed her mother and father and their dust. Her father had left when Lisa was eight, gone out west, and her mother became a recluse before she died of lung cancer. It was easy never to tell a soul about them.

So, her parents were dead when she landed in Houston in the early eighties, in a bland, nondescript neighborhood. Solidly middle class. Gary was loyal, dull except for his terrible temper, and the victim of early-onset balding. She knew it wasn't nice, but his hair, or lack thereof, repulsed her.

They divorced when Victoria was ten. Victoria was so sensitive then, she might as well have been a tuning fork, and for a while Lisa worried the divorce had ruined her. For years, Victoria slept with her mother at night, the child's warmth a comfort. Most days, Victoria came home from school in tears, disturbed by the minor cruelty of one girl or another.

The divorce didn't ruin her. Neither did Lisa's second marriage, two years later, to a cardiac surgeon who owned a home in Tanglewood. To the contrary, that marriage seemed to harden Victoria, laying a chitin over her creamy, adolescent skin. She'd never gotten pimples like other girls. That Victoria felt betrayed by her mother—it had been just the two of them for two years—was to be expected. But Lisa knew better. The marriage meant neither she nor Victoria would have to worry. About college, about paying for the wedding Victoria would eventually have, about any of life's requirements. And Lisa was lonely. She didn't want Victoria to grow up thinking this loneliness, this all-female household, was normal. And, most of all, there was the house.

Tanglewood: it felt like the center of things, yet the lots the houses sat on seemed enormous to Lisa. It wasn't privacy she craved, nor space, but she knew, the moment she saw the house, she would accept Lance's proposal. It was one of the older houses, with black shutters and a wide wraparound porch. Lance hadn't proposed yet, but he would. Men were as readable as books.

Tanglewood did not smack of carpet and coupons. It was not one but five steps above where she'd lived with Gary. Not River Oaks and not Shady Side—places she'd once dreamed of—but close enough. Her entire life defined by an exhilarating momentum. Lately, it was also tinged with exhaustion.

How different her mother's life would have been, had she owned a vacuum cleaner, Lisa thought whenever she saw hers.

Mornings, she liked to go outside and look at the other houses. She could just barely see them from her screened-in back porch. Flashes of stucco and brick through the neat row of sky pencils that bordered the backyard.

Lance opened the sliding-glass door. Lisa didn't turn or give any sign she'd heard her husband as he brushed her forehead with his dry, hot lips. She sat in the porch swing as wide as a bed and held her coffee carefully so it wouldn't spill.

"Bye," he said on his way out, and waited for her response.

"Bye," she said, and he was gone. They had not met each other's eye.

Victoria opened the porch door a minute later, as if she'd timed it. She'd told Lisa, when she was twelve, that she'd never think of Lance as a father, and she never had. There was no love lost between them. She held a cup of coffee from her own home, a street over. She had large, capable hands. Lisa had always admired them.

Lisa and her daughter had coffee together most mornings. Victoria held Lisa at a distance, and had since her mother remarried, but still, they were close. There were other mother-daughter pairs in Houston, of course. It was a big city that felt like a small town, especially in Tanglewood, where everyone gathered at the Houston Country Club for cocktails on Saturday evenings, where everyone's child went to Kinkaid, where everyone's husband left for work before the worst of the heat started and came home after it ended.

"Hi," Lisa said.

A pause. "Hi." Victoria seemed distracted. She was wearing the sleek lounge pants women her age favored. She was tall and fleshy but not fat; prettier than her mother, but not as confident. Victoria knew how to plan and host a five-course dinner party, invest in the stock market, and get the yardmen to edge the grass in a way they considered fussy, but she didn't know how to move through a room sexily. It was a quality that couldn't be taught, Lisa supposed.

"You sound sleepy," Lisa said carefully. She wasn't a religious woman, but she found herself praying lately that Victoria wouldn't get pregnant. *Lord*, she thought, *let her be smart enough to take the pill*. Her husband wasn't the kind of man to want to prevent a pregnancy.

"I am. Tired," Victoria said.

"Did he do it again?" Lisa tried to keep the tremor from her voice.

Victoria shook her head. "No." She sounded annoyed, dismissive.

"It's just—"

"Mom. It was a one-time thing."

Lisa nodded. She hated that word: *Mom*. *Mother* was unwieldy, old-fashioned. She would have preferred *Mama*, but Victoria hadn't called her that since she was a little girl, still losing baby teeth.

Lisa tried to look as if she believed her daughter. Her plan depended, for the moment, on her willingness to believe.

"So hot," Victoria said, which seemed to be an olive branch.

"Yes," Lisa murmured, "yes." She was eager to agree.

Victoria pulled a chair away from the table and slumped into it. Lisa was often struck by how young she still seemed, even though her daughter was thirty, married to a corporate attorney, in charge of a house. "Speaking of which, the yard is dry as a bone. The water restrictions." She sighed. "I'm tired of this drought."

Lance had returned, was plucking his phone from the counter. He lifted his hand in a silent wave; Lisa returned it. Victoria tilted her head but otherwise did not acknowledge Lance. They had never fought, but they had never loved each other, either. Lisa supposed she should be grateful that their relationship, if not intimate, was peaceful.

Lisa took a sip of her coffee. It was cold. Victoria seemed lost in thought. Well, Lisa had plenty of her own to think about. Her daughter who was beaten. Abused. When her own husband would sooner cut his hand off than lay it on Lisa.

Lance was cheating on her. With, Lisa was almost certain,

Patsy Olsen. Patsy had thick, bluntly cut silver hair. She was pretty and a decade older than Lisa. It was the way things had gone in their marriage for a very long time. But it wouldn't go on for much longer.

Victoria was now talking about volunteering and a woman they both knew who headed a committee. "Can you believe it?" she asked, her voice mildly outraged.

"No," Lisa said, though she didn't know what it was she couldn't believe. Their rhythm, long established, was off today. She glanced at her watch.

"We better get moving," Victoria said, smiling. Lisa was amazed at her daughter's happiness. Or if not happiness, light-heartedness. That she could grin, her big, pretty teeth flashing against her dark lip gloss. That she could utter such meaningless platitudes: "Mom." Less a name than a command. "It was only the one time. I promise." When Lisa knew for a fact she was lying. And anyway, it was never just the one time. Not in life. Not in any part of it.

Lisa patted herself dry after her shower. Her hair, her face, her throat. Lingered on her stomach, which grew softer and softer as the years passed. She wasn't a vain woman, which was lucky, because age had loosened the skin at her throat, creased her forehead, freckled the backs of her hands.

Victoria was vain, and so was Lance. Vain men were easier to be with. Easier to understand and anticipate and stay ahead of. So were women, for that matter.

Victoria's vanity had propelled her to her mother's house the week before, to borrow a pair of diamond earrings for a fund-raiser that night. She hadn't wanted to miss the annual Azalea Trail opening party. Black tie, and Victoria was going to wear her strapless dress and the ruby drop earrings. She and

Lisa had talked about it. That was one of their favorite things to do together—shop. Plan their clothes, as they called it.

But then Victoria had to change her outfit, and thus her earrings, at the last moment. "It doesn't look good," she'd said, which Lisa didn't believe for a moment. Because she'd seen the dress—it was flattering—but also because of the catch in Victoria's voice. Victoria's voice so rarely caught. The new dress featured an elaborate yet modest neckline.

The old dress was strapless.

Lisa glided through the day. She'd been squirreling away money for years, which wasn't as hard as it should've been. Now it didn't pay to be a cardiac surgeon, but when Lisa first married Lance, eighteen years ago, it had. A surgeon rarely touched a heart anymore, unless performing a transplant, and those, too, were rarer and rarer. Now cardiologists tended to the heart, with highly technical, nearly mundane procedures that had robbed cardiac surgeons of both money and fame. Houston had always been so famous for its heart surgeons, and now correcting an arrhythmia was as simple as threading a line through a groin to ablate the errant piece of the wildly beating heart. Denton Cooley had lived in River Oaks, of course. He must be turning over in his grave. Lance had trained with him, long ago.

It had happened to Lisa last year: an ablation, due to an arrhythmia that would not correct itself. The most painful part of the procedure had been the shot that numbed her groin.

Lance had been fucking someone else while she was at the hospital. An outpatient procedure. It killed Lance, that handling the heart had become so ordinary.

But Lance didn't cheat because he was no longer considered a god who cracked open human chests and held beating hearts in his hand. Who knew why he cheated? Lisa only knew why he didn't, and the distinction was important to her, if no one else. He didn't cheat because of her, Lisa. He did it because he was an animal. And for years, Lisa had looked the other way. And she would've continued to look the other way had Victoria not shifted at a certain angle that morning, allowing Lisa to glimpse the nasty bruise covering her daughter's armpit.

Such a strange place to hit someone. She knew immediately what it was. She'd raised Victoria to be better than this, the victim of such a cliché. It was like something out of the movies. He was beating her on private places, so no one would see.

And Victoria—she was so strong. Just last week she had forcefully but somehow gracefully made a hostess sit them by the window at Brennan's. Lisa had followed her daughter through the restaurant, feeling proud. It was difficult to reconcile the two halves—the Victoria who moved through the world with such authority, and the Victoria who allowed herself to be hit. Lisa felt like her brain was splitting in half. Seeing the bruise, she'd cried out, as if in pain.

She, not Victoria. She'd wanted to kill him.

Victoria had watched her mother. She'd seemed unsurprised by her reaction.

Lance came home for lunch, which he did sometimes. He liked to surprise her.

"Busy morning?" he asked while assembling two sandwiches. One for him, one for her. He was thoughtful.

He was good with his hands. Spread mayonnaise on the bread deftly, in one neat motion. Pulled out Lisa's chair while holding both plates—wide, white—in his free hand.

"Remember, we're going to Lake Austin," she said. "The spa." Lance nodded. "For a week. Will be so nice to get away."

"You deserve it," Lance said absently. He ate slowly, methodically. He would leave part of the sandwich on his plate. Lisa would not have married Lance if he hadn't owned this house, this house she would be sad to leave. Built in the thirties, updated every decade. It was the perfect house, both old and new, charming and convenient. Heart pine floors, sunrooms attached to every bedroom, a porch that went on for miles.

Nobody deserves anything, she thought.

She went for her regular walk at dusk. Homes in Tanglewood were expensive, expensively kept. She passed the Spanish-style villa with the red-tile roof, the white Tudor, the new three-story brick that looked like a university in miniature. Tasteless, but she saw the appeal. Building something bigger, bolder. More.

She saw the outlines of her neighbors in their kitchens. Mothers, nannies, maids. Lisa knew no one very well, though she'd lived here for years. It wasn't the kind of neighborhood to host block parties. Even if it had been, she wasn't the kind of woman to attend them. She and Lance were nominally social, but her husband's proclivities made things thorny. She was never sure who he'd fucked. Or wanted to.

She had Victoria. Victoria who had gone to the University of Texas and pledged Tri Delta even without the benefit of a mother—or any family member—who was a legacy. She was a first-generation college student, but no one who met her would ever guess. Victoria didn't even think of herself that way, because Lisa had never let her. Money had paved the way, to be sure. Lance's money. But Victoria knew how to move through these crowds, even though this—these gilded houses, these manicured lawns—was not her birthright.

In a month, it'd be too hot to walk at night. Lisa would have to get up with the chickens. A saying of her mother's. It was too hot now to walk. She did it anyway. She tripped over a piece of crumbling asphalt and looked up at a window, just in time to see someone—a nanny, a mother—grabbing the outline of a child by his or her arm.

She shivered, though it wasn't cold. There was violence everywhere. Dogs barked, disrupting the quiet. Insects buzzed, voices carried, cars flew through streets, ignoring signs telling them not to. Lately, she braced herself when Lance touched her. Or perhaps she'd been bracing herself for years.

After half an hour of walking, slick with sweat, she'd wound back to her street, to her daughter's street, and climbed the steps to Victoria's sprawling ranch. She wasn't winded.

Victoria opened the door before Lisa knocked. Handed her a glass of wine. Smiled.

Lisa entered her daughter's house. Remembered to smile back.

Sometimes it felt as if she were moving underwater. She went to the bookstore near Rice and bought books with covers featuring faceless women: their heads turned or severed at the eyes. Those were the kind of books she liked: preferably set in the past, about women and their troubles. Dropped into societies and marriages and families that didn't understand their desires.

She went to the grocery store and bought two loaves of the ciabatta Lance liked. Stood in the deli line and sent the turkey back, apologetically, when it wasn't sliced thinly enough. Went to the salon and luxuriated in what would be her last appointment for a long time. When her hairdresser massaged her scalp with a drop of oil, Lisa nearly wept with pleasure.

Other times—like now, at home, in her white-tiled bathroom, staring at her new bob—she felt thrilled. Titillated. An electric current running from her brain to the tips of her fingers. She now had brown hair, for the first time since she was a child.

Her plan was simple. She'd heard somewhere that simple plans were the best plans. She hoped it was true.

Her makeup had been disturbed at the hair salon, by the hair washing and the heat of the dryer. She took a pad soaked with astringent and drew it across her face, starting at her chin, moving upward in quick, deft strokes.

It had always been her nature to be gentle. When Victoria was a little girl, Lisa was good at untangling knots in her daughter's hair. Her instinct was to move slowly, to solve with patience instead of force.

A less patient woman would've left Lance. He wasn't flagrant with his affairs, but still there'd been a nurse who'd driven by their house too many times to ignore. And then, abruptly, stopped. A smear of lipstick on the back of one of his collars, hidden from his sight. Late nights at the hospital, even when he wasn't on call.

Lisa hated to think about the fight Lance and the nurse—she wore sunglasses, drove a Honda with an empty car seat in the back—must have had. Lance challenging her, invoking . . . Who knew what he invoked? Did he threaten her career? Her marriage? Did he say he loved his wife?

Lisa dabbed at the delicate skin beneath her eyes. Imagining the sex didn't bother her. It was the fighting that disturbed her—the intimacy that accompanied conflict.

Lisa lived in a beautiful home. Liked her life. Loved her daughter, who she was lucky to have living close by. She hadn't ever thought seriously of leaving Lance. Or demanding that he stop. She knew he wouldn't.

But the bruise. And then the photographs. One day, Lisa let herself into her daughter's house—a ranch, yes, but totally gutted and restored—with the key hidden beneath the stone turtle out back. Found the Polaroids. It undid something in Lisa, holding them in her hand, stacked in a neat square. She guessed that David checked Victoria's phone. That something physical, in this digital age, felt safer.

The photographs were lurid. The bruises against the pale skin—Victoria had always had such beautiful skin—reminded Lisa of tie-dye. Multiple variations of the same hue. An irregular pattern that somehow made sense.

She had put the photographs back into Victoria's trunk. The same trunk in which she'd hidden her secrets since she was a little girl: notes passed by friends, treasures dug up in the creek that ran through the backyard of their first home. A letter from her father, who was barely in Victoria's life.

Lisa startled back into the present: her white-tiled bathroom, with the dormer windows to let in the light. The light was not flattering, but it was useful for applying makeup.

It was Lance, opening the door in his firm way. He never hesitated. Lisa caught his surprise in the mirror's reflection; he rarely saw his wife without makeup.

She felt naked.

"You're home early," she said, resisting the urge to drop her head. Let him look at her. Let him see.

He shrugged. "Thought I might go hit some balls."

"We have the thing at Deb's tonight."

"I know." He made to go, raising his hand in a sort of half

wave, but then he paused. "You look nice like that. You look nice without all of the—" He ran a hand over his face, as if removing a mask, before he left.

She was moved. But she shouldn't have been. It was Lance's instinct, always, to make women feel good about themselves.

It was only later that she realized he hadn't noticed her hair, brown for the first time in years.

Victoria met David three years ago, while walking through the neighborhood with her mother. She was twenty-seven. He was a partner in a law firm, recently divorced, Victoria's senior by a decade. Lisa didn't like the decade part, but she liked David. He was quiet and seemed kind. The rumor was his wife had left him for her high school boyfriend, breaking David's heart. Now, of course, Lisa wondered why the woman had left. They had no children. And he adored Victoria.

When they'd been dating for a few months, Victoria had fainted, and David had taken her to the emergency room, calling Lisa on the way. When Lisa arrived, David was in a quiet fury, demanding that his wife be seen that instant. And she was.

David was quiet, but he was forceful. Taller and larger and less handsome than Victoria, with a weak chin and sandy-colored hair. Victoria had worked at a marketing firm when she met him. Not her passion, perhaps, but a good enough job. A way to get out of the house, at least. She'd gone to part-time after they married, then quit altogether. *You don't work,* she'd said to Lisa, *and you're happy.*

That was true, or true enough. But sometimes Lisa felt the world had passed her by. Especially once Victoria left for college. She had no purpose, had never had a purpose, except for her daughter.

But then Victoria moved to Tanglewood, and her presence brightened Lisa's life. They were each other's purpose.

The first surge of sickness, when Lisa was sixteen years old—she'd known what it was. Who it was. And everything after that, all her moves—up, up, up—had been for her daughter. She knew people—Gary's mother, for one—thought she'd gotten pregnant so she could escape Midland. But it'd been the other way around, entirely. She doubted she would have left if not for her child, her child who had made her life possible.

Lisa would've lived a lifetime with Lance. He would've retired, eventually. He was reluctant to leave work, said he didn't know what he'd do with his time, but Lisa and he both knew that the office and the hospital provided good cover for his extracurricular activities.

They still had sex. A few times a month. It was nice enough. She'd told him once, after the nurse had driven by, that if she ever got an STD, she'd kill him. They had been eating dinner on the porch. She didn't look at him when she said it.

"Okay," he'd responded after a moment, and they'd never spoken of it again.

Lisa's first plan had been violence. Lance had a gun—Lisa would use it to kill David. She'd stare him in the face and pull the trigger. She knew how to handle one; it was Texas. She'd grown up among men who hunted. She'd be arrested and spend the rest of her life in prison. Or maybe not. Maybe a good lawyer could prove self-defense, on her daughter's behalf.

But the risk of leaving Victoria—abandoning her—was too great. Victoria hadn't needed her mother in such a long time.

Her daughter had arranged an enviable life for herself.

Talked about having children soon. Liked to cook elaborate meals from old French cookbooks. Was developing an interest in wine. Was—Lisa had thought—happy. She loved her mother, but didn't seem to need her, not as she had when she was a child. But perhaps that was what it meant to be a parent: your child needed you until she did not. That's what Lisa told herself.

But then the bruise. And then the photographs. After seeing them, Lisa had left her daughter's home and vomited into a camellia bush.

She didn't know which part she found more alarming: that Victoria was being beaten, or that she hadn't told her mother.

A few days before they were to leave, Victoria dropped by the house with a book. Lisa was on the patio—she would miss this patio—drinking a glass of wine.

Victoria rested the book on the table, raised her eyes at the wine. "Cocktail hour somewhere?"

Lisa nodded.

"In that case . . ." Victoria went to the kitchen and returned a moment later with her own glass.

Lisa was so grateful her daughter wasn't pregnant, she nearly cried.

"The stuff you drink is shit," Victoria said. "All tannin." She wrinkled her nose. "But whatever," she said, and took another sip.

Lisa studied her daughter. She had a solid look about her: firm cheekbones and big hazel eyes. Her eyes had always been her best feature. "You look pretty today."

Victoria seemed startled. "Is something wrong?"

Lisa shook her head. Victoria picked up the book, flipped through it idly.

"Is it good?" Lisa asked, her voice fraught. She was near tears.

Victoria shrugged. "I hope so." She knew something was amiss. She did not know what.

They were going to run away. To a little town in Mexico where Lisa and Gary had vacationed once, years ago. They would come back once the dust had settled. Lisa had been to see her lawyer—a man with an underbite and a thick head of silver hair who'd come highly recommended—four times in the last week.

They would each—Victoria and Lisa—file for divorce in Mexico. Victoria had a prenup, of course (everyone did these days), but the attorney was certain they could void it, as long as Lisa got the pictures.

Victoria would sign the papers in Mexico, Lisa knew. In Houston, she had no interest in leaving David, but things would be different once they were elsewhere. Once they weren't in Tanglewood. Victoria thought, like Lance, that she and her mother were going to Austin, to a spa. Mexico would be a surprise. Victoria loved surprises, had since she was a little girl.

In Mexico, Lisa would take Victoria's phone so David couldn't reach her, and she'd explain their future to her daughter. She could imagine the words, what exactly she would say: *You're fooling yourself. He will never stop. You're too young to throw away your life like this.*

Platitudes, all of them. And all of them true.

Lisa knew Victoria would listen, once they were away from all this. It would be easier, for both her and her daughter, to be gone. To absent themselves from the lives they were going to destroy.

"Mom," Victoria said, "stop looking at me like that."

But she, too, seemed close to tears.

* * *

Her love for Victoria was the purest thing she'd ever felt, even now, thirty years later. Or especially now. She'd never loved another person so deeply, so obsessively. With anyone else she'd loved—her mother, a boy before her first husband whom she'd loved an unreasonable amount—there was a desire underpinning it all. There would have been no love without it. She wanted to touch, she wanted to be touched. She wanted to be made to feel a certain way. That want made her feel like an animal.

But there was none of that with Victoria, of course. Lisa's attachment to her drew from some well that had previously been unknown to her. She wondered, when Victoria was tiny, more a collection of scents and sounds than a human, if all parents, all mothers, felt this way. It didn't seem possible.

Victoria asked Lisa about her own mother once, when she was a child: "Did she love you like you love me?"

The pronouns confused Lisa for a moment. "Yes," she'd said, but not because she believed it.

They were leaving tomorrow, and it felt too easy. Victoria had come over that morning and talked about what she'd packed. Swimsuits. Sundresses, for dinner. She described a new one so vividly—striped, off the shoulder—Lisa could almost see it. And then she could almost see Victoria in their house on the beach, standing ankle-deep in the water. And a surge of something—happiness, excitement, some combination thereof—threaded itself through her brain.

Victoria seemed worried. Lisa thought she understood why. Her daughter had found herself trapped. She didn't know how to escape. Lisa would help her.

Lance didn't suspect a thing. Lisa had rented a storage

unit and put clothes into it and a few small pieces of furniture Lance wouldn't miss. Things she didn't want him to have.

Her jewelry and important papers went into a deposit box at the bank. One last trip to the lawyer's office.

She went into what had once been Victoria's room and lay on the bed. But no, that didn't feel like enough and, though she wasn't a woman given to melodramatic gestures, she took off her shirt and pants and lay on the floor. The wood was old heart pine. It bore many years of tiny, almost invisible scratches. A map of scratches.

She could feel her bones through the floor. The wood was cool, solid.

She would miss this house.

Lance was at the hospital. Victoria was at the gym. She was of the younger generation, which considered working out, beating the body into submission, as natural as brushing one's teeth.

Lisa went to the stone turtle, then let herself in Victoria's front door. David wasn't home. He worked insane hours, but she could feel his presence as she walked quietly through his home. It still felt like his, even though Victoria had added her own touches: paintings, antique furniture. But still, David's masculine leather furniture dominated.

She took the Polaroids without looking at them. And yet, the feel of them in her hand was a comfort. Thick and sturdy like an object, not a stack of flimsy photographs.

The pictures gave her hope. The past would be the past. The future, theirs for the taking.

She felt excited, despite the circumstances.

As she passed the guest room door, she heard a knock within. Then another. Some part of her thought it was David beating Victoria, though she knew that was impossible. David was at work. Victoria was at the gym.

She opened the door out of some sort of maternal instinct, her other hand clutching the square of pictures.

Lance looked at her first. For all his indiscretions, she had never seen him with another woman. Certainly not on top of one, as he was now, a look of pleasure slowly morphing into pain upon his face.

"Mama," a voice said from underneath Lance. The pictures slid from Lisa's hand.

Victoria had not called her *Mama* in so long.

ONE IN THE FAMILY

BY ADRIENNE PERRY
Museum District

"You have some experience with food prep?" asked Angus, the owner of Taco Heaven. He wore snake-skin boots and his jingle-jolly gut stretched a *Clutch City* T-shirt. Dad's age or a little older. For this informal interview, we sat outside Black Hole, next to the laundromat, so that Angus could smoke. Rancheras played on the laundry's radio, and I knew enough Spanish to get depressed by what those sisters were singing. Through the open door, the floral, pastel perfumes from detergents and dryer sheets mixed with Angus's smoke. Toxic, but when was the last time I'd done laundry in actual machines, not secretly in the Y's showers? Finals week. Now it was full-on June.

I said, "I washed dishes in the dining hall."

Angus watched me attack the iced coffee and Southwest quiche he'd offered at the interview's start. Raggedy, but dignified. Hungry. I knew how I looked. Trying to figure me out, Angus's wide forehead wrinkled. It looked like kind confusion.

"I had an uncle who taught history at your school."

"For real?"

"He's retired now. It's a good school."

I nodded without smirking. "For most people."

"What makes you special?"

No comment. I pushed my finger onto the crumbs and eggy bits on my plate. I'd eat whatever wasn't strapped down.

"Would you say you're any good with people?"

"I'm great with people."

"Re's an interesting name. Where's it come from?"

I knew what Angus was getting at and I wasn't going to make it easy for him. I showed him the backs of my hands. *R* (right hand) *e:* (left hand). "A nickname. Pronounced *rey*."

"Like a ray of light? Like shafts through clouds? Like the Virgin Mary?"

"Like a king. I have to send money home each month. Can you remind me how much the pay is?"

Angus hired me because he felt sorry for me.

That was fine.

Summer in Houston is like the dead of winter in Easthampton, Massachusetts, only hot instead of cold. In both places, weather traps the lucky people inside. I tried to explain this to our dad, but he's from Mississippi, so he already knew. End of my sophomore year and I talked about the heat because I didn't want to talk about why I wasn't going back. Not to school and not home. Macy had just returned from Afghanistan. When I say *just*, I mean a year. Staying in Houston was my way of pretending that everything would work itself out— for all of us.

The fusion-taco food truck was pitched to Dad as a paid internship. Small business administration, hospitality, team building, and sustainable food. Workday's end, I would wring sweat from my *Taco Heaven* T-shirt and pocket fifteen wet dollar bills in tips. End of the month, I had saved enough to send home four hundred.

Dad said inquiring minds want to know: Were my supervisors nice? What was I learning about bookkeeping and advertising, about how to run my own business? I'd look at

Wikipedia and memorize the difference between budgets and actuals in small business accounting. Make shit up—factoids about the history of tacos. Or Angus. I'd tell a story about my boss, say he was a felon who'd miraculously turned a corner in his life of crime, was mentoring me, showing me how to transform an idea into three edible dimensions. That was the summer I started telling grown-up lies. When your father launches a Kickstarter campaign to finance his oldest daughter's Sip-N-Puff, he doesn't want to hear that his other kid pays for a student membership at the downtown YMCA just to take showers and use the free Wi-Fi. He doesn't want to hear they've been stalking their ex-financial aid officer, or that they're sleeping on the street. No father wants to hear that. So I spared him.

Angus and I worked together five days a week. Taco Heaven employed no one else. Lemons and limes, edible flowers, and fruit dominated my workstation. Grilling and marinating meats, heating tortillas—Angus handled all that and chopped cilantro, whipped together salsas and fresh chutneys from mangos and allspice. I took orders and ran the register, cranked out a green-and-white awning, and, underneath it, set up an outdoor Ikea table plus two chairs for ambiance. Both of us cleaned. A winged hot-pink taco flew on the truck's black side.

Every Tuesday, Taco Heaven camped out at the Museum of Fine Arts, between the parking lot and the sculpture garden. A small man-made hill sloped up to a mini plateau behind the truck, where a magnolia and ponderosa pine threw shade. On the grass beneath the tree branches, during my breaks, I would stare out at the sculptures, watching the guards on their breaks. We echoed each other.

A bronze man made of rectangles ran down a slope near a sick-looking naked boy riding a horse. The horse had a tiny head on a wrestler's neck. *The Pilgrim*, the artist named the horse and boy, and I thought, *That's just like white folks*. Not the sculpture, but the value of things and how they're just for certain people. Gardens are green prisons and if I could steal that horse and sick boy and sell them to solve our money problems, I would. Without regret. If that's racist or wrong or something, right about now I just don't care.

A Tuesday was my first official day on the job, though I worked with Angus Mondays through Saturdays. The cicadas in the sculpture garden sounded like sirens for the buses and cars barreling down Bissonnet. A museum security guard sweating through his uniform leaned on the parking lot sign. The atmosphere inside the truck—how can I describe it? Stainless steel can hold onto heat with a death grip. A fluorescent light beat down like a tin hammer on the top of my head.

"Feels like a grown man tap dancing on your chest, doesn't it?"

"Something like that," I said, studying Angus's map. Every food item or utensil had a home. Angus had systems and, within the first hour, I fucked those systems up. I'd read the map upside down.

"If you weren't a girl . . ." Angus shut himself up. I'll give him that. He knew when to quit about that aspect. That first day, Angus didn't know what to make of me. But by early July, he was talking about his favorite butch cousin from Chicago, full-sleeve tattoos on her arms, big diamonds in her ears, girls practically throwing their panties in front of her. He said, "If you weren't a girl, you'd be toast."

Before Macy came back from Kabul, this would have gotten to me. I would have licked the counter to apologize. But Macy put the world to scale.

"Good thing I'm not really a girl."

"All right," Angus chuckled, "have it your way. I'm just saying: awareness. So nobody gets hurt."

I thought: *That is my fucking way.* I said, "I'll be more aware."

Angus cocked his head, searched my face, and waved a hand in front of his nose. "You've got what my nephew calls an *ice grill*, you know?"

"I have a decent sense of what my face is doing."

"You ever been in?" Angus pointed to the museum. A fat line of schoolchildren snaked through the doors. "It's an ugly building from the outside, but don't judge a book. Am I right?"

Museums don't intimidate me. Entering the MFAH lobby for the first time, I saw a Warhol self-portrait and a negative of myself, in the same moment. Against a black background, Warhol was pink, his hair stuck up like feathers in an Easter Sunday hat. A death mask expression on his face, like Macy's when we picked her up at the Hartford airport. How much would a Warhol like that go for? What gave *Warhol* value? If I could figure that out, I'd start throwing paint on canvases.

These were not observations to share with Dad and Macy on our video calls on Thursday nights, when the museum was free and stayed open until nine p.m. Pessimism would only confirm that I was in a bad way. They wanted to know what I had seen: Greek vases, gold leaf–topped linguist sticks, Mary with the Christ child, silver, photographs, capes made of Technicolor bird feathers. As their tour guide, I led them through the corridors and into the galleries, narrating what I saw, and I felt close to them. Like last summer.

Each Thursday, we ended the call with three or four passes through the Turrell tunnel. Dark platform above and, below, the hot-pink and red and violet and blue changing walls. The thin, lighter outline that passed to other dimensions. Macy would moan so loudly through the passage, I learned to put the phone on mute.

The ends of these calls were often awkward. Dad might ask, "You headed back to the dorm?"

One lie required another: "Yeah. I'll take my time walking back."

"What classes did you register for, again?"

"I don't think I said. I have neurobiology and art history. Still figuring out the other two."

"Financial aid is all straightened out, then? We haven't got anything in the mail."

"I'll double-check."

I'd stopped going to school since the spiritual nut-kicking of trying my fob on doors to my dorm, to the gym. Instead, I decided to walk down Graustark to Mr. Larson's house and stare at his condo from across the street. He didn't live far from the MFAH, and even closer to the Menil. Lights on timers, the pool's motor circulating lazily. No mail delivery as far as I could tell. On Mondays, a cleaning woman might come by. Polished concrete, a window like an icicle going from the first to the third floor. I was waiting for them to come back.

Near the Rothko, I sprayed heavy-duty insect repellent all over and lay beside a fence, out of view, using my backpack for a pillow. Same routine every night. At first, I couldn't sleep. The A pitch of mosquitoes. The fear of frightening someone. Kids who looked like me were treated savagely. Routinely. I wanted to trust the people who lived this close to Rothkos, but that was too generous. In the early morning, when it was cooler, I calmed down and slept. I dreamed that Angus had installed a grill inside the Turrell tunnel and I had shrunk to fit the grill. The kitchen setup didn't bother the guards. Angus seared my back, browned my front. Poked my thighs with a spatula to make sure I was done. Then he chopped me up, slid me into a corn tortilla, and handed me over to Larson with a wedge of lime.

Ninety-nine degrees and 100 percent humidity. A gray haze all around and pollen and ozone advisory warnings. Droning on Montrose and Bissonnet and Main. I have never been in a desert, and I know Pakistan is not the desert, but I saw a photograph of Pakistan in a *Washington Post* left at the Y. There were cypress trees shaped like wizard hats. Distant mountains. A small gray swimming pool with, I'm estimating, a few hundred men. Pants on in the water. Hottest day on record in Pakistan. A scientist quoted in the article said these heat waves pushed people to the limits of their thermal comfort. Absolutely. Brains cook at that temperature, just like the brain of a customer standing in the Taco Heaven line in Houston in July. Just like our brains inside the truck. The men in the picture looked shocked, as if standing in front of a body that had just collapsed in the street. But I was probably projecting. They might have been having a great time.

Tuesdays were usually slow, but the week of July 4 meant family time at the museum. Angus hustled on four orders of Indonesian tacos and three fried chicken tacos with waffle casings. I wiped down the counters and refrigerator, then hopped out front to double-check the customer experience. "Order up!" I delivered the tacos to a couple with their in-laws. The mother handed me ten dollars to bring more Topo Chicos. How did she know handing people cold drinks was my favorite? I loved to hold bottlenecks covered in condensation, to feel the glass slip through my fingers. *I'm the Red Cross*, I thought. *I'm saving people.* I was bettering the lives of people who hate. In Houston, people were friendly on the surface, happy on the surface. But they hated their lives, themselves, each other, same as back home. Same as everywhere.

I went behind the truck and put cold fingers on my face.

"Do you know how to cook?" Angus asked.

"I can boil water."

He was being nice, making conversation, but I didn't want to talk in that metal animal mouth reeking of onions and garlic and meat.

"You could learn to do a little more than that. Based on what I've seen, you could do short order most places and some besides." That was nice to hear. "Not that you'll want to, when you get back to school."

I got up and went inside the truck, paired plastic forks with plastic knives, wrapped them in their paper napkin blankets, and put them to sleep in a plastic tub. Angus kept talking and I saw it coming—a sermon—whether I wanted it or not.

"Food was waiting for me. My uncle Ross married this woman Cecilia. There's this picture of her from the seventies wearing a tight Astros T-shirt, and I always think, *That woman changed our diapers and spanked our butts!* She was sweet, Cecilia, but she had a temper."

"Are you following me, Re?"

What I think Angus went on to say:
"Uncle Ross never took any shit. You know? But Aunt Cecilia. She could really cook. Breakfast, lunch, dinner, pastries. Everything. My uncle starts cheating

What I think I went on to think:
Sometimes I don't want anyone to talk

it's like Angus is sitting there

on her with this woman in the downstairs apartment. I'm not saying it's right, but the worst part is the woman starts talking about Cecilia. She starts saying bad things about her cooking and how she can't cook well enough to keep her man.

"Aunt Cecelia tells Uncle Ross, *If that bitch—pardon my language—says one more thing about my food, I swear to god!* This other woman, she says something, and you know what Aunt Cecilia does? She makes some cyanide. This is the truth. She makes cyanide from apple seeds and peach pits and puts it in Uncle Ross's chicken cacciatore. Aunt Cecilia told the judge she planned to put broken glass in his food, but she realized that was too cruel. Did she want to kill him? No, she said she just wanted him to think about the choices he was making. And I guess he did. Uncle Ross tells the judge he deserved it. The woman downstairs moves out and Uncle Ross helps Aunt Cecilia start a catering company.

talking ███ and he's so ██████ sweet, but I'm like, *Shut the fuck up* █████ █ it's nice, on one level, █ ████████████ I never want to be that kind of dude—promise me—and I ██ ████████ there's this ████ Bitch crossed the line ██████████████ ██████████████ ████ stuff going on promise me you won't be that kind of dude █ ████████ home ██████ ████████████ ████████████ ██████████████ ███ I should have gone home and just ██████ they cut me off, ██████████ █ ███████ █████ █ can totally relate to Cecilia, ██████████ some bullshit, ████ it's fucked up Dad won't ██████████ like Cecilia wouldn't take that ██ poison ████████ $3,500 is like ten months ███ job at least until Dad ████████████ ██████ take care of Macy █

Where had I been? Thinking money, thinking Macy. "Why are you telling me this?" Angus looked hurt. I laughed, to play it off. "I'm never going to eat your food again."

"If I didn't feed you, you'd fly away." Angus wiped his face with a rag and threw it in the day's laundry. He handed me two limes. "Work. It'll make you feel better."

I destroyed the lime's skin on the mandolin, making zest and a citrus smell I loved to hold to my nose. Finished that and started with the inventory. Angus took a pencil from behind his ear and checked the inventory sheet. "You mean to tell me you don't have an Aunt Cecilia in your family? Come on, you know you do."

What he meant by that, I don't know.

March of sophomore year, I made an appointment to discuss my financial aid package. A day of cold rain hushed campus, the raindrops pressing down tender leaves, new flowers. I walked through puddles just to hear the *swish-glub*, to remind myself of walking through puddles with Macy when we were small and both mobile.

On my floor, a sister-girl from Kentucky described Brandon Larson as *a fat, bitchy Mark Twain*. She said I should see if I could meet with someone else. As gray light came through his office window, I could see the resemblance to Twain, mostly in the hair and mustache.

"What are we here to discuss?"

"Did you get my father's letter?"

Larson turned to his computer. "Give me your student ID number. Ah, René Garraway."

"I go by Re."

Click. No eye contact. "Yes, I see the letter here." *Click.*

"Like my dad said in the letter, we can't afford to pay that amount." I pointed to the aid award letter. "The amount listed here."

"Now that your sister is so ill."

"Yes. My father had to leave his job to take care of her."

"What your father is doing is noble, I commend him, but your financial aid is based on the previous year, and your mother's earnings were significantly higher last year too."

"My mom won't give anything. She doesn't have anything."

"Her income is modest, but she and your stepfather have a significant amount in assets. Your parents have joint custody?"

They did, but we'd lived with Dad exclusively since we were four and seven. Mr. Larson's cell phone rang. "Sorry." He stood by the window, facing the crush of gray and green just beyond the glass. I wanted to draw back the curtain of leaves and push him into it. I thumbed through notes for my women's studies test without gaining any traction. I was too busy eavesdropping on the conversation.

"What would I like?" I looked up, thinking he was talking to me. "Janine. I expect you to do everything you can for her. I mean, yes, that's what we're asking, what we've been asking. For how long now?" While he listened, he hummed. "What kind of surgery? I understand. I understand it costs. Everything costs. Haven't I been? Right. We're prepared. Yes, she agrees."

His daughter or his wife? Maybe a sister or a niece. Was it cancer or heart disease? Something rare? A brain injury? Something like Macy? Mr. Larson was going through troubles too. That we might share a pain warmed me like hot pudding.

"Sorry," he said, sitting down. He checked the applications on his computer with shaky hands.

Should I or shouldn't I ask? I found myself asking: "Who's Janine?"

"Our bichon frise. The vet has been trying to figure out what's going on. He was half suggesting I put her down, but the money we've already poured into medical costs . . . If we do this gallbladder surgery, she might have another year. That's worth six thousand. We're probably throwing good money after bad, but . . . Sorry about that," he said again, though nothing about him seemed sorry for me. I doubted he had any idea what six thousand dollars would do for our family. I'd never heard people talk so lightly about so much money before I came to this school.

"Maybe I could speak with someone else?"

"They're just going to tell you the same thing. You always have the option of a loan."

"I can't take out any more in federal loans."

"I was suggesting a private loan."

"My dad doesn't want me to . . . We don't want to do that."

"I appreciate that. That position, and it's a special one to take. It's your education, after all. College is an investment and, I understand, an expensive one for many families. All families have sacrifices to make. You don't have to decide this second." He handed me his card to end the conversation.

It was easy enough to get his address. Where could I send a *Get Well* card for his dog?

A grackle floated off the bus stop. An Oxford-blue suit, European cut on a big man, approached Taco Heaven. Dad called suits this nice *revenge suits*, purchased after a first paycheck or on the occasion of a breakup. But this was probably one of many revenge suits. Did the suit's owner have a face? Sure. But all I saw was a smudge where eyes and a mouth should be. God had licked his thumb and rubbed this man out from the neck up. White hair and a bushy mustache came slightly into focus.

For the last ten minutes, an older woman with a light shawl had struggled with her order. She was peering at the menu when the suit cut in front of her. He gave me the up-and-down, the same look I get in bathrooms. Angus was on break.

"I believe the lady was first," I said to the suit.

"She doesn't look ready to order."

I recognized Larson, back from vacation. I should have placed him right away. Did he recognize me? I was wearing gloves, so he couldn't see my name.

The woman raised her eyebrows. She said, "Actually . . ."

"Give me a Jamaican jerk taco, a bahn mi taco, plus an agua—"

I said to Larson, "Let me grab her order and then I'll take yours."

"But I just told you what I want."

Ice cracking over a thin puddle—that was the expression traveling across the woman's face. "I've lost my appetite." She put a five-dollar tip in the jar and walked away.

When Larson placed his order, he spoke slowly, insultingly. It was the kind of voice kids used to mock Macy last summer.

"I heard you twice the first time," I told him.

Angus came back inside, scraped down the grill. "Everything good here?"

"Maybe you want to think about who you have up front," Larson said.

"Or," I said, "maybe you want to think—"

"Why don't you take your break now?" Angus interrupted. "I can take this one. You're so wet you're shaking, Re."

I was sick of it. So sick. Of the cutting in line. The looks people like Larson gave people like me and Macy. My school. The heat and the rashes on my arms from sleeping on the ground.

A bronze sculpture of a ripped man walking with no arms

and no head. Who knew where? The sorry bastard. A giant had pinched off his limbs and left him to wander around with no strength. The bubbles in the Topo Chico popped in my mouth. I hadn't changed. My shirt clung to my binder.

"I thought you said you were good with people," Angus said when he came out, throwing a dry *Taco Heaven* T-shirt on my shoulder.

"That guy wasn't people. He works at the college."

"Do you know him?"

"He didn't even recognize me. What a dick!"

"Can't you avoid him at school?"

I shook my head. "I don't even know. I don't think I can go."

"Why wouldn't you?"

We sat beneath the magnolia, suffering. I took out my phone, went to the gallery, showed Angus two pictures of Macy. A before and after.

"I'm sorry for your sister."

"Maybe I should go home."

"You never know," Angus said. "I knew a kid like your sister. We were all out together in Austin, off the Greenbelt, and people were diving, drinking. It was getting dark. You had to know where to jump and he didn't know. Broke his neck."

"My sister's neck isn't broken. What do you know about my sister?"

"Nothing. I'm just saying."

The guards let us use the bathroom on the first floor. I wanted to cry in private, to change clothes and rinse my face after. As I walked into the men's room, Larson came out. He looked at me with the same cocked head Angus had at my interview and that day he said I was lucky to be a girl.

In my stall, the same stall I always used, I changed shirts. Just outside the door, a pair of shiny brown leather shoes came into view. There was a knock and I heard Larson's voice: "René Garraway?"

I didn't respond, hardly breathed.

"Is that you, René? I think you've made your point."

I put my face down in my lap so he couldn't see me through the space near the hinges.

People like Larson make life harder. They hang around asking questions, making assumptions. They think I'm trying to make a statement when I piss. I'm not. I just want to piss. Is Larson trying to make a statement when he pisses? No. How much time lapsed, I don't know. The glare off his polished shoes disappeared. I heard a faucet, then the door opening.

"Miss. Please use the other restroom." The voice of a security guard from the door.

I wondered, as I sat there, waiting for them to go away, what Cecilia was thinking when she put the poison in Uncle Ross's chicken cacciatore. Not enough to kill him, but enough to make him think.

Dad always said that in the fall, men either want to fuck something or they want to kill. Fall was two months away, but I had the urge.

At the Y, I did a search for cyanide. This led to a search for tasteless poisons. A stunning catalog of horrible deaths people had imparted to their wives, animals, coworkers, lovers, and rivals greeted me. In England, a man made ricin from castor beans and used it to kill his boss and another business partner. Cyanide came in powder form and the gas worked just as quick. Uncle Ross should have died. She just wanted to scare him, because she could have killed him easily. Arsenic, for instance. No taste, no odor. For many murderers, those qualities weighed heavily in arsenic's favor. Antifreeze. In one article, there was a picture of a green street gutter. A tabby cat tipped its face down to drink its death. How small a dose would I have to give to hurt without *really* hurting? The information on wikis and websites contradicted each other. Two teaspoons for a child. So, a tablespoon for an adult? I wouldn't do it. It wasn't real. A curiosity, that was all.

On my day off, I walked to H-E-B to buy a money order. Four hundred dollars to send home. After the money order, I walked the aisles, imagining what I would buy to eat when I had money someday. I grabbed a sample tortilla at the bakery—warm, oily, and salty—and ate it while touching fruits and vegetables. Pink salmon and frozen scallops and lobster tails. Waters. Milks in the dairy case. In the aisle for home goods and insecticides, a yellow antifreeze bottle. I left the aisle for a sixteen-ounce Mountain Dew, went back for the antifreeze, and paid at the self-checkout.

On Friday nights and weekends, bands played on a small outdoor stage to the right of the grocery store's entrance. When there were no bands, it was shaded and a good place to sit. The Mountain Dew's cold and sugar hurt my teeth, but the flavor . . . Delicious and weird. Mountain Dew tastes like nothing but itself—just like me. When the Mountain Dew was gone, I walked to the edge of the parking lot and poured antifreeze into the empty bottle. I left the antifreeze jug tucked behind a grassy bush sprouting hard white flowers. Clouds stacked like skyscrapers pushed south toward the gulf.

Did I really want to hurt people? No, not badly. Actually, yeah, just a little. But not seriously. Just a fright to make them appreciate life, just as I had been forced to do through Macy.

I walked through several neighborhoods. I passed bungalows and brick homes, but also construction sites. In Houston, if something is old, people want to rip it down, put in a condo, a steak house.

I needed a hat but didn't have one. The sun swarmed like bees around my head. I went into the Rothko and pretended to meditate until six, when they kicked everyone out.

I was feeling lost until I saw Larson's house. There was a dog with curly white fur in the yard. This was Janine. She looked sluggish, like me. I could help her. Larson stepped out onto his stoop and called her in. The two crepe myrtles in front of his house had scattered the ground with pink confetti.

It took a few days of going back at dark, to wait and to watch. He let her out at ten, but didn't come out with her.

I took a small Tupperware from the food truck and filled it with the poison. I pushed it through the gate, standing back in the hot dark, to watch Janine drink. Forced myself to watch her finish.

I waited for Larson. I knew he would come. It wasn't fate so much as tacos. The next Tuesday at the MFAH, he appeared. The longer line forced him to wait. I told the next customer I'd be right back. The Mountain Dew bottle was warm in my backpack. I scooped ice into a plastic cup, poured in a tablespoon of the antifreeze, and covered it with limeade.

When it was Larson's turn to order, I said, "Sorry I was so weird the other day. It took me a second to recognize you."

"I knew it was you right away, René."

"How'd everything work out for your dog?"

"Not great. Did I see you the other day, on my street?"

"I like to walk. Do you live nearby? What can I get you?"

The limeade, I told Larson, was on the house.

I watched him eat two Thai chicken tacos at the Ikea table. I watched him drink a plastic cup of water while some feeling, like hair in a drain, clogged my gut. Fucking with a dog was a bullshit thing to do, right? I tried to imagine what Macy would say if she could speak. As Larson stood up, he shook the limeade to say thanks and goodbye.

"Let me make you a fresh one," I said.

"This one's fine. When they're too cold, it hurts my teeth."

He waited at the crosswalk for the westbound traffic to pass. I told Angus I had to pee. By the middle of the crosswalk, Larson had sucked down the limeade. I followed him into the museum. Near the Islamic art galleries, he rested on a bench. *Should I say something to a guard?* I could have said something to Larson, but Angus was expecting me back at the truck. I walked outside into thick air.

Within thirty minutes, an ambulance arrived.

"What's going on over there, I wonder?" Angus said.

A customer with a broad, flushed face leaned on the truck. "I was just coming out. Some guy fell down. They're trying to help him."

"Who was it?"

"Search me. Guy wearing a suit. Lots of thick white hair."

Angus turned. "Do you think it's the guy from your school, Re? What did he have?"

"A couple of tacos and a limeade. And a glass of water."

"Let me go see," Angus said. "You never know. It could be something. Hold down the fort."

I am still too close to the feelings. To describe them. I remember my heart pounded when, a few minutes later, the police cruisers parked behind the ambulance. I remember my hot and sour mouth, my curiosity. Another part of me, the part that could move, tucked the Mountain Dew bottle back into my bag and grabbed the cash out of the register before leaving.

* * *

August brought Hell's furies. Walking over asphalt hot enough to melt, I became a blister. Red, shiny, and taut. Between the Y's water aerobics classes, I slipped into the pool. Cold and chemical, it stripped away my skin, my cells. Given enough time, I would be stripped to bones.

In the locker room, I shook a bottle of shaving cream and rubbed the foam over my head. My own face was a blur, a smudge in the mirror, like Larson. I'm sick. No, I'm not. I filled the sink with water and pulled the razor in straight rows across my scalp. After each pass, I cleaned the blades, and it reminded me of shoveling snowy walks. I missed snow now, though I hated it then. The old men shuffled in from the sauna and turned cool showers onto their curved backs. Their loud voices were a comfort. They didn't mind me. Called me a nice kid as I hand-washed my boxers and binder in the sinks.

When I was done, I sat on a chair outside of the locker room and stared at the picture Dad had sent earlier that week. It came with a text: *Remember the pool? Wish we could see you before school starts.*

We'd all gone to Walmart to buy an aboveground pool. I'd pushed Macy in her chair into the clothing section and rubbed different fabrics softly along her cheek. In the overgrown backyard, Macy watched us put the pool together and I filled it with the hose. We let the water warm for a day. Then it was ready and I stood in the pool.

"Light as a feather," Dad had said, lifting Macy from her chair and setting her in my arms. Macy gasped at the feel of the water, let a long moan out of her faintly purple mouth. The inside of a mussel, the sea, Macy's thin brown legs twigs scissoring in the water until my *shhhhhh* calmed her down. Behind me, I could hear Dad saying, "You're good to your sister. You're good."

Standing in the museum's shadow, I watched Taco Heaven from across the street. Angus had hired someone to replace me, a tall and lanky man who would have trouble standing in the truck all day. I waited to see Angus come out, but there was a small line and he always liked to stay ahead of a rush. Another half hour and I would go. At the sculpture garden's edge, the bamboo waved as squirrels crawled up and down its narrow green trunks. In the middle of the Montrose and Bissonnet intersection, a man wearing a neon vest wove through the traffic, holding a cup. *Veteran. Spare change. Anything helps.* I waited the first half hour and then another and wasn't surprised that, the whole time, no one gave the man anything. He was fast with his cane. Maybe he'd been hit, like Macy. Eventually, the line at Taco Heaven disappeared.

I took a drink of water, thinking I would give it another half hour, when the replacement walked across the street to use the bathroom. He scooted across the crosswalk holding something in his hands. Maybe trash? Maybe Angus had seen me and this guy was bringing me something to eat. I looked away, bent down pretending to tie my shoe. I saw the man's raggedy New Balance sneakers and stood up to look at his face. Fortyish, but younger-looking than Dad. He had a gap between his front teeth and wore his *Taco Heaven* T-shirt small.

"You look just like he said you would."

"Who said I would?"

"Angus. He says don't come back around here."

"Who are you?"

"Vaughn," the man said. "I'm the new you."

"Why did he send you? Why won't he talk to me?"

"I don't know. I got nothing against you, but you got to get." Vaughn peered at me hard, sweat pouring off his face. "You been through some things, huh? Well, I don't know nothing about it, but you look young and smart enough to pull yourself back from that edge. I got to get back." Vaughn handed me five dollars. "You know how Angus do."

"Tell him I'm sorry," I said.

The truck wobbled as Vaughn slipped inside it. The cicadas sounded like buzz saws and I dug a finger in my ear to get rid of them, but that only made the buzzing stronger. After noon, the shadows moved like ships on gray water. The heat held me close. But Angus would come out soon. Angus would come out. I was sure he would, once Vaughn told him I was sorry.

THE USE OF LANDSCAPE

BY ROBERT BOSWELL

River Oaks

I magine that thieves move into a house while the owners are away, and the first thing they do is mow the yard, trim the hedges, tend to the landscape—make it seem that they belong while they plunder.

This was Cole's plan precisely, only the house was Madelyn's body.

The Criminal Element:
Tariq, who owed Cole.
Herta, who loved Cole.
And Cole, who loved no one.

Why Tariq Owed Cole:
Cole, out of the goodness of his heart (and with the idea that it might be useful to have Tariq in his debt), drove a stolen 1998 Chevy Camaro over Tariq's friend-turned-snitch Sunny, while Tariq, snugged away in a holding cell, possessed the state of Texas as his alibi.

Why Herta Loved Cole:
He was handsome, decisive, clever, lively, and heartless.

Why Cole Loved No One:
He didn't know how.

* * *

"The girl is the center of the group," Tariq explained. He bartended at the Azure Lounge, an upscale tavern with divey pretentions on Westheimer just below River Oaks Boulevard. In Houston, River Oaks equaled royalty: money to make Rockefeller envious, mansions to make Gatsby blanch. "They show up three, four times a week—after gym, before dinner, late at night. Rude bastards who tip for shit. Usually three or four of them, sometimes five. Ordinary looking, except they've got that sheen that comes from money. You know that sheen?"

Cole had lived in Houston all his life. He knew that sheen.

Herta said, "You can't spend sheen." She was not from Houston. She was not from anywhere.

"Not to worry. Madelyn lives with her dad right on River Oaks Boulevard," Tariq said. He, too, was a native Houstonian, by way of Lahore. "They're loaded."

"Money with a pedigree," Cole said.

"Yeah," Herta agreed. "Not just any mutt can move onto River Oaks."

Cole and Herta shared a house two neighborhoods east, in Montrose. They sat at the kitchen table and passed around the covert photos Tariq had taken at the Azure: Madelyn Glancy in tennis gear, in yoga pants, in a gold lamé dress that bunched at her neck.

"That dress fits her body," Herta said, "the way a newspaper fits a fish."

Cole fingered the picture, tracing the woman's head. Madelyn Glancy had a rather long face.

"Don't say like a horse," Herta said, reading his mind. "It's not accurate. People just say that."

"More like Virginia Woolf," said Cole.

"I hated *To the Lighthouse*," Tariq put in. "Why do they force that mopey white woman on every English major?"

"Here we go," said Cole.

"Because she was a genius?" Herta suggested. "Because she was the best writer of her generation?"

"I got a black eye reading that book," Tariq went on. "Fell asleep and hit my beer with my face."

"You may get another," Herta said. "I have a first-edition hardback that'll crack your skull."

"Don't argue with her," said Cole. "She reads."

"I gave up reading after college," Tariq said dismissively. "Even before."

Cole raised one finger to make them focus. "Let's see the other photos."

Tariq speculated that Madelyn was sexual with a boy in the group, a pudgy wide-butt with a hipster haircut. "They don't seem like a real couple," he said, "but I think they do the nasty sometimes."

"I can distract Pork Chop," Herta said.

"How?" Tariq asked. "They ignore everybody."

"Use a little personal landscape."

"Am I supposed to understand that?" Tariq asked.

"I will show him my buttocks," Herta said. To Cole, she added, "This is why I don't like adding partners."

"You can't show your ass in the Azure," Tariq said. "It's a respectable bar."

"Stand up," she said.

"Here we go," said Cole.

Tariq obeyed.

"Good boy," Herta said, rising but losing her balance, catching herself just before her face hit the floor.

"I didn't know girls actually wore those," Tariq said.

"Every woman under forty wears a thong." Herta righted herself as she spoke. "Haven't you ever gotten laid?"

"Pakistani girls don't wear them."

"Yes they do," Herta said. "Mormons wear them. Nuns wear them."

Tariq turned to Cole. "So after Butterball breaks up with Madelyn, you move in? Catch her on the rebound?"

Now it was Cole who glared.

"You guys are so touchy," Tariq said.

"Look at this picture." Cole indicated Madelyn. "Elaborate haircut, plucked brows, painted nails. Wearing gym clothes but also makeup and mascara. If she's screwing fat boy—"

"Pork Chop," Herta said.

"—that's good news. Think she'll hesitate to dump him for me?"

Cole got up from the table to pose. He had a casual, alluring way of standing, as if he were about to tip over backward. A child looking up at him wouldn't see his head, just the promontory of his chest. Adults would note eyes the color of an overcast day and the delicate purse of the lips, as if he were considering extraordinary things. He was clean-shaven, free of sideburns, and carried the retro odors of Lucky Strikes and Old Spice.

"Here's the kicker," Cole went on. "She's vain enough—and rich enough—to believe I might actually be attracted to her."

"I think she's kind of good looking, anyway," Tariq said.

"That's only 'cause she's bitchy to you," Cole explained.

"Have you even read *Mrs. Dalloway*?" Herta demanded.

The Azure Lounge was cool but close, like mentholated smoke. Heavy drapes the color of a bruise shut out the world. Through slits where the curtains failed to overlap, yellow blades pierced the room. Tariq stationed Cole and Herta near the entrance, where the drapes parted a sliver.

"Incoming," said Cole, and Herta moved into position.

The group arrived boisterously, Madelyn leading, with three boys trailing. Herta, who'd situated herself perfectly, dropped her leather wristlet between the passing of the first lug and the arrival of Pork Chop, permitting only him to see the length of her legs as she bent. Then she jumped up and into him, as if he'd goosed her.

Pork Chop uttered a series of *wha, wha, wha* sounds, as if suddenly transformed into a helicopter.

"Oh, sorry," she said, patting his chest and dropping her purse again. "I'm such a klutz!" She started to bend once more, but stopped herself and crouched demurely, offering an exaggerated frowning-smile for Pork Chop alone.

Simultaneously shocked and smitten, the fat boy could manage neither expression nor locomotion until the trailing boy of their group prodded his shoulder, and Pork Chop reluctantly hoofed it to their table.

Herta handed Cole a copy of the *Houston Press*, taken from the stand by the door—the presumptive reason for her stroll. Wrapped within the tabloid's pages was Pork Chop's wallet.

Cole went into action, aiming himself at Madelyn's group. He paused on his way to swoop down, pretending to snag the wallet from the floor. The periphery of his vision flashed red, as if a trigger in his head were half-depressed—a sensation he understood as pleasure. "Hi there." He copped a pose and smiled, eyeing Pork Chop. The group circled a table but were not yet sitting. "When my sister inadvertently *tackled* you—" he paused to laugh and roll his eyes; he hated eye-rolling, but rich people loved it, "you dropped your billfold."

The three males self-frisked, dogs with fleas. This was their greatest worry, and they had to lay hands on their money.

Cole handed the wallet to Pork Chop, who riffled through his cards and cash, saying, "She's your sister?"

Cole and Herta did not look anything like siblings except that each had a cunning nature that lent a cast to their eyes and set their heads at an angle, and these shared traits were easy to mistake for familial bond.

"Thank the man," Madelyn Glancy told her portly pal. Her eyes never left Cole's. "Can he buy you a drink? Your whatever—*sibling*—too. Have I seen you here before?" To Pork Chop, she said, "Put your money away. Where are your manners?" She rolled her eyes for Cole's benefit.

Cole had rolled his first. He couldn't hold it against her. He said, "You guys have room for two more?"

Tariq's First Words to Cole:
"This is supposed to be funny, right?" They'd exited a classroom at the U of Houston, Tariq brandishing *The Importance of Being Earnest.* "Funny ha-ha?"

"It's funny," Cole assured him. "I can tell. Want to help me boost a car?"

"I don't know 'bout that."

"From the faculty lot."

"All right then."

What Cole Speculated about Tariq:
That he never thought twice about anything, and this was his greatest asset.

Herta's First Words to Cole:
"Oh, is this yours?" Her hand was on his wallet. His hand held her wrist. Anvil was happy-hour crowded.

He leaned close. "How many billfolds in that purse of yours?"

"I don't have a bookkeeper," she replied.

He led her to a booth where, after a few drinks, he discovered that her skills were hard-earned. Her résumé included a six-month stint in Shakopee Women's Prison in Minnesota, but she'd never been arrested in Texas, and never anywhere under the name Herta Oberheuser.

Cole had no criminal record. His ID was legit, if odd—his whole name was simply *Cole*. His mother insisted it was all he needed.

"What about your dad?" Herta asked.

"He was in Kuwait when I was born."

"They still alive?"

"They were the last time I saw them."

"Which was?"

"Five years ago," he said. "Maybe six."

"Where'd they move?"

"Nowhere." He named the address of his childhood home.

"That's like a five-minute drive."

"Without traffic. It can back up there because of the off-ramp."

"I've never met anyone like you," she said.

To which he replied, "Let's steal something together."

She counted it as the most romantic moment of her life.

"What's your actual name?" Cole asked before they left Anvil. "Nobody is really named Herta Oberheuser."

"It rhymes with something found in nature," she said.

"Belephant?" was his only guess.

What Cole Speculated about Herta:
That she must have attended college—you couldn't do any-

thing without a degree these days—but not in Houston, which was the only place he knew.

And that she loved him, which meant she'd be loyal. Up to a point.

What Cole Speculated about Himself:
That his only gifts were his looks and charm. And his ruthlessness, he supposed, but this acknowledgment made him feel immodest.

"Vodka tonic," said Cole. "Stoli." To impersonate the wealthy, one had to be picky, but when Tariq returned to say they were out of Stoli, Cole couldn't think of another brand. "Whatever your house vodka is, I guess."

"It's absolutely barbaric," Madelyn interjected. "From reject potatoes grown in Oklahoma or Kansas. Without the best potatoes, you get inferior vodka. Russia has the best. Or Idaho. Which is why the capital of Idaho is Moscow. Oh, don't just stand there, Tark, get the man a Cirôc and tonic—and use your best tonic, Fentimans, if you've got it, or Schweppes from a bottle. A small bottle, freshly opened, not from that abominable squirter."

She continued her monologue after Tariq departed, extolling the virtues of several liquors, many of which Cole knew for a fact were indistinguishable from one another, but he listened and nodded, feigning interest.

Well, he *was* interested, so he was feigning something else.

"This is just what I need," he told her when she finally paused, "someone to give me a clue." He showed as many of his teeth as he thought she could handle, then asked if she knew the way to a person's heart.

"I don't know the way to anyone's *heart*," she said, as if it were an unattractive organ like the bladder or rectum. "Most people I know aim a little lower."

Did that mean they aimed for simple affection? Or the groin? She was hard to read. In any case, she kept talking. Across the table, Herta already had her hand in Pork Chop's hair. A priest sat in the next booth, drinking whiskey, talking to a woman in a dark dress. She might be a nun. Cole wondered if she wore a thong.

"Get me another of these," Madelyn told Cole. Tariq was working both the bar and the tables, which made him slow. "And don't let him forget the lemon peel. I like a good peel, and these guys, you have to watch them or they cheat you."

By *these guys*, Cole wondered as he walked to the bar, did she mean workingmen in general or Pakistanis in particular? Whatever else one might say about Cole, he was not racist. He disapproved of all humanity equally.

According to their research, Madelyn Glancy was amply wealthy now but also heir to the family's money, and her mother had recently kicked. Her father was the only stumbling block, and he was off in Europe—a *grieving tour*, Madelyn called it. The term would trouble Herta but did not interest Cole.

"You want her drink extra strong?" Tariq asked. "Yours extra weak?"

"Just regular," said Cole. "You know the priest and nun?"

"The priest, sure, Father Silverman. I don't think that lady's a nun."

"*Silverman*? He's a Jewish priest?"

"What do I know from Jewish?" Tariq deadpanned. "The woman, take a look when she gets up. She's got a tattoo on her leg."

"Still could be a nun."

"Like it's a Jesus tattoo?" Tariq set the drinks before him and waved away payment. "Add it to my share."

Prior to this scam, Cole had only ever worked one rich woman, a good-looking widow in her fifties. She gave him a watch that he hocked for $750, but the real money came from her checkbook. Herta copied the woman's penmanship perfectly, and they paid off their debts and bar tabs. Cole sent money to a handful of phony businesses that Herta set up online. By the time the woman cut him off, he'd stolen close to twenty thousand dollars. Yet she didn't have him arrested. She could afford financial loss better than embarrassment.

Tedious Madelyn Glancy was worth a great deal more than the Rolex woman. Cole girded his sensibilities and headed back to the table. His was hard work, but it was the life he'd chosen.

"I want you to take this back," Madelyn said after a single sip. "Tell him I can *taste*. I have a discerning tongue and a developed palate. This is *not* Cirôc. He's charging you for the good stuff and pouring rotgut."

"Sorry," Cole said, "I didn't think to track that."

"They're always looking to cheat you," she went on without pause. "Especially to cheat *me*. They think I can afford it, and, big whoop, I *can* afford it, but I don't let it happen. My eyes are like an elephant's memory: they never forget."

That makes no fucking sense, Cole thought, rising, smiling.

"She says this isn't Cirôc."

"She's a piece of work," Tariq replied.

"Pour it into a different glass. Add a dollop of the cheapest shit you've got," Cole said. "Vodka's vodka."

"There you go." Tariq nodded to a departing couple, the priest and woman. The tail of a dragon descended her leg, its body vanishing under her skirt. "Lucky dragon," he added.

"They have forked tongues," Cole replied. "In the Chinese tradition, at least."

"You're a fount all right." Tariq slid papers onto the bar.

"What's this?" Cole asked.

"The report you fucking made me write. I know you can't take it now, but tell Herta."

Cole examined the pages: *Virginia Woolf's Use of Landscape in* Mrs. Dalloway. He shrugged apologetically. "It was the only way to shut her up."

"I want a full third."

"It's three pages."

"Single-spaced."

"Fine, Christ, give me the drink. Wait, did you get this off the Internet?"

"Fuck you. I was an English major."

"She'll know, and she'll have your balls."

Without looking down, Tariq wadded the papers and threw them away. "I still want a third," he said, delivering the drink.

"Then do your work," said Cole.

The party moved to River Oaks. Madelyn's house was not big by neighborhood standards—barely the size of an ocean liner. White columns divvied up the front. Sycamores and live oaks shadowed either side. The living room was roughly the size of a Walmart. Not a Walmart Supercenter, Cole noted, just the ordinary store. They aimed themselves at a cow-colored leather couch as long as a limo.

"A whole herd of Holsteins committed hari-kari to be this family's sofa," Herta said.

"The wealthy have that effect on cattle," Cole replied. "It's why they're forever running for office."

Cocaine on a silver tray passed from lap to lap. "We have different dads," Herta was saying. "I'm an Oberheuser, he's a Cole."

"Herta Oberheuser?" one of them said. "Wasn't there a Nazi with that name?"

"Probably," Herta said. "Our family has long history of betting on the wrong nag." She changed the subject: "Isn't it funny we say *lose* our virginity?" When in doubt, talk sex. Boys loved girls who talked sex. "Like it's a rowdy dog that got off its leash? Should've kept that damn virginity in a kennel."

"How else could we say it?" Madelyn pressed.

"Whopped my virginity upside the head," Herta said.

"Poisoned it," suggested Cole. "Murdered that twit."

Pork Chop's face reddened at the grinding of wheels inside his thick head.

Herta adopted an accent. "Give me virginity da boot, I did."

"Hanged it from a mighty oak," offered Cole.

"I let someone else have it!" Madelyn said, thrilled to contribute. "I let him or her have it!"

Herta smiled and leaned to whisper in Cole's ear. "This is like filching marbles from first-graders."

"Yeah," said Cole. "Fun."

"Did I tell you what happened at Affirm today?" Madelyn asked. Affirm was her gym. She described the day's activities in excruciating detail, a saga that lasted nearly twenty minutes. Summary: she exercised.

They waited until one a.m., then drugged everybody.

Herta helped Cole carry Madelyn upstairs, her arms looped around the girl's knees. They dropped her onto a wide bed in a girly room with Madelyn's name spelled on the wall in seashells.

"Jesus," Herta said, tugging on Madelyn's skirt. "What a narcissist."

"Not narcissism," said Cole. "Egomania." He unbuttoned

Madelyn's blouse. Tariq was right: Madelyn was long in the face but attractive nonetheless. Especially unconscious. Not that it mattered. Cole recognized beauty but could not comprehend what it was supposed to do for him.

"Self-absorption is a classic symptom of narcissism," Herta argued. She tossed the skirt aside and tugged on the woman's panties.

"Narcissists have a delusional sense of grandeur," said Cole. Her bra was the type that hooked between the cups. He unhooked it and pulled one cup free. "Egomaniacs operate from a deep sense of self-doubt and anxiety. She blares her horn so people won't examine what's under the hood."

"Ooh," Herta said, "I like that."

"Don't think I didn't notice the underwear."

"Granny panties," Herta acknowledged. "Don't tell Tariq. It'll undercut my authority." She crossed her arms and studied. "Leaving the bra on is a nice touch. Maybe I'll have Pork Chop's boxers hanging from one ankle."

"That's cliché," Cole said. "It's beneath you."

Herta poked at the woman's exposed breast to measure the wobble. "Enhanced, but nicely done. Top-notch work."

"You can tell by the angle of the nipples," said Cole. "They aim too insistently up. No need to touch."

Downstairs, they separated Pork Chop from the other unconscious saps and lugged him out the door in the direction of the car that answered his key's beep—a Mercedes the blue of an unobstructed night sky.

"I hope we never drop the term *horsepower*," Herta said. She had Pork Chop's feet. "Have you ever wondered how people who live in countries without horses make sense of it?"

"This fat bastard is heavy as a horse." Cole's arms were wrapped around Pork Chop's chest. He had to waddle to carry

the lump. Cole did not like waddling. "There aren't any countries without horses."

"Ethiopia, maybe. The Sudan," she said. "Do they have a
conversion to *wildebeest power?*"

"I don't think wildebeests are found that far north," said
Cole. "More likely to encounter a horse than a wildebeest in
the Sudan."

"You're being intentionally pedantic to squelch my con-
versational gambit," she said.

"Tariq will want to *drag* Pork Chop across the yard to
your bed," said Cole. "Don't let him do it. Make him lift. Mr.
Chop's got to think he walked into your bedroom on his own.
He can't have gravel in his sneakers." Pork Chop's sneakers
looked to be made from the pelts of endangered animals.

"I can handle Tariq," she said. "Don't you fret."

Headlights appeared up the boulevard, a couple of cars ap-
proaching slowly. Cole and Herta ducked beneath the hedge.
Sour sweat from Pork Chop's underarms reminded Cole that
humans were merely stinking animals, which led him to think
about meat. "She really should have provided snacks."

"Tacky," Herta agreed. The headlights of the first car
swept past. "I think we enjoy this—even though it involves
tasks like toting this human tuba—because our shady inten-
tions darken the things we do, and that darkness lends them
weight. Which is to say—"

"Here we go," said Cole.

"Our objectives *mascara* the activities."

"Too girly," said Cole.

"You wear mascara."

"Only when I'm working."

"I'm talking about work," she said. "I'd like to hear you
do better."

Cole sighed. "Each of the stupid things we do with these rich turds is bearable because the promise of money cuts through the odor of shit."

"That's bad in so many ways, I can't count them all," she said. "It's vulgar without being funny. And you can't literally smell money."

With gentleness, Cole set Pork Chop's head on the ground. He took a quarter from his pocket, rubbed it vigorously between his palms, and offered a palm to Herta, saying, "Smells like blood."

It did smell like blood, and something about this made her happy. The effort he made, she supposed. "You're not the perfect boyfriend," she said. "For instance, I know sooner or later you'll decide to kill me." She raised her hands to still his protest. "I'm not perfect either."

The second car turned onto San Felipe and Cole said, "Lift."

"We were going to, *obviously*," said Cole with a soft laugh, "but you were just too drunk. It didn't feel right. Then we passed out."

Madelyn, who'd wakened naked with her head on the Cole's chest, said, "I don't remember . . . Well, I do, of course I do, just not every detail."

"You recall what you said to me?" His full smile was a chasm few heterosexual women could safely navigate.

"Oh god, was I crude?" Madelyn asked, delighted. "Sometimes I can be crude. Crude, crude, crude. Oh, my head, opening my mouth to talk is all I need to send a shuddering pain right through my temples. Here." She touched a temple. "And here." She touched the other temple. "It really hurts and my *stomach* . . ."

"Let me see your head." Cole massaged her temples.

"Oh my," she said of his touch. "Where was I? My stomach . . ." She prattled on.

As it happened, her stomach impressed Cole. The plan called for her to vomit on his chest, putting her in his debt, but she managed to rouse herself and make it to the toilet. The hangers-on—they might still be on the cow-couch downstairs—got knockout drops, but Madelyn and Pork Chop were given extra doses to make them toss. Cole wondered about Herta, confident Pork Chop upchucked on her. She was good with a plan.

"Your hands are so yummy," Madelyn said. "Where was I? Oh, yes . . ." The blather renewed. So far, Madelyn's stomach was the only thing about her he found impressive. "Okay then," she said, monologue running down, "what's this terribly clever thing I said?"

"You said, *I covet you.*"

"I said *that*? I love it! I just adore it! And it worked, 'cause here you are."

"Here I am." His fingers worked her skull.

"I hate it when people are always worrying about money," Madelyn said, brushing her hair, attired now in a peignoir that hazed her body like smog. "Money is overrated."

The brush, he noted, was gold-plated.

He and Madelyn had sex the first time in the shower—a tiled stall the size of a car wash. Afterward, he massaged her back and butt and legs, her head and legs and soles. The second go was on the bed, and—for almost a minute—she lost herself in the act, he could tell. It was noon now, and Cole needed to see his partners. "Can I borrow your Volvo for an hour?"

"It's not a *Volvo*," she said. "Do I look like a mother of

snot-nosed toddlers? It's an Audi RS 7—not a TT or an S5, but an RS 7—a car *built* for the autobahn. Have you ever driven the autobahn? Texas thinks it knows something about speed, but the autobahn, my god, would you believe I cruised at two hundred miles an hour? And it felt like fifty? Smooth as silk."

He did not believe two hundred miles an hour, and *smooth as silk* was a cliché. "Smooth as thirty-year-old Scotch," he appended, teething at her still.

"My dad has *fifty*-year-old Ardbeg, the peaty stuff, which is what he likes. If you like it smooth, we can go to Richard's Liquors on Kirby . . ."

"Dick's Liqs?" began Cole, but she talked over him.

". . . a two-minute commute, tops. I've timed it. Why don't you wear a watch, anyway? As for car privileges—"

"I just want to get clean clothes," he interrupted. "I'll be right back."

The driver's seat of the Audi was softer than his bed, but what difference did a car make, really? Cole was not materialistic. He just liked money.

"How's Miss Bend-n-Squat?" Herta asked before Cole shut the front door. "Off contorting at the gym? Paying to crook her expensive thighs?"

"You're too sedentary," said Cole. "You don't like to think of people exercising."

"Exercise is for people who don't read," she said. "They do nothing of consequence, so they lend meaning to *planking*. The term pretty much sums them up."

"You're formidably sedentary."

"I've never seen you in a gym."

"There's no money in them," said Cole.

"What you guys talking about?" Tariq entered from the kitchen, dressed for the afternoon shift at the Azure Lounge: white shirt, dark pants, thin black tie.

"Work," Herta said. "Madelyn."

"She performs in bed like a porn star," said Cole. It was not a compliment. "Makes stupid faces, ridiculous sounds, speaks absurd banalities."

"*Pound me down like ground round?*" Herta suggested.

"It was the boringest sex I can recall."

"I hate when you say things like that," Tariq said.

"At least she performed," Herta said. "Pork Chop came in my hands. Not that I'm complaining."

Cole produced a single, folded page, and they moved to the desk. Herta scanned the page. She had a talent for forging documents, imitating signatures, pickpocketing, disguising herself, adopting accents. Cole was just good at taking things—like the statement page from Madelyn's bank account, which held $73,987. They would use its corporate logo and page layout in the letter they sent Madelyn, and include her account number, phone number, address, and Social Security number. The letter would announce a security breach. *Do not change your password online. Do not access your account online at all until you have changed your password. Call the automated system to make the change. Speak clearly and follow the prompts. Calls must be made from the number associated with the account.* Cole had already attached a recording device to the phone in question—the pink number in Madelyn's room.

Her father's study, Cole informed them, was locked. Neither he nor Herta knew how to pick locks. He made a mental note for Herta to learn. "When the old man gets back from Europe, he may be in the market for a trophy wife."

"I can do trophy," Herta said.

"We need money now, though," Tariq said. "Didn't you skim their wallets?"

"Those clowns track each penny like bloodhounds after a scent," Cole said.

"Did you mean that to be funny?" Herta asked.

"We have to be patient," Cole said. "See how much Madelyn's good for, and the same with Pork Chop."

"Even *he's* calling himself Pork Chop now," Herta said. "That's how much he loves me."

"I have needs," Tariq said. "Like finding a boring sex partner of my own. And, you know, *food*."

"There's pastrami in the fridge," Herta said. "Jerk off. Make do."

"Anyone in this country motivated by anything but the accumulation of wealth is a chump," Cole said. "Every piece of the culture makes the argument."

"What about that movie we watched?" Herta said.

They'd streamed *Love Actually*. Her choice.

"The cinematography was adequate," Cole said.

"It would've been better with more nudity," Tariq chimed in.

"You didn't see it," Herta accused.

"It's something you can say about any movie."

"It was about *love*," Herta insisted, "not the preeminence of money."

"Yet they all had thousand-dollar haircuts," said Cole, "cute lofts, beautiful clothes. The real message: money matters."

"You're going to wind up cynical if you're not careful," Herta told him.

"Sex is a sucker's game."

"You've really got to think more about your metaphors," she replied.

"It's a means to an end."

"There you go again."

Cole didn't do drugs and drank only in the line of duty. He didn't *get* music. He didn't really *get* sex, either, although he would now and again condescend to screw Herta. What he liked was theft. That and money, but not for what it could buy, most of which did not interest him—simply for the sake of money itself.

Herta liked first-edition books by authors she loved. Ideally with signatures. She also liked good food and nice clothes. She wouldn't mind a BMW.

Cole took one of her books from a shelf. "I do not understand how this brings you pleasure." He waved a first edition of *The Optimist's Daughter*. "You've already read it. Yet you buy a fantastically expensive version because it has a scribbled name that *maybe* the writer put there. It's a fetish."

"How would you rather I spend my money?"

"Give it to me," said Cole.

At the same instant Tariq said, "I'll take it."

"As for you," Herta said to Tariq, "I read what you call an essay. At least you understand it's a great book."

Tariq shrugged. "Not my very favorite, but decent."

"What's your very favorite?"

"*Pet Sematary*," Tariq said.

"Here we go," said Cole, but his phone quieted them—a text from Madelyn: *Let's eat at Uchi!! And then head back to my place for private fun!!!*

"I'd like to shoot her in the head," Herta said. "One shot per exclamation point."

"If you shoot her in the *head*," Cole said, "there's no point in multiple shots."

"Uchi is major bucks," Tariq said, adding: "Get the gyu-toro yaki."

"She'll expect me to pay," said Cole. "How can we redirect her?"

Herta took his phone and wrote, *No to Uchi!!! Can't wait that long to hop into your giant hooter!!!!!!!!!!!!!!!!!*

Cole erased the message. "That she doesn't understand irony doesn't make her a bad person."

"Yes it does," Herta replied.

I've ordered pizza for delivery, Cole typed. *So we won't have to get fully dressed when the food arrives.*

"It's not a cheese knife," Madelyn said that night, after sex but before pepperoni slices, "it's a *rocker* knife."

"Ah, yes," said Cole. "Of course." They stood at the kitchen counter with the pizza box and a round of cheese from her refrigerator. She was unhappy with the pizza. *Everyone in Houston with a palate orders from Pinks,* she'd said. "Anyway," Cole went on, "it's the perfect knife for the Brie."

Madelyn huffed. "It's not *Brie*." Her head quaked with emphasis. "It's *Camembert*." She rolled her eyes.

Cole plunged the rocker knife into her neck. Madelyn's eyes rolled all the way around until they were, at last, staring inwardly.

"She talked too much," Cole explained. He was on the phone with Herta.

"Boy howdy," she said. "Let me tell Tariq. He's scrounging the fridge." Cole heard her call out, "Change of plans!"

A moment later, Tariq's voice at a distance: "Well, crap."

Herta returned. "And now, o wise one?"

"The backyard is the size of an airport," Cole said, "and wild in the way back."

"We'll be there in ten minutes."

"Don't park nearby."

"Twelve minutes."

"There's pizza."

"And *Camembert*," Herta said.

"It's spattered with blood," he said, "but I can carve around it."

"There's something in those bushes," Tariq whispered. They labored near the back wall of the estate, shoveling by moonlight. "I swear to god."

"But you're an atheist," Herta said. "So that means nothing."

"It's an expression," Tariq said, "that indicates sincerity."

"Not if the expression itself is a dishonest representation of who you are."

"Dig," said Cole. "It has to be deep." He dropped a stack of pavers at their feet.

"Look over my shoulder at those bushes," Tariq said. "There's something in there."

The back wall of the estate held dense ground cover and a mad scatter of hawthorns, live oaks, and sweet gums. Cole lifted one of the pavers and flipped it at a pocket of myrtle. A white-faced creature hit the ground without so much as a squeal.

"Eww," Herta said.

"A ghoul!" Tariq whisper-screamed. He jumped from the hole and behind a tree. "What is that?"

"Opossum," said Cole. "I didn't even hit it."

"It's playing possum?" Tariq asked.

"Opossum can't play possum," Herta said. "It's just *doing its thing*." After a moment she added, "I don't like knowing it's alive. So close and all."

"Then we should hurry." Cole yanked the shovel from her hand and headed for the creature.

"Don't kill it," Herta said. "I changed my mind."

Cole sighed. "Sentimentalist." He gave her back the shovel. "This is why you tolerate coarse commercial tripe like *Love Actually*."

"What are we doing with those bricks?" Tariq asked.

"The paving stones go over the body to deter animals from excavating," said Cole. "I'm going to check our work inside."

"It's good," Tariq said. "I've cleaned maybe a dozen crime sites, and except for one, my record's perfect."

"That sentence makes no sense," Herta said, digging. "You can't say perfect *except for*. It's either perfect or it's not."

"What did you miss at the imperfect site?" asked Cole.

Tariq shook his head. "I prefer not to talk about it."

Simultaneously Cole and Herta crossed their arms.

"Yeah, fuck, all right," Tariq said. "I got up all the blood and skull chips and brain goo, but I left one item I shouldn't have, that's all."

"Which was . . . ?" Herta asked.

Tariq shrugged. "The body."

"I think that's called *a significant oversight*," she said.

"It was wrapped in black plastic, and I got used to seeing it, you know? Like it became part of the landscape. I cleaned the holy fuck out of that place."

"But forgot the body," Herta said and laughed. Cole, who rarely laughed, smiled broadly. Herta turned to him. "You ever think how *oversight* has opposite meanings?"

Cole pointed behind them. The opossum was gone.

E-mail from Madelyn to her father:

Dear Dad,
I decided to follow your lead and roadtrip!!!

*I got so tired of my Houston bunch, just like you said I
would!!!*
I've gone to Mexico!!!
I thought about inviting friends but decided to wing it!!!
I'm so brave!!!
I'll write again when I've got a hotel with wifi.
I hope you're feeling better about Mom being dead!!!
Love!
Madelyn

"I think you've slipped into parody," Cole said.

"I'm the one who studied her e-mails," Herta replied.
They strolled through the Plaza de Mercado in downtown
Matamoros, across the border from Brownsville. "Some stuff
you can't parody." She wore Madelyn's big floppy hat, scarf,
and sunglasses, as well as one of her blouses—a distinctive
polka-dot number. She stood in the shade of a palm tree to
take a selfie.

Cole examined the photo and shook his head. "Make the
face," he suggested. "Move deeper into the shadows."

In her passport photo, Madelyn offered a moue—not
to seem pouty, in Cole's analysis, but to give her face more
shape. Whenever Herta showed the passport, she was careful
to make the same expression.

"That's her sexy face," Herta argued, "not for her dad."

"He's seen it a lot, though," Cole said. "He'll assume she's
sending the pic to her friends too."

"I guess." Herta moved farther into the shadows for the
next photo.

In texts to her friends, Madelyn would say that Cole broke
her heart and she needed travel. They were spending from
Madelyn's bank account, using her credit cards. They had

transferred her money to accounts Herta set up, which was how they'd given Tariq his share. "And what if Pork Chop, who's nursing his own broken ticker, texts to say he wants to join Madelyn down here?"

Cole thought for three seconds. "Tell him to bring a lot of cash."

Text from Madelyn to Pork Chop:

> *Laptop stolen!!!!! Everyone here is out to take what they can!!!! Going to dash down to Can in for better ocean. Let's get together when I get back. Just me and you!!! I'm ready to try. Love you!!!!!*

"Going to *Can in?*" Cole asked.

"That's what autocorrect gives you for Cancún," Herta said.

"Nice touch," Cole conceded. "You're kinda dicking with ole Pork Chop."

"I know." She laughed. "It makes me so happy. I've got an even better one coming up for Dad."

"Don't make me read it," said Cole. "I trust you."

Madelyn's text to a girlfriend included a photo that showed Herta-as-Madelyn nuzzling Osvaldo Cuevas, who cleaned the pool at the Hotel Alameda de Matamoros, where Herta was staying. *He's so ethnic!!!!!*

Cole stayed across town at the Best Western. He didn't want the inevitable investigator to hear that Madelyn had come to town with another gringo. "The problem with Mexico," he said, "is I don't know how to steal from people here."

"We don't need to steal from anyone here," Herta pointed out. "We have all we need stealing from Madelyn's rotting corpse."

"Exactly," said Cole. "It's boring."

The plan called for Madelyn to rent a car and drive all the way to Cancún. There, she would e-mail everyone about a jungle trip she was planning with a guide whom they'd make absurdly sketchy. Then the e-mails and texts would stop.

"*Juan* is not a sketchy name," Herta said. "*Adolph* is a sketchy name."

"You can't name a Mexican guide Adolph," said Cole.

"It'll be the one odd detail that'll convince them," Herta insisted.

"Whatever. You're the one who likes to think."

"Are you depressed or something?"

"I'm never depressed," said Cole. "Just bored."

"Here's something that might interest you. What if Adolph holds Madelyn for ransom?"

"Hmm."

They were walking on the beach and the setting sun caught in the waves' curls, shining white within them like oceanic smiles.

"How much do you think we could get?" asked Cole. He took her hand.

Facebook post on Tariq's page:

Any of you guys read Orlando? Gotta wild tranny angle.
I'm on a mad Woolf kick. What should I read next?

PART II

Peaceful Hamlets, Great for Families

A DARK UNIVERSE

BY LARRY WATTS

Clear Lake

Curtis Simon maneuvered his year-old Nissan 370Z into a parking space in the strip center on Egret Bay Boulevard. On the window in front of him, he saw a bumper sticker proclaiming, *Proud supporter of the Clear Lake High Falcons.*

Curtis thought of his days at Clear Lake High, which was three miles from where he sat at that moment. Back in school, he'd rubbed shoulders with the children of astronauts. That was back when it was first announced that Houston would annex Clear Lake. Curtis's parents dragged him to their Saturday marches to voice their objection to the annexation. He was always embarrassed by their activism or anything else that exposed him to public display. The astronauts and their children didn't participate in that sort of things. They seemed to consider it an activity for the lower strata of society. And he'd lived anonymously in that strata, until he met Jennifer.

Jennifer was born in Galveston—born on the island, or BOI, as the locals said—which put her as close to royalty as the local hierarchy offered. She was self-assured and popular. Willing to be and beautiful enough to be the center of attention in any situation. That would create problems for Curtis, though he didn't know it at the time.

They'd met as students at the University of Houston.

While Curtis was handsome enough and excelled in math, he was shy. Jennifer needed a calculus tutor, and he relished the opportunity to share his expertise. They began dating.

After graduation, Curtis landed an accounting job with a prominent NASA contractor. Jennifer skillfully groomed him to become a husband she could control, who would let her lead her life as she pleased. Curtis put his math skills to use in the stock market. Within a few short years, his and Jennifer's financial well-being no longer depended on a paycheck. Until recently, he reflected as he sat in his car, marrying Jennifer had seemed like the greatest achievement of his life.

Curtis reached for the ignition and turned off the engine. He opened the door and unfolded from the low-slung sports car, carefully avoiding the many potholes in the parking lot. He stood at the glass-fronted office in the middle of the retail center that seemed otherwise devoid of tenants. The sign on the door declared in large red letters: *DONOVAN AINSWORTH, PRIVATE INVESTIGATOR.*

Curtis took a deep breath and opened the glass door. A bell jingled, announcing his arrival. There was an unoccupied dusty desk just inside the office. From the looks of it, no one had worked at the desk for some time.

Just as he was becoming uncomfortable standing in the empty office, he heard a toilet flush. A door opened from a narrow hallway at the back of the room. A man about his age, forty-five or so, raised his hand in a half-hearted greeting and walked toward Curtis. The man appeared to have slept in his clothes. From the pained expression on his face, he might have been hugging the commode a few minutes earlier, rather than using it for traditional purposes.

"I'm Ainsworth. What can I do for you?" he said in a hoarse, less-than-welcoming voice.

"My name's Curtis Simon, and I'm looking for help," Curtis muttered as he held out his hand.

Ignoring the outstretched hand, Ainsworth reached for the chair behind the desk and rolled it into an open space before plopping his body into it. "Pull up one of those other chairs," he said, pointing to three chairs positioned in a semicircle in front of the desk. "If you want help, you're going to have to be more specific than that."

Curtis dusted the seat of the chair closest to Ainsworth's and turned it to face the other man. As he sat, he wondered if he'd made a mistake. He felt vulnerable with no desk between himself and the man he hoped would keep him out of prison. He realized, however, based on the detective's greeting and apparent attitude, that telling his story was necessary if he didn't want to be thrown out of the office.

"My wife's been murdered," he mumbled, clearing his throat before continuing, "and I think the police believe I did it." Lips tightened, he studied Ainsworth's face in anticipation of a useful directive.

After a few seconds of silence, Ainsworth leaned back in his chair and asked sarcastically, "So, do you think you could give me a little more detail, or is it all a big secret?"

"No, no, it's not a secret. I . . . I just wasn't sure you wanted to hear more. My wife was shot in the head as she was getting in her car in a hotel parking lot on Bay Area Boulevard. It happened three days ago. The police have questioned me about it every day since. This morning, the detective asked me why I killed her. I'm not a murderer and, if I was, I would never have killed Jennifer. Marrying her has been the greatest accomplishment in my life." Curtis's voice was pleading and his face twisted in anguish. "Can you help me?"

Donovan Ainsworth would take the job, even if the prospective client had only a few bucks, because not one other person had jingled the bell on his front door for two weeks. But Curtis Simon didn't know how desperate he was for a client.

"I'm not cheap," Ainsworth began, "but if you've got a $5,000 retainer, I'll try to help you."

For the first time in the conversation, Curtis showed an inkling of confidence. "No problem, Mr. Ainsworth. Will you take my check?" He reached for the inside pocket of his sports coat.

The two men spent the next hour discussing Curtis Simon's life. Ainsworth learned that Jennifer had an affair less than a year after their marriage and that she'd engaged in several more trysts in the years since. Curtis knew the particulars of some of the conquests. In fact, he'd considered one of the men his best friend. But nothing Jennifer did had been enough to cause him to end the marriage. He loved being married to her. Curtis chose to bury himself in his work in the hope that she would eventually mature and recognize the shallowness of flirtations with other men. He told Ainsworth he believed Jennifer had recently become involved with an astronaut, Brodie Bancroft.

As Curtis walked out the door, Ainsworth glanced at his watch. Still time to get to the bank and deposit the check. He wasn't worried about it bouncing, but about several checks he'd written in the last few days. One was for the office lease. Since he'd been kicked out of his apartment for failing to pay the rent there, losing the office would mean sleeping on the streets.

After making the deposit, Ainsworth returned to his office. Past the bathroom, at the end of the hallway, was a room just large enough for an army cot, a small table with a George Foreman Grill, and a refrigerator, on top of which a microwave perched precariously. Under the table was a cardboard box containing Ainsworth's drinking supplies. He retrieved a relatively clean cocktail glass and a bottle of Scotch. It was Johnnie Walker Double Black, the one extravagance he allowed himself, even if it meant hot checks and no food. At nearly fifty bucks, the bottle was more than twice the cost of what he referred to as bar Scotch.

Sipping the golden liquid at his office's dusty reception desk, Ainsworth spent a few minutes pecking on his computer keyboard and learned that Bancroft had flown on the final mission of the American Space Shuttle program, on the orbiter *Atlantis* in 2011. He was a throwback to the old days, when astronauts were former test pilots—raucous, hard-drinking, and living life as if it would all be gone tomorrow. But *Texas Monthly* magazine had published a profile on Bancroft, noting that he had settled down since his marriage to a Houston socialite.

Two days later, Ainsworth discreetly obtained copies of the reports on the ongoing murder investigation from an old friend who worked homicide cases at the Houston PD. From these, he learned Jennifer was shot with a 9mm pistol. The slug had been recovered in good enough shape to be matched to a weapon, if one were to be discovered. The reports indicated that Curtis had told the detectives everything he'd told Ainsworth, including his suspicions about astronaut Brodie Bancroft. When interviewed, Bancroft acknowledged that he knew Jennifer, but denied a relationship beyond casual acquaintance. Ainsworth concluded that Curtis Simon was the focus of the homicide investigation. There appeared to be no more than a passing interest in Brodie Bancroft as a suspect.

After reviewing the reports, Ainsworth spent a few minutes on his computer and had Bancroft's address. He wasn't surprised that the man whose personality was much like that of the sixties-era astronauts lived in Taylor Lake Village, a small, elite community where some of those older astronauts still resided.

The following morning, he drove to the Village and located the stately lakeside house where the astronaut lived. It was easily worth a million, maybe two or three. He could imagine why Bancroft might want to deny an affair. He had a lot to lose.

As Ainsworth circumnavigated the block to make a second pass by the home, he spotted Bancroft ahead of him, pulling out of the circular drive onto the tree-lined street. He easily identified the astronaut because Bancroft was driving a Mercedes SL 450 Roadster with the top down. His face matched the photo in the magazine article Ainsworth had looked at again just before leaving his office. He fell in line behind the Mercedes.

The driving surveillance was short-lived. Bancroft's sleek convertible pulled into a convenience store/service station at the corner of Kirby Drive and NASA Parkway, just blocks from where he'd spotted the astronaut leaving home. Ainsworth parked beside the convertible and waited for its driver to exit the store. When he returned, the detective approached Bancroft, identified himself, and asked if they could talk. His request was immediately rejected with language that clearly expressed the astronaut's displeasure. The diatribe ended with a threatening demand that the detective stay away from Bancroft's neighborhood and family.

Donovan Ainsworth returned to his office, not shaken in the least by the astronaut's aggressive behavior. He poured a half glass of Scotch and pondered the murder of Jennifer Simon. He was certain that the focus of the investigation needed to be redirected toward Brodie Bancroft. That would require another visit with his client.

"So why do you suspect that Bancroft and your wife were having an affair?" Ainsworth asked as soon as Curtis was seated.

"Two days before she was murdered, I saw them drinking coffee at the La Madeleine Café on Bay Area Boulevard, just down the street from where she was killed," Curtis murmured.

"And . . . is that it?" the detective asked. "Nothing else?"

Curtis looked uncomfortable. "She has a history. I told you that. I just know her. I thought you were on my side."

"Here's the deal, Curtis. There's nothing about Bancroft that has piqued the interest of the police so far. If you want me to try to get them interested in him, I'll have to set up a surveillance on his activities. If I do that, we'll blow through your retainer in a day or two. I'll need another five thousand if you want a surveillance. Even then, I'm not promising you anything." Ainsworth suspected he'd be off the case momentarily, but the retainer he'd already received would keep the rent paid and the Scotch flowing for a month or two. To his surprise, Curtis Simon reached for his checkbook.

"No problem, Mr. Ainsworth. Have you been to the scene of the crime? Would there be any reason to take a look at where it happened? I'm happy to increase the amount if you believe it will help your investigation to examine the parking lot where she was killed. I'll do whatever it takes to make sure I'm not the suspect." Curtis paused with pen in hand, which hovered over the checkbook.

Before he responded, Donovan Ainsworth pondered just how low he'd fallen. His head ached from too much Scotch.

Though he was relatively sure there was nothing in the parking lot the cops had overlooked, especially several days after the murder, Ainsworth knew the words with which he would reply. "Well, if you want an in-depth look at the crime, rather than just trying to get the focus off you as a suspect, that will require more money. Let's say $7,500 additional. That should get us close. I'll let you know if there's more needed."

Curtis Simon wrote the check without comment. As he handed it over, he took a deep breath. "When do you think you'll be able to survey the crime scene, Mr. Ainsworth?"

The detective said, "I'll be out there first thing in the morning, probably before ten. Why do you ask?"

Curtis retreated with slumped shoulders and diverted eyes. "Oh, no real reason. I just feel like I can't get on with my life as long as the police think I was involved."

Ainsworth stood, anxious to get the tortured little man out of his office. He had considered offering him a drink, but decided a quick exit was the better plan. Once Curtis was gone, he could nurse the Scotch bottle the rest of the afternoon.

Curtis didn't need encouragement. He jumped from his chair.

"I'll let you know if there's any progress tomorrow," Ainsworth said, following his client to the door.

The next morning, Ainsworth slept late. After Curtis had left his office the previous evening, he'd finished a fifth of Scotch. He slept until after nine and only woke then because the garbage truck in the alley made a lot of noise emptying the giant container there for his office and other nonexistent tenants.

He prepared a cup of black coffee, topped it with a splash of Scotch, and drove to the hotel identified in the police report, where Jennifer Simon was shot in the parking lot. On the way, Ainsworth thought over his last few years, how he'd gotten to this point. He'd been a young cop in Houston for eight years when he was dispatched to the call that ended his career. The call was made by a mother, concerning the rape of her daughter. When he arrived at the scene, Ainsworth found a mother waiting at the curb with that five-year-old girl. The girl had blood on her legs; her dress was ripped. She stared at him with eyes that said no one was home inside her pretty head. She'd been viciously raped and sexually abused by the mother's boyfriend. He was still inside the house.

Without waiting for backup, Ainsworth had walked into the house, pistol in hand. He found the boyfriend in the little girl's room, beside the bed. A butcher knife lay on the bed, within the man's reach. This memory triggered Ainsworth's hands to clench into fists, and a bitter taste of bile burned his throat. He had raised his pistol and shot the man twice. As the body crumpled onto the floor, Ainsworth used the barrel of his pistol to push the knife off the bed, to the floor beside the man's still body.

The inquiry was over quickly. An older child, the brother of the little girl, had heard Ainsworth enter the house and followed him to the door of the bedroom. Once the boy gave his statement, Ainsworth was suspended from the department. Luckily, there was quite a lot of support for him when the shooting made the evening news.

He made a deal with the district attorney, who didn't want to try a case against a police officer who had shot a pedophile only minutes after the man had raped a child. Ainsworth pled guilty to manslaughter. The little girl didn't have to testify. He received a six-month jail sentence and a short probation. The district attorney was elected to another term without opposition.

After the conviction, Ainsworth couldn't get a private

investigator's license, so he worked under the auspices of an attorney who was an old friend. Even so, since leaving police work, he'd been on a spiral toward self-destruction, pulling himself out of the bottle just enough to survive whenever he lucked into a case. This time, it was one that would pay well. After that, he would drown himself in whiskey until another case came along. Or . . . well, who knew what turns life might take?

He parked in the hotel's lot. Although the shooting had occurred early in the evening, the police had shown a photo of Jennifer Simon to all three desk clerks on shift that day and night. None of them admitted to having seen her before. Ainsworth wasn't sure he would accomplish anything more than adding to the billable hours on his client's tab, but Curtis had nearly begged him to take more of his money, so he'd walk the parking lot and interview the desk clerks again.

According to the diagram attached to the report, Jennifer's car was parked in the middle of the parking area behind the hotel. Ainsworth walked the entire lot and found a quarter on the ground next to a minivan loaded with fishing equipment. But he discovered nothing of interest to the case. He made a pass around the lot's perimeter, which was separated by a thick hedge from another, larger parking area for commercial businesses along the boulevard. The hedge was not well-trimmed; wind had blown newspapers and fast food wrappers against the line of vegetation.

Ainsworth strolled, thinking the grounds crew was shirking its duties. The sun emerged from behind a cloud, and he noticed the glint of an object struck by its rays. He leaned over, pushed branches aside, and discovered a Smith & Wesson 9mm pistol on the ground, next to the trunk of a bush. Looking back toward the area where the shooting had taken place, Ainsworth realized he was as far from that location as one could be while still in what could be considered the rear parking lot of the hotel.

Ainsworth called his friend in the homicide office, told him what he had discovered, and agreed to wait for officers to arrive. Minutes later, a patrol car pulled up. The officer wrote down the information regarding why and how Ainsworth had discovered the weapon, placed it in an evidence bag, and drove away.

There was little for Ainsworth to do on the case until ballistics tests were run. True to his effort to maximize billable hours, he spent the next few days tailing Brodie Bancroft around Houston. Bancroft met no women except at a garden club event where he spoke. He either wasn't a player or had suspended his extracurricular romantic liaisons while the murder investigation proceeded. After a week of following Bancroft for three hours each day and billing for eight, Ainsworth ended the surveillance. It wasn't conscience that prompted him, but boredom with the astronaut's routine.

Two weeks after he found the pistol, Ainsworth sat in his office just after noon, sipping on his third drink as he half-heartedly watched an old episode of *Bonanza* on the television set he'd purchased with Curtis Simon's second retainer. The show was interrupted by a breaking news alert, indicated by the words *Breaking News Alert* flashed on the screen and several beeps loud enough to get the attention of every living thing within earshot, including the cockroaches that had been scampering about the detective's feet.

There'd been a break in the Jennifer Simon murder case. High-profile—some would even say famed—astronaut Brodie Bancroft had been arrested. Officers had recovered the weapon used in the crime and learned it had been purchased by Bancroft several years earlier.

Later, Ainsworth watched the evening news. The astronaut's attorney denied his client had been involved in the murder or an affair with the dead woman. The attorney claimed Bancroft had placed an ad in a local weekly to sell the pistol. He said Jennifer Simon responded to the ad, and they met at the La Madeleine Café to complete the transaction, for which there was no written record.

Donovan Ainsworth garnered some local attention during Bancroft's trial, but squandered it on getting a few free drinks instead of increasing his client list. Curtis Simon reaped much sympathy as the betrayed spouse. Brodie Bancroft was convicted and sentenced to life in prison. The judge gave him two weeks to get his affairs in order before imprisonment. Bancroft's socialite wife filed for divorce.

Ainsworth sent Curtis Simon a final accounting of his time on the case, including his court appearances as a witness. It came out to an additional $2,000. There was no objection.

The morning Brodie Bancroft was scheduled to report to begin his incarceration, his attorney found the astronaut's body in his Mercedes SL 450 Roadster. The suicide note read simply: *I didn't kill anyone. I didn't have an affair with that woman. I will not go to prison.* Ainsworth heard about it from his buddy in homicide.

He drove to a convenience store and bought a *Houston Chronicle*. Back at his office, he read the details of the suicide. After a few minutes of contemplation, Ainsworth called Curtis and asked him to drop by the office.

When the introverted accountant entered the room, he held out his hand in greeting, just as he had the first time the two men met. Again, Ainsworth ignored the outstretched hand and told Curtis to have a seat. Then he began.

"I know what you did, Curtis. You shot your wife with the pistol she bought from Bancroft."

It was impossible to detect any reaction. Curtis's body shrank into the seat as if he were trying to hide, but that was how he'd always sat. "Mr. Ainsworth, I'm surprised you would think such a thing. What would make you believe that?"

Ainsworth noticed, then, just a hint of a smile on Curtis's lips. Or was it a smirk? It was accompanied by a vague sense of self-confidence the detective had barely seen in any of their previous meetings.

Curtis continued: "You have no proof of anything. I will concede to you and only you that I suggested Jennifer needed a weapon for self-protection and showed her an ad in the newspaper. But your accusations are just that. And, of course, I would deny even this conversation, if asked."

Smiling broadly now, the accountant stood, nodded his head at Ainsworth, and walked toward the door. He paused, turned back, and added, "You know, I shouldn't have had to suggest you look at the murder scene. You should have gone there the day I hired you." With that, he was out the door.

Ainsworth walked to his makeshift home at the back of the office and reached into the cardboard-box liquor cabinet.

He'd never regretted killing the abusive pedophile, though it had cost him his career. The little girl's face had been with him every day since. Now, it would be replaced by that of a swashbuckling astronaut.

He poured a full cocktail glass of Scotch, and thus began the rest of Donovan Ainsworth's miserable life.

XITLALI ZARAGOZA, CURANDERA

BY REYES RAMIREZ

Spring

Xitlali leans on the bar at her other job as a Mexican restaurant waitress, five hours into her shift, feeling the bags under her eyes deepen. A customer waves her over to his table, to pay the tab for four margaritas and three cervezas, drunk and alone on a Tuesday at five p.m. He has a sad aura about him, thick and gloomy-colored like cough syrup.

"Ah-kee ten-go el dee-naro."

"I speak English, sir," Xitlali says.

He hands over cash and barely leaves a tip. Xitlali yawns and doesn't bother to offer a blessing, as much as it seems he could use one. *Dios mío*, she thinks, *prayers and alcohol are the two most abused inventions in human history. Any method to not completely accept this reality will do.* That's when the phone in her pocket vibrates. She walks outside and answers.

"Curandera Zaragoza, we have an assignment for you. Es urgente."

"It can't wait?"

"We tried calling other curanderas, Xitlali. No one else wants to touch this."

"Why is that?" Xitlali asks, leaning against the brick exterior of the Mexican restaurant and watching out for her coworkers.

"This client is gay. The other curanderas say they cannot save a sinner from himself. We know it's short notice, but can you take it?"

"Ay, pues . . . of course. If evil does not discriminate, why would I?" Xitlali says as she pulls her notepad from her back pocket. Desgraciadas. "Digame."

"Jose Benavidez has been experiencing a haunting. Says that every night, while walking home from work, there's a presence that follows him. Won't say what exactly. Says he might encounter it again tonight."

"Has there been physical interaction?"

"No."

"Bien," Xitlali mutters, scribbling onto her notepad. She can sense his energy already, tense yet weakened by anxiety. Pobrecito. "I'll be there as soon as I can."

"Bien, bien, bien. Mira, the code is 1448 to get into the gate. Complex is called Cherry Pointe. Apartment 13."

"Gracias. Que Dios le bendiga."

"Que Dios le bendiga, Curandera Zaragoza."

After closing all her tabs and sneaking out of the restaurant an hour early, Xitlali jumps into her 2004 Ford Taurus with over 138,000 miles on the engine and leaves for the complex, fifteen minutes away. The air is thick with blaring lights like cheap knockoff suns. Every stoplight turns red, as though trying to slow her reaching Jose Benavidez. Xitlali uses these short pauses to turn and sort through her messy backseat, littered with clothes, various documents, and crumbs from the many dried herbs she uses day to day. *I gotta make time to sort through all this shit. Always something.* Juan Gabriel sings sadly through the radio.

As Xitlali pulls up to the apartment complex's box to enter the code, she can feel music and taste food grilling. She's so hungry she can't think of the code. Notepad out, she looks for the page, flipping through scribbles on other cases she's solved.

Mayra Montevideo—Heights
Curse from a lover
Space purified with Sage, Oracion

Salvador Trujillo—Midtown
Rashes from bad energy
Recommended oils and scents
Referred to Curandera Gabriela Herrera who specializes
in herberia, Oracion

Muriel Falfurrias—East End
Fevers
Blessed her belongings & space, Oracion

Xitlali gains some confidence, remembering she helped solve these cases and many more in her other notepads. *This will be no different . . . but I have a bad feeling.*

As she parks, she sees where the sounds and smells are coming from. In the apartment complex clubhouse a quinceañera is underway. Xitlali can tell from the strobe lights, cumbia pounding out from speakers, the drunk uncle standing before a grill loaded with carne asada, and a young woman in a light-blue dress with rhinestones lined vertically on the bustier, sequins and pearls in a swirl design on her belly, the gown raining down the rest of her body like thin tissue. Her silver crown peeks out of her hair, styled in a bouffant. *She's gorgeous.*

A grand sadness yearns out of her heart. Xitlali hasn't

spoken to her own daughter in twelve years. She tries not to think about it. There used to be a picture of her daughter on her dashboard, but Xitlali took it down awhile ago, so as not to be reminded. *Bad energy for the job.* She looks at the spot where it was, a patch of plastic darker than the rest of the dashboard. *Twelve years. Not a word. I can't do anything about it right now. Twelve years, carajo.* Her tire bumps into the curb, waking her from her trance.

Xitlali gears up: three vials on a chain around her neck (one full of sage, one of holy water, and one with a tiny doll made of wire and various colors of string), ajo in her pocket, and a case of tools and containers with crystals, holy water, and herbs.

What makes Xitlali special is that she goes deeper than most curanderas. Rather than just addressing the symptoms of a haunting or bad energy, she investigates what caused the problem. Her clients love this about her.

She finds apartment 13 and knocks. She can feel a headache coming on from hunger, and her ankles are swollen from standing around all day.

"Yes?" a man yells from behind the door.

"Xitlali Zaragoza, curandera."

Locks clink sharply behind the door.

"Come in, please," the man says. He's light brown–skinned, in his early thirties.

"Jose?"

"No, he's my partner. I'm Rolando. I'll let him know you're here."

There are unframed photographs all over the walls, ranging from portraits to landscapes to abstractions, some color, some black-and-white. One in particular stands out to Xitlali: a shoulders-up portrait of a young man. He peers at the camera—

beyond it, at you—and his eyes portray a deep lethargy or an accepted sadness. If there's a difference. Xitlali stares into the picture, entranced by his eyes, which are unblinking, watching ceaselessly. *You cannot return the gaze. His gaze has power over you. That is its beauty.*

"Ms. Zaragoza, you like my self-portrait?"

Xitlali looks at the young man in the picture and the young man now standing before her. They are the same person, except that the one before her has eyes and an aura that aren't as strong.

"Oh, yes. I love this piece," Xitlali says.

"I took it after I had a nightmare," Jose says, rubbing his neck with his right hand.

Xitlali pulls out her notepad and pen. "What is this dream?"

"Can we sit down?"

"Yes, of course. But the dream. Digame."

"Why? It's nothing really."

"If you want me to help you, you must answer my questions. Everything I ask, say, and do is to help. Entiendes?"

"Yes, of course. I'm sorry."

"Don't be sorry. Go on."

"It starts with me in a room, surrounded by mirrors. I'm wearing jeans, a white shirt, and these really tall high heels. I'm staring at myself. I can't leave or move, and I work myself up into a panic. Then my father appears and looks right into me. I can't talk. I can't do anything. Then I wake up. It's funny—in that self-portrait, I'm trying to make the face he made in the dream."

"Why do you think you have this nightmare?"

"Well, because it really happened. My dad walked in on me wearing heels and gave me this angry look. In the dream it's more melancholic, but in reality it was rage. Every time I have that dream, it reminds me of how disappointed he was in me."

"Was?"

"We stopped talking when I came out, and he died a few years ago. We never really reconciled." Jose's eyes well up. His partner rubs his back with one hand, but Xitlali can sense anger and helplessness from within Rolando.

Xitlali feels the same sadness from earlier creep up within her. *He must feel awful for never reconciling. It causes bad energy. I know the feeling. Shit, not right now, Xitlali.* She concentrates on the job. There's a lingering feeling of regret haunting Jose. *If I can find a connection, we can finish this quick.*

Rolando speaks: "This all just seems like a lot of nonsense."

"Whether you believe it or not, this is causing tangible pain and dislocation. You dismissing it only feeds the evil power. Your bad energy is wasting our time," Xitlali says. Rolando is startled.

"I'm sorry, Ms. Zaragoza," says Jose. "Rolando doesn't believe in any of this."

"Ya. It's okay. Look, take me to see where this happens. Then I can make an accurate assessment."

As they head to her car, Xitlali sees the party still going. She sees the birthday girl hiding behind a sedan, drinking a beer. She and the girl meet eyes for a second. Xitlali looks away. *You only get one quinceañera.*

She drives Jose to the movie theater where he works, a few blocks away. Its bright lights fight with the night sky, long enough to attract families, couples, and loners to sit in silence together and watch. Jose has explained that he works as a ticket attendant, sometimes as late as one thirty a.m. He walks home alone after, in the odd time before the bars set the drunks loose, but after the certainty of the buses still running, sometimes yes and sometimes never showing up, the homeless sleeping under the bus stop kiosks. Xitlali parks in the back of the theater lot, close to the street.

They walk down Westheimer, a long, long street that always smells of burnt rubber and carbon monoxide, occasionally interrupted by the aromas of foods from all over the world: Mexican, Japanese, Indian, Brazilian, Vietnamese, Chinese, Guatemalan, etc. Passing cars honk and muffled strip club music whispers through the streets. The streetlights produce a yellow glow. As Xitlali walks, she feels the looming sensation that a truck could swerve into them at any minute, or a car could pull up and drunken voices from within call them spics, dirty Mexicans, job stealers, illegals, then step out of the car and ruin you. *A lot of dark energy here.* White bicycles and crosses dot the sidewalks, memorials where Houstonians were run over. *Conduits by which the dead speak to the living.*

"Why doesn't Rolando pick you up from work?"

"He's a bartender," Jose says. *That explains a lot.* "So I walk along this big street, and then I get this feeling that something is following me. I get closer to home, and this feeling of dread fills me."

"And?"

"This little stretch of road that connects Westheimer to my apartment. This is where the thing starts to follow me."

"Have you ever seen it?"

"Yes. It's hard to describe," Jose says, rubbing his head with his hand, trying to stimulate thought.

"Look, I understand it's hard, but I have to know what it is. Otherwise, I won't be able to help you."

"Okay," Jose says, massaging his left bicep with his right hand.

This smaller road only goes a quarter-mile, and it wallows in a murky darkness. Garbage fills the ditch alongside it. The sidewalk is cracked with no indication of future repair. There's no more sound from Westheimer.

"It's when I walk on this sidewalk that I hear them—these footsteps—*clack-clack-clack*," Jose says.

Xitlali can sense the fear running up his spine. Blood rushes into his head, reddening his ears and cheeks. "And what do you see?"

"I'm going to sound insane."

"Mira, I've seen and heard crazy. Digame."

"I-I look back and there's this . . . this dog. A brown-coated, white-bellied pit bull with a human face . . . this face of extreme grief. It follows me, and it's crying. What's making the clacking sound are the heels it's wearing. Bright red heels. It can walk perfectly in them, on all fours. It's sashaying, dancing even, like it's mocking my fear." Jose trembles, a sheen of sweat on his face.

Xitlali nods. "Yes. I can feel a dark presence here. Let me inspect the area." She pulls a flashlight from her bag and uses it to illuminate sections of the sidewalk, like a prison guard searching for a convict. There it is: another white cross, surrounded by McDonald's wrappers, cigarette butts, and tall weeds. Xitlali approaches it and feels her pulse quicken, skin becoming cold. *Yes, this is it.* The cross has something written on it, smudged by time and rain: *Gabriel Mendez.* Xitlali is light-headed from the hunger and humidity and finds it harder and harder to think. *Virgen, ayúdame, porfa. Dame la fuerza.*

"Pues, Jose, I think I know what's happening. There was a death here—an unresolved one. Many dark feelings have lingered here and grown. It seems someone mourned this death for a moment, but not enough to give this spirit peace." Xitlali rubs her temples to ward off the forming migraine. "Could be because people around here move a lot. Or they lost hope."

"What does that have to do with me?"

"You're already spiritually fatigued and carry traumas. That makes it easy for this spirit to feed off your fear and pain," Xitlali says. *I know, joven, because I, too, have a past to reconcile. Who am I to lecture anyone on that?* "You being tired after work and the fear the night instills in you make it easier for this spirit to take advantage. It's why it manifests into our reality, wearing the heels from your nightmare. It knows what gets to you. I will give this spirit peace. However, you have to make peace with whatever is happening in you, or it'll only be a matter of time before something else happens. I can't help you with that, but I know you can do it. You must. Do you understand?"

"Yes. I understand," Jose says.

"Bueno. I need you to help me purify this space."

Xitlali takes the holy water from a vial on her neck and sprinkles it over the cross. She pulls some of the weeds out and collects the garbage from the ground. Jose, as instructed, places candles around the cross and lights them. Xitlali says her prayer: "*May God bless this space, la Virgen ayúdanos, porfa, forever and always, con safos, safos, safos.*" She takes the sage from her other necklace vial and burns it so it emits a fragrant smoke. She hands a piece to Jose, then makes the sign of the cross on herself, thumb touching left shoulder, right shoulder, forehead, and heart, then a kiss to seal it all in.

When they're done, Xitlali can sense Jose's energy lift from his new peace of mind. She has him sign forms and gives him her bill.

Later, after she's dropped Jose at his apartment complex, she sits in her car for a while to write notes.

I see more and more of these crosses along the streets. How many have been forgotten? How many spirits linger within the streets, within their cracks? As more of these traumas happen and stay unresolved, the more these restless spirits will roam within our reality and demand our attention, using our fear and anger. This spirit was more grotesque than usual and knew Jose's traumas, even though Jose did not seem to know the name on the cross. Are these spirits becoming more desperate to agitate us?

Xitlali reaches down to take off her work shoes. She gets another call. She sighs.

"Bueno?"

"Curandera Zaragoza, we have another assignment."

"I can't. I'm exhausted," Xitlali says, running her fingers through her hair.

"This is an emergency. You're the only one who can handle this case."

Puta madre. "It can't wait?"

"It's a woman and her children, and they're desperate."

Evil never rests. I can't turn down a mother and her kids. I wouldn't sleep.

"Digame," Xitlali says.

"Trailer park out near Spring called Strawberry Glen. Contact's name is Petra Ruiz. Three daughters. Recently separated from her husband."

Fucking Spring? "Got it."

Xitlali leans her head back and breathes in deeply. She turns on the car, opens a vial and sniffs the sage inside, rubs the exhaustion from her eyes, and drives. She looks at the road in front of her rather than at the spot where the picture of her daughter used to be.

* * *

During her drive, the purple sky becomes black. Xitlali has never been to this part of town before. She had heard about these recently established communities on the outskirts of Houston, where many Latinx families, immigrants and non-immigrants, settled down to provide underpaid labor and expendable energy to the growing needs of white middle-class suburbs of Spring, the Woodlands, etc. At its outer edge, separated from the rest of the suburb by a band of tall pine trees, is the trailer park where her next client lives. The trailer park is so new that there are still logs stacked from all the freshly cleared trees, and proper streetlights haven't yet been installed. Generators on wheels power scattered lamps throughout the dark plot. Cicadas scream through the hot night. Xitlali can imagine who lives here: the cooks and busboys that work in Spring's restaurants, and the women who clean the mansions and schools. They live close enough to get to work, but far enough for those who benefit from their work to feel safe.

Xitlali drives slowly around the trailers, trying not to linger too much and cause concern. She doesn't have to wander long. A woman sits outside the trailer with her three daughters in patio chairs, weeping, her tears falling into her bowled hands.

"Señora Ruiz? Are you Petra Ruiz?" Xitlali asks, getting out of her car.

"Sí, sí. Gracias a Dios," Petra cries, shaking Xitlali's right hand with both her own.

"Señora Ruiz, por favor, let's go back inside. It's very dark out here."

"No. No me meto con mis hijas. It's not safe in there."

The oldest daughter, around fourteen years old, has a sheathed machete in her lap, the handle resting in the grip of her bitty fingers. She looks restless, eyes peering far into the night and her torso rocking back and forth in her blue pajamas. Her aura is dim and purple. Her sisters are playing near the trailer's little light, shrouded in moths, giggling as they serve invisible tea at a small pink table. Their auras are bright and yellow, oblivious to what's happening.

Xitlali remembers her daughter at that age. She didn't play with tea sets, but collected crystals and spent hours organizing them, naming them, enchanting them, getting to know each and every one. She used to beg Xitlali to bring her more during her supply runs. Then, at some point, she stopped. She turned fourteen and said she didn't want a quinceañera. She would argue with Xitlali about it and give her that look— staring at nothing, especially not at her mother. Once she left a crystal on the windowsill, burning in the sun. That's when Xitlali knew: her daughter didn't want this work. She showed it through little things: not watering her herbs, her crystals gathering dust, her eyes rolling when Xitlali tried to teach her prayers. *Until she left for college. And then, well . . .* Xitlali forced herself to stop this train of thought, pulling out her notepad and pen. *Anyways.*

"Let's begin. The sooner we finish, the sooner everyone can go back to sleep."

"Bueno," Señora Ruiz says. "Okay, pues, let's not talk too close to mis hijas. Mijas, voy a hablar con la curandera. Aqui voy estar. No se mueven de aquí."

"Sí, 'amá," they say in unison.

Xitlali and Petra walk to the end of the trailer. Petra leans against it and takes out a pack of cigarettes. She offers one to Xitlali before putting one between her lips and lighting it with a match. Her aura is thick and pulsating with anxiety, mostly purple and bordered with red.

"Pues, mi marido left about . . . hace two weeks, ya." Petra's eyes fill with tears. She wipes them away and takes a puff of her cigarette. "Y, pues, this started a week after he left."

"What happened?"

"On Monday, I came back into my house after seeing mis hijas off at the bus stop for school. I was getting ready for work, when I felt this presence watching me." Petra takes another drag of her cigarette, her exhaled smoke resembling a ghost's hand moving through the air. The smell of the smoke exacerbates Xitlali's headache. "I couldn't shake the feeling. Like someone invisible was standing in the corner, watching me. I thought I could even see it in the corners of my eyes, sabes?"

"Lo siento, but what do you do for a living?"

"I clean houses in the neighborhood nearby."

"Okay. Go on," Xitlali says, marking in her pad. *Typical work around here, I hear. I've been there.*

"Sí, pues, it got worse as the week went on. While we were sleeping, I'd wake up to hear breathing that didn't belong to my daughters. When I looked into the darkness, the breathing stopped, as though to hide itself. Soon, things started falling off the walls, and I started having these headaches that make me imagine the craziest things, like my daughters dying. Or from back when my own mother was sick—I think about her dying and I can see her right in front of me, dying all over again, with her graying skin and cracking voice. I'm scared it'll get worse. Mi hija, mi mundo, my oldest tonight started crying, and I asked her, *Qué pasa, mi linda?* She couldn't tell me. What if she's seeing the same things? Tonight, she woke up screaming, saying she had a horrible nightmare that she doesn't want to tell me about. I brought the girls out here and called your agency. Ay, Señora Zaragoza, I can't let it get any worse. There's something muy, muy evil in this trailer." Petra's cigarette is now two inches of ash, ready to crumble. She struggles to get another from her pocket.

"And this all started happening after your husband left?"

"Sí, señora. Where is he? He would know what to do. I can't afford to move out of here alone."

"If you don't mind me asking, why did your husband leave?"

"Pues, la verdad es que . . . there's a lot of reasons. He had problems with drinking and he didn't like this place because it's so small, and we started to argue a lot. What made him leave was that I told him my boss, un güero, kissed me and asked me to have sex with him. I said no, of course, but he made me promise not to tell his wife. Yo no digo nada a ella. I don't want any trouble, me entiendes?"

Ah, I see. She's powerless at work.

"My husband told me to quit, but I said that we just moved here. The schools are good in this neighborhood and mis hijas deserve that. It reached a point where, when he got drunk, he would keep bringing it up. He said if I wasn't going to quit or let him confront my boss, it would hurt him as a husband and man. I said no, qué no, and, well, se fue."

Shit. It goes beyond the workplace. The source is her boss, but the chain continues at home. "I see. Bueno, whatever is making you see these visions could be something strong at work. I will investigate. Your husband may be involved. You don't know if he's come back? Like while you are at work?"

"I wouldn't know. Mis hijas stay with a neighbor until I get home from work at six en la noche."

He can come and go as he pleases. "Okay, I'm going inside."

Xitlali enters the trailer. She turns on the light and it gives a yellow tint to everything in the room. The trailer is small:

a kitchen area with a sink, table, and hot plates; living room area with a love seat, shag rug, and HD television; and the bedroom area where futons and blankets are spread across the floor, disheveled from sleep. Xitlali sees that all the pictures on the walls are warped and worn, and all the crosses look loose, ready to fall. *The good thing about this case is there isn't much to inspect.* She's tempted by the tortillas on the counter and the soft blankets on the floor. All the day's fatigue spreads through her muscles and bones like a possession. She has the urge to sit down, just for five minutes. *Get it together, floja! Porfa, ayúdame Dios.*

In the bedroom area, Xitlali feels a presence—a strong energy pushing against her. The energy travels up her arm, into her head, as though someone put a wet cloth on her brain. *Not good at all. I can see how they get visions. To someone not ready for this, it'll cause some bad shit. I have to find the source.* Xitlali looks under the futons and on the walls to see if there's any point of connection for a spirit or a conduit of evil energy. *Right there!* On a wall next to the futons, there is a hanging black-velvet blanket with a snow tiger majestically standing at the top of a mountain. Xitlali notices a bulge near the bottom, where the blanket meets the floor. She lifts the blanket and sees an egg.

The egg is white and seems to be breathing, the shell straining and relaxing, almost seeming to emit a wheezing sound. Xitlali taps on it, and a muffled sound resonates. She grabs the egg and its shell seems to stiffen, as if it doesn't like being touched. It feels less like a shell than a layer of warm skin. *What the hell is this thing?* Xitlali picks at the shell. The white peels off and the egg begins bleeding. The egg's energy surges through her body. *Fuck!* She feels it release more energy. She can't fight it . . .

I can see someone, off in the white distance. It's my daughter! I see her as she is now. She's so gorgeous. Her brown hair is long, reaching down to her lower back. She's aging like me, Dios mio. I don't miss her father's nose. She's wearing nice jeans and a green sweater. Ay, she's always wearing the wrong thing! It's summer! Ay, mija, why do you always wear a sweater in the summer? Pues, I guess it doesn't matter. She's here! Mi vida, she's here! She seems to be talking to people. I'm going to walk up to her and surprise her. Mija! It's me! Tu mamá, la unica qué tienes, mi vida! Dígame! Tell me everything. Oh, how I've missed you. Digame todo. Qué pasa? What are you doing now? Where do you work? Where do you live? Are you seeing anyone? You're not married, are you? And your studies? Hey, por que . . . why are you looking at me like that? That's no way to look at your only mother. Twelve years and this is how we start? No me mires asi. Mija, where are you going? Where have you been? Please, mija. Don't go. If I reach out to you, will you hold me? I'm trying to hug you, mija, but you only go farther away. Please stop looking at me like that. Please stop going away. I can't take it. No seas cruel, mija. I can't see your face. I can't. I can't—

Someone bangs at the trailer door. Xitlali opens her eyes and finds herself lying on the floor, on the blankets.

"Señora Zaragoza! Is everything okay?"

"Yes!" *How long was I out? Holy shit, that was strong.* Xitlali sits up and rubs the tears from her face. She sees the egg lying where she dropped it, on the blanket next to her. *Whoever did this really wanted this family gone.*

She takes a pair of tweezers from her bag and uses them to remove the tiny doll from the vial on her necklace. She places the doll on top of the egg, says a bendición, and gives the doll time to absorb the egg's energy. Then she burns sage near the doll and egg. The smoke surrounds the egg but doesn't touch it, pushed away by dark energy. Xitlali waits a bit, then uses the tweezers to pick up the doll and hold it near the burning sage. Like the egg, the doll repels the smoke. *The energy transfer was a success.*

She puts the doll back into the vial. She puts the egg in a black pouch with sage, rosemary, and hierba santa. She blesses both, egg and doll.

As Xitlali steps out of the trailer, she thinks about advising Señora Ruiz to leave. But she knows that if the woman could do so, she would've already. There's no use telling her the obvious. *There's only so much we can come to terms with. Así es . . .*

Instead, she says, "Someone cursed an egg and placed it near your beds, Señora Ruiz. It was a strong curse, done by someone either inexperienced or evil. Your daughter must have slept too close to it tonight, causing her nightmares. I got rid of it, but someone put it there. I don't want to say it's your husband, but that's the only person I can think of. He may have paid someone to place the curse. I don't know. What I'm saying is, it's gone for now, but he might do it again. You need to talk to him and tell him he's hurting your daughters."

"Thank you, Señora Zaragoza. Gracias, gracias, gracias," Petra cries.

"Claro, señora. Bueno, let's all get in a circle." The family gathers and Xitlali has them clasp hands. *Do they know any of this? Is it better for the little ones to not know? Perhaps if you don't believe in these things, they have less power over you. Maybe it's best if my kind die out. Ay, mija . . . maybe you were right.*

Xitlali recites the prayer: "*May God bless this house, la Virgen ayúdanos, porfa, forever and always, con safos, safos, safos.*" She tells Señora Ruiz how to purify the trailer with sage, hierba santa, and rosemary, every day, for as long as they have to live there.

Señora Ruiz signs the standard form for purification services and pays the bill in cash. "Gracias, gracias, curandera. If it weren't so late, I'd invite you in for café."

"'Sta bien. Take care of your hijas. Their fear only provides more dark energy for evil spirits. Love them. Dales todo."

"Claro que sí."

In her car, Xitlali watches the Ruiz family walk back into the trailer, one by one. She wonders if they will be safe.

Her gente, spreading into spaces where they weren't allowed before. Opening new traumas and wounds that will take years and lifetimes and generations to even diagnose. New manifestations of spirits, dark energy, and evil entering into our reality, evolving within these transitions. Then comes the work of accepting past truths. Reconciliation. She will always have work. There will always be a need for her services.

I'm so tired.

Xitlali drives back into the city on the great spine of the freeway that connects the suburbs, where people like her work and clean, to the skyscrapers, where people like her work and clean. The drive feels like a dream, the passing billboards and landscapes acting as newsreels for the imagination. Over yonder, the light from the sleepless metropolis fights with the darkness of the cosmos above.

Xitlali will drive these freeways many times over the coming years. She will take her daughter's picture from the glove box and tape it, again, to her dashboard. It would behoove her to come to peace with herself, her past, with what she's done. That's another story. For now, Xitlali Zaragoza, curandera, will rest as much as she can until her next assignment.

PHOTO ALBUM

by Sarah Cortez

Downtown

There's a place I remember perfectly without a photo. A hotel lobby, with its shabby wingbacks and dirty octagonal floor tiles just inside the wide doors. Dust motes circling in hot afternoon air. The smell of chlorine on my skin as I walked from the car through the broiling downtown sidewalks' reflected heat. The stolen keys in my pocket. Hot metal grazing my thigh at each step. I was crazy with longing, crazy to feel his quick rise. He wasn't there anymore. That's what the old clerk at the front desk said, his eyes going too bright, going down to where they shouldn't. *Okay,* I said. *Okay.* I wasn't going to die.

This picture is the new house Dad bought us, close to the airport, near his work. A bare yard with no trees, scattered grass; a neighborhood with almost no people. My small tan-and-white dog dead of a broken heart. Old English. A clean pad of concrete for a circular patio in the back. A built-in vanity for Mom with two shades of brown tiles shaped like leaves. Daddy also bought Mom a new car. For her long commute—too long to ride the bus anymore, as she'd always done. She didn't even try to plant flowers in the flowerbeds this time.

He wouldn't let me take a photograph of him. Once I even brought my Instamatic upstairs to his room. Late-afternoon sun across the short golden hairs of his belly. Sparks of the sun's fire in each lower curlicue. His blue eyes blazing with a light I couldn't define and didn't need to. Sheets pushed off the foot of the bed, onto a dismal braided rug. Strong, tanned fingers girding my pelvis. Wordless time spent with a man who didn't need words to convince me to be with him. I remembered him from before, when he'd worked for my dad doing yardwork, then at the airport hangar. *You gotta give people a chance*, Dad liked to say. *Everybody deserves a chance.*

Oh, that's Frankie Petras, the boy I had such a crush on back in grade school. We were both so shy. He had blue eyes too. He never would've asked me to steal. I think the only conversation we had in twelve years of grade school was the day Kennedy was shot. We talked by the bike racks after school, where we'd prayed for hours for a miracle. We prayed until they pronounced him dead—the man we'd seen the day before at Rice. Frankie started crying—a thirteen-year-old boy crying in public—as we stood holding our bikes. I stood mute, watching fat tears squeeze from under eyelids he tried to shutter with a thumb and crooked index finger. A few moments later, he turned without a word, undid his bike lock, and pedaled away without once looking back. His body, a slender torch burning, consumed by grief and betrayal. At home that night, none of us could speak of it. And what would've been the point? There were no answers to the whys. Nothing beyond our sadness and loss.

Our confirmation class between the front pillars of the church. After Mass, the men talked in groups, without their wives and kids. Clean-jawed, still-athletic World War II vets like my dad. Grim and silent, they returned to walk us to the cars. Every Sunday became a litany of defeats—more families driven out by the blacks as they block-busted South MacGregor, someone's watch dog murdered, the Sakowitz mansion sold for pennies. You see, even the Jewish families moved out, fled to Braeswood. Mom would try to talk about something cheerful as we drove home. Beneath her summertime straw hats, I'd see her forced smiles in Charles of the Ritz's reddest lipstick. Only grunts from Dad's side of the car, if that much. We started going out for breakfast after church, instead of cooking at home like we'd always done. The smell of pancakes and bacon frying in cast iron no longer felt safe. Anything could happen, at any moment.

I wish I had just one photograph of our old neighborhood before all this started: The enormous white antebellums along Braes Bayou, with acres of undulating beauty beneath long-armed oaks. The large yards, restful. Every spring, I waited to glimpse the azaleas—a six-foot-tall solid wall of vibrant pink next to the long white porches. We lived several blocks south of there, in the middle-class section where all the streets were named after the South's beauty: Charleston, Tampa, Shenandoah, Allegheny, Ozark.

Near the end, I couldn't walk half a block down our street to my friend Miriam's. Mom still hadn't learned to drive and refused to go to the neighborhood grocery without Dad. Her lips were pursed and eyes serious all the time, especially when she thought I wasn't watching. When Dad got home from work, he wouldn't drink his highball. *I have to be ready*, he'd say. *I don't know when they'll come.* The voices who called us at night had promised rocks, firebombs, bullets. The voices of people we'd never met. Did we pass them at the grocery store on

Saturdays? Did we sit with them on the downtown bus? Were these the husbands and sons of the black ladies who called me *honey chile* and smiled in radiant friendship while patting my cheeks?

I don't have an outside photo of the place he lived. A run-down three-story hotel downtown on Caroline. Painted-over yellow-brown brick. Squares of glass windows on the first floor as if it had a diner inside. Red neon on the outside advertising *Pecan Waffles* in block letters—food that didn't exist. That wasn't why I stopped. His room was on the second floor.

His strong, sinewy arms were perfectly tanned. Nails split from the yardwork, the lawn mowers and the tools. But always clean khakis with a crease when I was there. A thin belt around a trim waist. An ease of movement that, even back then, I would've described as graceful. Calm. Purposeful. Never rushed. A strong tongue. The barbed wedge called loss cutting into my sternum from underneath, where no one could touch its excruciating facets—not even him. Besides, we didn't talk much. That's part of why I remember so clearly when he told me to get a copy of Mom's car keys—both of them, ignition and trunk. We could drive to his folks' farm— farther south, near Victoria. He'd introduce me to his mom. I'd just have to make up a reason to get away for a Saturday. I did sports—it'd be easy. *Piece of cake.*

Those damn high school photographs. Crooked grins and a patchwork of colorful optimism and plans for bright futures, full of achievement. The hidden truths of hatred and fear I'd learned during that last year in our old home. All of it swallowed but stuck partway down your gullet. Terror that what you retched up would be your heart. The one thing you wanted:

to be truly dead so you'd forget all those childhood things you loved that had been taken away by people you didn't even know well enough to hate. Your heart, the only thing you'd convinced yourself you could kill with no one noticing.

See how straight my mother is standing? That strained smile. In every photo. That ugly wood paneling we thought was so modern. I showed him that photo once—our little family in the new den. Behind us, the gilt-edged rows of the World Book Encyclopedia stand at attention. He kissed me up the side of my face while extracting the photograph from my fingers. *I'm your whole family now.* Then he pushed me back on his bed and raised my skirt, lowering his lips to where they always went the second I was inside his room. *I'm your everything, remember?*

Yes, yes. I always said yes.

Oh, that was our dog at the new house—a hunting Lab for dad. He was a sweet dog—born during a norther in February at the first house. Four of the litter froze to death before we could get a heater into the garage for them. I got home first and could've saved them, but I was scared of the mewling puppies and couldn't face the blood leaking everywhere in heavy clumps. So I didn't go closer—just shut the wooden door and walked back to the house. I sat in the empty house listening to the sleet hit the windows. Too old for dolls, uninterested in reading books, I just sat in the kitchen watching the grayness outside. I didn't call anyone for help.

One of the pups who survived became Dad's. They spent a lot of time together on weekends—gone to the hunting lease. In the evenings, after work, Dad would toss a burlap dummy for the dog to retrieve in the narrow backyard of the new house. The dog always eager, no matter how many throws or how much slobber trailed down his glossy black fur. Dad was silent in the evenings, always silent by then.

This photo is back at our first house—the one we had to leave. Those flowerbeds were wrested from Houston's famous black gumbo. Bright-headed hydrangeas, lavender and light blue, coaxed into bloom. Mom and I on our knees weeding every Saturday afternoon. There's no photograph of Mom pulling weeds and crabgrass in her sweat-soaked pin curls. We only took pictures on Sundays, after church. That one day full of photogenic smiles and homemade pancakes, hot syrup and leisure. Even that one day ultimately wrecked, like all the others, by the cruising cars of men with two-by-fours and baseball bats.

The last Easter in our little house, in the front yard by the big picture window. Remember Jackie Kennedy and her color-coordinated pillboxes? Mom let me pick out a white one with a short veil. I still have it. The dress was also white. A square neckline showing my tanned collarbone. At thirteen, I had a collarbone like the First Lady's—elegant, bones showing nicely. That's what Mom said. She also said I was *beautiful*, but I knew it was the lie of a fond mother. Hopeful too. Above all else, hopeful. *Boys your age are intimidated by your looks—that's all.* I was surprised when she said this. No one ever asked me out on a date, so she couldn't be right.

I don't remember posing for that Polaroid. It must've been taken by Pat, the girl who lived next door. She was a few years older than me. She loved to come over in the evenings with that camera while Mom fixed dinner. But this one was taken during the day. See, I'm holding a beach towel and leaning on the gray tiles of the kitchen bar. I tanned like it was a religion. Oiled and glistening, I became a long stretch of sweaty muscle. I remember being proud of my flat brown stomach. Green beans for dinner—that's how I did it. Metrecal cookies at lunch—nine of them in a packet of crisp cellophane. For days on end.

Here's another one of the front yard, from farther away. That other picture window was the dining room where I did homework every night in grade school, until Dad said I had to sit in the kitchen, farther back in the house. The phone calls were bad then. The blacks wanted us out. Threats in a deep bass voice: *We gonna burn you out. We coming tonight.* Mom didn't cry, not that I saw. But every meal was ushered in by her urgent questions: Had any *For Sale* signs appeared on our block? Had I been threatened walking to or from school? What were the next door neighbors doing? Hard-eyed, Dad promised we wouldn't sell. He promised. I kept quiet at dinner and lingered in other rooms whenever the telephone rang. The one time I heard a man's voice full of hatred was enough—his voice reverberating inside my bones, permeating the marrow. It was a thick voice, full of intention and spite. I put the phone into its heavy black cradle slowly, so he wouldn't know I was scared. No point to crying. No one had answers to the questions I could barely think clearly enough to ask, but that always hung in the air: *Why do you hate us? What have we done wrong?*

That one is out of order. Me, a fat baby. I look like my dad's father—bald, same shape of head. See how I'm straining toward the edge, off the gray countertop? I knew what I was doing; I wanted to step off. Bright air would hold me—I was sure of it.

* * *

In the background of this photo, you can see a large picture window, off-center to the left. My first bedroom to myself. A reward for turning thirteen. It hurt to grow breasts, remember? That embarrassing growth of new hair that felt every breath of breeze, every sashay of fabric across its light-brown fineness.

From the front yard, you can't see the gardenia bush, tall as a man on the side of our little house, just beyond my screen windows. At night, in early summer, the scent as heavy as a wrestler on my chest. White waxy flowers fragrant enough to eat, whispering all their secrets into humid air. The night's friendships between creatures of earth and grass, air, and bayous were heard in a long murmur of comforting sounds. I missed that in the new house—the sound of night. A/C shut off everything.

Mother's mahogany vanity in our little house. The curved front and large round mirror. I'd wait for impenetrable darkness in my still bedroom, decorated in my favorite colors—a splurge after turning thirteen. June bugs crawling on the screens, gardenias outside spreading their white lips. My hands on my breasts and nipples eventually became his hands. I'd raise my baby dolls and throw off the sheets. Dream his lips, recall his blue eyes. Shame, the greatest catalyst; and the forbidden geometry of a grown man, the most irresistible attraction on earth.

That's Mom's brand-new Olds in the driveway. My dad only bought Oldsmobiles, and he only bought green ones. I stopped by a hardware store on Telephone Road to get the keys copied. Then I hid them in the piano bench. Every time we ate dinner, I waited for my mom to ask me why I had an extra set of her car keys. After all, she handed me her only set to drive to school when I needed them. I couldn't figure out a good lie. The only truth I knew was his mouth on the mess of fine hair he loved. A ceaseless tongue.

Yeah, that's my new school, after we moved. A tedious commute through Houston's small Downtown, then west, out 59 South. We'd just left our little house. Found a newly built one farther out. Cute freshman beanie, huh? For those days, twenty-three miles each way to high school was long. I did okay at first, but then I started failing. Me, the honor roll kid, failing: algebra I, world history, and British lit. Mandatory tutoring after school—I couldn't see him on the way home anymore. Mom arranged carpools with older girls, so I could stay late at school. *Pecan Waffles* winked at me in red neon along Caroline every afternoon as I sailed past in some preoccupied upper classman's car. I dug fingernails into my palms so I couldn't feel what I was feeling. His window was always open, one panel of limp curtain hanging out into Downtown's exhaust fumes. Those seniors were all in love with serious boyfriends they only saw on the weekends—we were an all-girls school. We sang along with the Beach Boys on the radio, and I pretended my ideal boyfriend would be a surfer like them—blond, cute, plenty of freckles, and tiki-god cool.

End-of-year swim party in May. Country club pool. Our two-pieces, so daring. We're all holding in our breaths trying to look thinner. Guess I liked bright colors—look at the hot pink against neon green and white stripes.

That day, alone, I stopped by his hotel. The damp swimsuit kept me sweating and on edge. The stolen keys were in the left front pocket of a seersucker cover-up. My hair, still wet from the pool's shallow end.

I'd been planning what to say, what to do, but I hadn't planned for the old clerk's drooping shoulders and brutal, hungry eyes. I hadn't planned for a turning away of all my precious treasure.

He done gone, and be glad of it, girlie.

He had to be upstairs. I was sure of it. How could he not be? It had only been three and a half months. The cracked linoleum on the stairs beckoned. The loud horns of outside traffic scraped at my skin. Flies buzzing against the sunny front windows worked at breaking through their dirty glass prison. But I was impaled by the fierceness of the old man's voice, the insult of his frank stare at my damp crotch. All this told me what I already knew—my time here was over. No need for the lie already in place, about the softball training camp this weekend. No drive south, my legs sprawled across the front seat and his right hand laced in the hair between my legs.

I walked back to the sea-green Olds parked at the curb. I looked up at the disgusting pink curtains one last time. The keys clinked in my flimsy pocket. Before I cranked the ignition, I sat up straighter. Mom's words floated through my head: *Smile, honey. Don't scowl. Through thick and thin, keep smiling.* I punched the radio buttons and kept the music loud all the way home. *Piece of cake, little rake.*

This photo he never knew about. His empty hotel room. A room where we stopped time. One wooden chair, painted blue. Smudged panes of glass on western-exposure windows— two of them looking out on tar-papered roofs dusted with pea gravel. Dust motes. Awful pink curtains blowing in the breeze. A mattress covering a box spring that looked like someone had been murdered or given birth on it, with blackened stains dripping down one side and at the foot.

For years, I dreamed of his family's house—the one I never visited. He's driving. He parks the car on an oyster-shell road and we cross sunlit weeds toward a small white clapboard. A shaggy farm dog barks, displaying ferocious little teeth, then relents and shows his belly. As we get closer, the sky darkens. He reaches the front door and opens it while grabbing my hand and tugging me forward. I walk inside, and it's my childhood home—the home we loved more than ourselves. The unadorned walls and hardwood floors. The pale-green net curtains in the sunroom that float in afternoon breezes while I nap. In the backyard will be the rosebushes whose flowers are crushed red velvet, full of scent. The garage will contain the small tan-and-white dog's bed and Dad's decoys for duck hunting. Dark green 7-Up bottles—ready for Dad's nightly bourbon and 7—will stand in emerald beauty in rows of wooden cases. Dad will be there, whistling as he putters in shirts the same pale colors of his eyes—greens, blues, and grays. At the end of the street will be the weeping willow. Its green-gold leaves trailing the ground, the parchment where we kids write our giddy pleasure, walking home from school each day.

No one can find me. I won't ever have to leave.

PART III

MINUTES FROM DOWNTOWN AND NIGHTLIFE

PART II

WHERE THE ENDS MEET

BY Deborah D.E.E.P. Mouton

Acres Homes

The fridge is empty. Nothing but an expired jar of mayonnaise and a half-eaten box of baking soda at the back of the icebox. I have $14.38 in my bank account. I'm praying that a check I wrote for the light bill doesn't clear for a few more days, and the disconnection notices are stacking up. I haven't worked in almost a month. Ever since The Dump opened a new location down the highway, the furniture store I drive for has had a hard time keeping up sales. No sales, no need for a deliveryman.

I try to make ends meet by picking up odd jobs. I worked for a bait-and-tackle store for a while. I loved being near the water. It made me feel like I was doing the Lord's work, like one of the apostles in the New Testament. But eventually, the long commute to Galveston killed me. Some days, I deliver feed for local farms north of here. Other days, I use my box truck to haul books for the Shepard Library. It never pays much, but it's kept my belly full . . . until now. I've always depended on community referrals for my next job, and I recently got a tip that this new restaurant may be looking for a deliveryman.

I lace up my Adidas. I put on my last clean white tee, though clean may be relative, slide on my black hoodie, and grab my keys. I jump in my truck and say a quick prayer that they're launching a catering business. Yeah, that would be steady work. I could see myself making big deliveries on Saturdays before the game or Sundays after church. My mom raised me to believe that God would provide for me.

Just off the feeder road of I-45, I see it. A building with boarded-up windows and graffiti gang tags, but the presence of cranes and dumpsters makes me think it may be under renovation. I park in the empty lot. I think this building used to be a Frenchy's Chicken—the one my mother used to go to on her way to Bush Airport. It still has the weathered yellow-and-teal awning outside and I'm sure it still reeks of stale grease. Next to where I've parked, there's a single black truck near the service entrance. It isn't big enough to haul nothing—it's one of those just-high-enough-to-not-drown-when-the-service-roads-flood trucks. To each his own. This is what it's come to. I say another prayer that He'll make some money show up, just in time, like he's done for me so many times before.

I exit my truck and try to find an unlocked door or a welcoming face. I tug on the service entrance—no dice. So I head for the main customer entrance. Before I get there, I hear keys jingle around the corner. I follow the sound to an old Cajun pimp-looking, redboned man trying to open an emergency exit door near the drive-thru. We lock eyes, but before I can say a word, his brown hands turn into a nervous frenzy and he darts for the back of the building. I chase after him, trying to explain that I just want to discuss business. I lose him for a moment, then hear something bang into the industrial dumpster. I slowly approach and look behind it and see the man cowering, his hands up in surrender. I guess the sight of a large blue-black man in a hoodie in the middle of January is still frightening, even at two in the afternoon. He just keeps repeating in a thick accent, "Please don't hurt me. I'll get you the money." I should've known then that something wasn't right, but the rumble of my stomach drowns out any sensible logic.

I explain, "Sir, my name is Jamaal. I live down the street and am looking for some work. I have seven years of driving experience and—"

"Did Daveon send you?" he interrupts.

"Who is Daveon? I just heard you needed a deliveryman."

"Oh. Uh . . . sure!" he says. He seems to be gathering his dignity as he stands up, wipes the tears from his eyes, and straightens his dress shirt. "I thought you were someone else. I'm Mr. LeFleur. I'm the owner here. We can go discuss it in my office."

He grabs his keys from the ground and heads back toward the emergency exit. When we enter the building, there's this weird smell. It takes me back to the sea, but this time something about the familiar stench is off. It reminds me of the fish spot that went out of business by the old community center on Montgomery. Someone was always getting sick from their food. One too many cases of food poisoning and the city shut them down. It's a strong, pungent odor that almost knocks me off my feet. I search for the source as I wobble behind the counter, through the empty kitchen, to a small office near the back.

He tells me I can have a seat at his desk and I plop down hard, trying to regain my balance. His office is composed of a large mahogany block with stacks of papers overflowing off every side. He tells me to excuse the mess. He explains that he has a large shipment coming in, and all of this is the paperwork he has to file by the end of the week.

"So what exactly do you specialize in here?" I inquire.

He rolls my question around in his mouth for a second

before replying, "We provide an exotic experience for some of the top foreign executives. You know, the Fortune 500 types. We deliver some of the most delicious cuisine for every palette. Ever worked with that type before?"

"No," I reply. "But I don't think it'll be a problem. What's the pay?"

"We pay by the delivery. Three hundred dollars a load, and we pay out at the end of every week. Would that work for you?"

He must not be able to smell the desperation on me through the other nose hair–singeing aromas in the air. I ask how soon they're looking for someone, and he tells me that they need someone to start this weekend, when the shipment comes in. It sounds perfect. I'd be able to work a long day and get some extra money before the lights are cut off. With any hope, I might even be able to afford a case of beer. I tell him I'll take it. He says he'll see me Saturday around three p.m.

I borrow twenty dollars from my mom to get me through the week. She's just happy I have a new gig in the works.

Over the next few days, I try to conserve my gas, only venturing out when I need to. I pass the restaurant a few times. There are never any additional vehicles around. There are no signs that the renovation is progressing. With the holiday coming up, maybe they're on hiatus. As long as they make sure I stay paid, they can look however they want. I wonder if it'll be enough to get the used Cadillac parked in front of Mr. Johnson's place over on Bradmar. I bet I could even put rims on it. Something real clean.

Saturday finally arrives, after a night of me barely sleeping because I'm excited about the new job and the easy money. I got a text this morning telling me to drive my truck to the restaurant for pickup. While two men load supplies into my truck, Mr. LeFleur brings me back to his office to fill out some standard paperwork. I wait in the hall while he finishes up a phone conversation. I hear him yelling and the smell of raw cod starts to swell again. Just before I pass out, he pulls me into the room. He explains that I'll be carrying *precious cargo* and gives me a slip with an address to take the delivery. He says the package will need to be handled delicately. I'll have his two men riding with me: one in the cab next to me, and the other in the back with the delivery. He tells me I'll back the truck to the loading dock at the delivery address and allow the other two guys to unload it. He instructs me to stay in the vehicle so we can get back on the road as soon as possible. "Time is money," he insists. If that means squeezing in additional deliveries today, I'm down for whatever weird procedure he has in place. I just want to make sure I'm not sharing my three hundred with these other two musclemen. He assures me I'm not.

I head back to my truck. One of the men, who speaks in nothing more than grunts, is already sitting in the passenger seat. He has a large tattoo on his face and answers to the name Slim. He's anything but slim. His weathered jeans and wifebeater under what seems to be an old-school Members Only jacket look like they're going to bust out at any second. The other man is much more refined. He has on a navy suit and carries a large metal briefcase. Since he never gives me his name, in my head I just refer to him as Suits. It isn't until I see Suits that I start to think I might be getting into something illegal. I joke with him that he looks like he's dressed for a massive drug deal. He laughs. I don't know if that makes me feel any better.

The drive is only supposed to take an hour, round-trip.

The address is off Richmond, near all the great nightclubs and high-end restaurants. Makes sense. I turn on some music on the way there, thinking it'll help Slim open up. He just grunts, shakes his head in disapproval, and turns it off. I wonder what kind of food could be so important that it needs three grown men to deliver it.

We arrive at a gentlemen's club about a quarter to five. Following Slim's directions, I back the truck up into the alley next to the club's back entrance. Slim gets out of the cab and I roll down my window to enjoy the cool air. This isn't the kind of place I imagined we were headed. The building has no windows and only two entrances. Muffled music can be heard each time the back door swings open. I hear the back of my truck slide open and a struggle to move the cargo. I wonder if I can step out of the cab and smoke a Black while I wait on them to unload. I reach for the door handle. Slim suddenly appears by my door, reaches through the window, and grabs my arm. He twists it and grunts for me to stay put. He stares me down like he'll hurt me if I leave. Then I realize he isn't here for the package—he's here for me.

I tell him that I don't plan on running. That seems to put him at ease and he lets me go. Just then, Suits comes up to Slim and says they have a problem. One of the packages is stuck and they can't get it moved. I offer to help and they both reply with an adamant no. Slim tells me he'll handle it and urges me to stay in the cab.

Now, I've always been one for following the rules. But you get the itch to smoke, it has to be scratched. I slide out of the cab just as soon as Slim is out of sight. I find a little corner where they can't see me from the back of the truck. The Black & Mild smells of cherry, even through the packaging. It's been stressful, thinking about how money's going to work out, not knowing if this new gig would be a good fit or if I'd have to find something else quick. Sometimes you just need to watch something burn in your hands. There's always been something beautiful about destruction. The ashes gather on my shoes and I feel myself relax.

About halfway through the third smoke donut leaving my lips, I hear what sounds like trouble. There's a loud ruckus coming from the loading dock. Maybe one of the packages has slipped off the truck. I hear the two fellas in what sounds like an argument. I want to help, but I wasn't even supposed to be out of the cab. I wait to see if the yelling subsides, but it just grows louder and louder until I have no other option but to intervene.

I round the back of the truck, and I will never forget what I see at that moment. There, tangled between the men's four arms, is a girl. She can't be more than thirteen, though you can tell by the red lipstick and heels she was going for much older. Her heavy makeup is smeared and her mascara is pooling around her collarbone. She's the kind of groggy that only exists at three a.m., after too many drinks, flopping and flailing like a fish fresh out of school. Her legs are a bundle of seaweed knotting in and out of themselves. To my surprise, in her stupor, she shows an amazing amount of strength. I'm impressed with how she's leveraged her lean elbow into Slim's throat. Her other arm is wrapped around Suits's neck. It's then that I notice Slim and Suits have seen me, but they aren't angry. They need help.

Suits gestures wildly at the tire of the truck. I look down and see something on the ground behind it, catching the light of the setting sun. I look closer and realize it's a syringe. Suits's face is a deepening shade of midnight as he jerks his head at the girl and tries to pry her arm off his airway. He wants me to inject the girl. I can only guess that the syringe holds some sort of sedative. I reach down and grab the stopper. It feels like God's eyes are on me as the seconds pile high.

Am I this kind of man, willing to shoot up someone's child with only God-knows-what for a paycheck? My mother crosses my mind. I wonder what she would think if she saw me here. Then I think of my piling bills, the disconnection notices, and the debt-collector phone calls. I see Mr. LeFleur in my mind with a blank check in his hand. I think about the fridge and all of its hollow depression. There isn't enough time to make the right decision. Is she more important than my hunger? I've been a good man up until now. Doesn't that count for anything?

I know I have to make a choice when I see she's all but free from Slim's grasp. I say a quick prayer: *God, you know me inside and out. You know that I am always seeking what is good and kind. I believe You will and have already provided for me. See my heart tonight. Amen.*

I stab the needle into her thigh. I watch her body jolt and her eyes roll back like the tide. Then her arms go limp and her gill-cheeks sink back down, and she's asleep.

Slim yells, "What took you so long? Now help us get her back inside."

I've been so busy watching them, I haven't looked into the back of the truck. There are four more girls, wrapped in net-like twine. They look unconscious, like they don't even know they've been caught. Two of them still in their school uniforms. I help net our escapee and stow her with the others.

The ride back to Acres Homes is mostly silent. I understand now why Slim doesn't want any music. There's no soundtrack for this kind of journey. The whooshing of the tires against the road reminds me of the gulf. Slim mentions that's where the girls are headed: out to sea. We get back to the restaurant about thirty minutes later than scheduled.

Mr. LeFleur comes storming out, demanding to know why we're late. I stay in the cab, still in shock over what the day's held. I watch in the side mirror as Slim and Suits get out and try to explain everything to Mr. LeFleur. I see his face changing from infuriated to concerned. He looks over at the cab of the truck. He fumbles some papers around in his hands, scratches his head, and slowly walks over to the passenger door as the guys empty the remaining catch out of the truck.

I notice that some of the girl's hair attached itself to me as I was helping her back into the truck. I instantly feel dirty. I remember the last time I went fishing with my father and ended the night covered in scales. Too many to count. I don't know how to wash any of this off.

Mr. LeFleur opens the passenger door and leans in, his arm on the seat. He peers up at me and slides an envelope against the torn pleather. "I'm gonna toss in an extra hundred dollars for all of the trouble tonight. Things like this rarely happen," he says. "Hey, but for this kind of money, we all have to take some risks."

I just sit there, still and silent.

He chuckles. "Sometimes things like this just come with the job. I have more merchandise coming in tomorrow. Pays double. I doubt you'll have another day like this, but I can't make any promises. Shit happens, you know?"

I look him in his eyes. All the fear he had when I first met him is now gone. He's much more confident—almost cocky. Like he's roped me into his net and knows I couldn't get out if I wanted to.

He pats me on the knee and says, "See you tomorrow?"

I take a deep breath and whisper, "Sure thing, boss."

TOLERANCE

BY TOM ABRAHAMS

Third Ward

There was something about the rain in Houston that seemed to leave a film on everything. The more it rained, the slimier it got. And when it rained a lot, like it had this week, a city built on a swamp tended to flood. That storm named Harvey had shown the world what Houstonians had long known: flooding made the slime break loose, made it impossible to ignore.

It was eleven thirty on a Thursday night.

The bitter aftertaste of Citalopram was caught in my teeth like a paste, so I sucked out the remnants with my tongue and licked my lips. I was up to forty milligrams a day. At least that's what my hook-up told me it was. It didn't seem to make a difference. Nothing did.

So I closed my eyes; the drum of thick, cold drops beating rhythmically on the roof of my '95 Chrysler urged me to sleep. I hadn't slept in a while.

A knock on the window drew me from the trance. A gray-haired man with a clean shave and a tan trench coat pressed a badge against the glass.

"Hey," he said, "you the new guy?"

I cracked the window. "Yeah," I said. "Unless there's more than one new guy."

He swiped the rain from the window and motioned past the Chrysler with his head. "The body's down there. The sergeant's waiting on us."

He backed away from the car and I shouldered open the door. It creaked and hitched, but opened wide enough for me to climb out and onto the pavement. I slammed it shut with my hip but didn't lock it. What was the point?

The detective offered his hand. "I'm Bill Waters. Homicide."

"John Druitt."

Waters smiled and led me from the parking lot across Allen Parkway to the aluminum statue of a kneeling figure called *Tolerance* that overlooked Buffalo Bayou. The milky light that glowed at its base cast an eerily judgmental form, so I looked away and trudged closer to the bayou's muddy edge.

Waters slowed his pace, digging his heels into the mud for balance. "You were vice before?"

"Yeah. Five years. Handled sex trafficking. Takes its toll."

Waters chuckled. "So you moved to dead people?"

My foot slid in the grassy mud and I skated a couple of feet down the embankment. "Dead people don't feel anything," I said.

Waters shot me a glance with a furrowed brow. His lips curled upward and his nose crinkled like he smelled something rotten. I'd seen that look before. It came from people who thought they had me figured out. He didn't, even if he thought he did.

As we descended the slope toward the coffee-colored bayou that snaked through Downtown and Buffalo Bayou Park, I used the cuffs of my consignment-shop blazer to wipe the droplets from the swell under my eyes. The rain gave the wool blend a sooty odor that lingered in my nose.

"According the sergeant, she was weighed down," said Waters, "but all this rain must have shook her loose. The bayou's up a good couple of feet."

I ran my fingers through my hair and shook free the water. "Who found her?"

"Jogger."

"In this weather?"

"Marathon's coming up in a week," said Waters. "People are obsessed."

The closer we got to the bank of the bayou, the louder the rush of water. Above us was a split bridge called Rosemont. The steel-and-concrete spans crossed the water in a V shape and resembled a train trestle more than a pedestrian bridge.

Under the bridge, within the confines of flapping yellow tape tied to a bridge piling and two young pine trees, was a hive of activity. A drenched rat of a man stood shivering off to one side. He had the narrow frame of a runner and the anxious disinterest of a man detained.

Past him, in the sloppy bank of the rising water, was a trio of wetsuit-clad divers. One was bent over, his back heaving as he worked for air. Another was on his knees next to the woman's body. The third stood watch, as did half a dozen rubbernecking patrol officers. Dead bodies attracted flies.

I stood there for a moment, lost in the rush of the bayou. It was hard not to listen to the gurgle and wash of a swollen bayou and not wonder, in the muddy parts of my mind, if the water would ever stop rising. I'd heard others voice the same fears over bitter coffee and undercooked migas. They'd huddled close to each other, leaning on the chipped laminate of late-night greasy-spoon bar counters. They'd absently stirred their half-and-half and whispered about the rain as if it could hear them, while lightning had flashed and the feeder roads had filled with oily water.

"I called the dive team on the way here," said Waters, shaking me from my thoughts. "Gets us a head start."

The woman was on her back. Her dark hair covered her face. She was clothed in a torn pink dress that clung to her body in a way that would have been unflattering on a breathing woman.

Waters planted his hands on his hips and faced me. "So," he said, "I don't know if they told you this when you applied for the posting or when they interviewed you, but in homicide, we split the duties. One of us takes the scene, the other takes witnesses. What do you want?"

"Scene."

Waters pursed his lips. "All right, I'll talk to the jogger."

He slopped over to the thin man. A uniformed sergeant wearing a wrinkled vinyl poncho waved me to the body. Angry raindrops slapped the bayou with a growing intensity. I stepped close to the sergeant.

"You the new guy?" he asked.

I knuckled water from the corners of my eyes and nodded. "New to homicide."

"Crime scene folks are on their way," he said.

I thanked him and moved past him to the body. Her stomach was bloated under the dress in a way that made her appear pregnant, almost. Her skin was grayish green, and something had nibbled at her bottom lip and hanging tongue.

The skin was loose at her fingers and on her feet. There was the beginning of a scar on her left shoulder—a small, partially healed burn in the shape of an X. There was a two-foot length of orange rope tied around her right ankle. The rope was knotted at one end, torn and frayed at the other.

Her neck was a different color than the rest of her mottled body: varying shades of purple, concentrated in a thick line that ran across her throat.

I pulled a wet notepad from my coat pocket, made some rudimentary notes, and pressed myself to my feet. Waters was standing behind me.

"Not much from the jogger," he said. "We'll have to canvas the apartments across the bayou for witnesses or surveillance cameras."

I wiped my nose with the back of my hand and looked at the dim outline of multistory buildings through the curtain of rain. They stood watch over the bayou. A couple of the windows glowed yellow from the lights inside; rich people living above the muck, warm and comfortable in their castles. They never flooded. They never waded against the current of rising water, holding their lives above their heads in trash bags.

"She's a hooker," I told him. "Probably trafficked."

Waters's eyes narrowed. "How do you know?"

I pointed to the wound on her shoulder. "That's a brand. There's a group that runs a house off of White Chapel. It's industrial and they have one of the buildings there. Maybe a block east of the Southwest Freeway. There's a cantina in the front, girls in the back. All of them have those marks on their shoulders. We keep busting them. Doesn't matter. They find a way."

Like the bayous.

Waters rolled his eyes. "Lucky SOB."

A sharp breeze swirled around us, whistling against the frame of the bridge and sending a chill from my neck to my lower back. I shivered and pulled the soaked jacket collar against my neck.

"How so?" I asked.

"You call scene," he said, "and in five minutes you've got good information on who she was, who the perp might be, where we go for leads. It's almost like you handpicked it."

Almost.

Waters's phone chirped against his hip. He wiped the screen with his thumb and answered the call. While he talked, I stepped back to the body and examined the rope at her foot.

The knot was good. It was a bowline, the type of knot that held its shape and didn't shrink or expand. The other end, the frayed end, was ragged. It probably rubbed back and forth against something sharp until it gave way. The killer couldn't have anticipated that. The local weatherman hadn't accounted for three days of nonstop rain, the most since four feet fell in four days during Harvey. That storm was the stain you couldn't wipe clean.

Waters slid his phone back onto his hip and crouched next to me. "CSU pulled up," he said. "They'll start snapping pictures, taking videos. They'll do all the measuring. You think we need to expand the scene?"

I shook my head. "Nah. She didn't drown. At least not here. She's got ligature marks on her neck. She was dumped upstream. The killer didn't think she'd break loose. We're not going to find anything here."

"I agree," said Waters. "Good call. Once CSU is finished, they'll call the medical examiner. They'll send a team to finish up here. Then she'll go to the morgue."

"Then we get out of the rain?"

Waters chuckled. "Something like that. Hey," he said, thumping me on my arm, "since it's your first case, you get to buy me coffee."

"Sure," I said. "Coffee. Beer. Jack. Whatever you want."

"I like you already, Druitt."

Delete. My favorite key on the computer is delete. It erases all my mistakes. There should be a delete key in life, something that helps hide from the rest of the world the things you've done but regret. Something that masks the errors with your real intent.

I was holding down they key, racing the cursor back to the

left side of the screen, when Waters sidled up to my desk. It was three thirty in the morning on Friday.

He toasted me with his cup of coffee, the Styrofoam stained brown at its edges. "You're not going to believe this," he said. "You need to go to Lake Charles and gamble, brother. Your luck is ridiculous."

I'd been to Lake Charles. I'd gambled there. I'd lost.

"What?" I said. "I'm almost finished with the rep—"

"We got somebody who knows our girl. Says she saw her Monday night."

"I thought we weren't heading over to White Chapel until after we have cause of death," I said. "Then going there with a warrant. Don't want to blow our wad needlessly. Right?"

Waters sat on the edge of my desk and drew a sip of the coffee. He was slurping what had to be his fourth cup. "We didn't go. She came to us."

"What's her story?"

Waters smacked his lips and set the coffee cup on my desk. "Got picked up in a sweep," he said. "Had a scar on her arm. Mentioned White Chapel to the arresting officer. Buddy of mine downstairs tipped me. I had her moved for a Q-and-A."

I saved my unfinished report and followed Waters to the elevator. We rode it to the floor where we do interrogations, talk to witnesses, and argue about the designated hitter and instant replay.

The woman was waiting for us in a small room with gray walls and a rectangular two-way mirror. She was rocking back and forth in her chair, one knee bouncing up and down. She was picking at her cuticles with her teeth. She had stringy brown hair that looked wet even though it probably wasn't. There was a faded tattoo of Betty Boop above her left shoulder blade. On her arm, there was a thick X-shaped scar.

I stood off to the side and let Waters start the conversation. He spun a chair around and straddled it, leaning on the back with his forearms.

"My name's Bill," he said. "This is my partner John. I heard your name is Annie. I also heard that you know about a girl who went missing. One of your friends."

The woman stopped chewing on her finger but kept it in her mouth. Her red-tinged eyes danced back and forth between the two of us, seemingly unable to focus on either. Her pupils were dilated.

"You high?" I asked.

The woman pulled her finger from her mouth and sat on her hands. She curled her lower lip between her teeth and bit down.

Waters gave a disapproving glance. I guess this wasn't how we were supposed to start. He softened his voice and tried to hold the woman's gaze. "You're not going to get in trouble. We really just need your help."

"It's Spice, isn't it?" I asked. I could spot a synthetic marijuana user like nobody's business. She had the jitters, the paranoia, and the sallow skin color. "You're using right now. I can see it."

Waters leaned back from the table and glared at me. He swung his leg over the chair and motioned me into the corner of the room. His jaw was set. His eyes were wide with anger. He spoke through clenched teeth. "What are you doing?" he asked. "We've got a lead here and you're intimidating her. You think she's gonna talk if she thinks we're gonna lock her up?"

I looked past Waters at the woman. She ran her fingers through her greasy hair and then picked at a small black gauge in her right earlobe. She swallowed hard and raked her teeth along her bottom lip. She couldn't sit still.

"Good cop, bad cop," I said. "Always works."

Waters raised an eyebrow. "So I'm the good cop?"

"Without a doubt."

"I don't think that's what we're doing here," he said.

He shook his head and resumed his one-sided conversation with the woman. He kept offering her useless niceties, promised her some cigarettes or coffee. Maybe a Shipley's donut or a hot dog from James Coney Island down the street. Whatever she wanted.

"How about another hit, Annie?" I said. "That help?"

She glanced at me, checked with Waters, who was frowning, and then looked back at me. She nodded.

"No problem," I said. "You just need to help out Bill here. He thinks you might know something about the woman we found in the bayou last night."

Annie stared at me. Her lips were pursed. She was stuck in pause mode for a moment, fixated on me, and then she nodded again.

Waters pinched the bridge of his nose and squeezed his eyes shut. He sucked in a deep breath of air and exhaled. "Okay," he said begrudgingly, "you tell us what we need to know and we'll see about getting you some of what you need. Deal?"

She nodded once more and Waters pulled his phone from his pocket. He unlocked the screen, tapped it a couple of times, and slid it across the table to Annie.

She glanced at the phone and closed her eyes. "Her name was Mary Ann," she said. Her voice didn't match her appearance. It was timid, almost sweetly apprehensive, the product of a life spent at the behest of others. She looked younger when she spoke. "She was new."

"New to what?" asked Waters.

The girl shrugged. "Everything."

Waters leaned in, his voice softer, matching hers. "Drugs? Sex?"

"She was from Connecticut," said the girl. "New London. They brought her last week."

"Who?"

The girl hesitated. She peered over at me, as if I could give her approval. As if I was the one holding sway over her. She bit on her cuticle, nibbling on the loose skin before working it free of her nailbed.

I nodded.

She looked back at Waters and ran her hand through her hair. "EastEnders," she mumbled.

"The gang?"

She lowered her head and tugged at the gauge. "Yeah," she said. "They have places where they keep us."

"Like White Chapel?" asked Waters.

She nodded.

"How would she get out?" he asked. "I mean, if they put you in these places, they must keep an eye on you. How did you get out?"

She tucked her hair behind her ear. "They keep some tied up. But most of us, they keep us high. You know, they give us stuff. For free. So we stay close."

"What if you try to run?"

"Nobody does," she said. "They'd kill us. I've seen them kill girls. You know, give 'em too much stuff. OD 'em on purpose."

"Did Mary Ann try to run?" asked Waters. "How'd you know she was missing?"

Annie glanced at me and then shook her head. She looked back at Waters and her eyes widened. Her head tilted to one side and she shook a finger at me. "I think I know you," she said. "I've seen you."

Waters swung his attention to me, a quizzical look on his face. He leaned back in the chair and folded his arms. "You know him?"

She wagged her finger again and narrowed her beady little eyes. "It's the hair," she said. "And the eyes. I know I've seen you. On White Chapel. You've been in there. Drinking at the bar."

She was right. She'd probably seen me. She might have handed me a Jack and Coke. She might have given me more than that. Sex trafficking. Takes its toll.

"Yeah," I said, unfazed by the accusation. "I've been in there. I worked trafficking for five years."

"Drug trafficking?" Annie asked.

"Human."

Waters, apparently satisfied with my explanation, shifted in the chair and planted his elbows on the table. "How did you know Mary Ann was missing?" he asked.

"I heard people talking. Nobody had seen her in a couple of days. They'd dropped her off. She got picked up by some dude in a beater. Never came back."

Waters scratched his chin. "Did she run away?"

Annie shrugged. "I don't think so. I don't really know. We worked different spots. I'm Old Spanish Trail. She's Third Ward."

"You think you could show us where in Third Ward she worked?" I asked. "What corners?"

Waters nodded his approval. "That'd be great, Annie."

"You think I could get a bump?" she asked, scratching the Betty Boop above her shoulder blade. "I'm coming down."

"If I get you the bump," I said, "you'll take me there? The spots where the EastEnders drop off the girls?"

Annie checked with Waters. "Sure," she said. "As long as nobody sees me in a cop car. I don't want nobody seeing me with cops."

"Not a problem."

Waters hopped up from his seat. "Can I talk to you?"

He motioned for me to leave the room and led me into the hallway. Annie just sat there picking at her cuticles.

Waters stood uncomfortably close to me. "Couple of things," he said under his breath. "I can't sanction you giving her synthetic pot. I don't know what kind of crap you got away with in vice, but that's not what we do here. She's already a shaky witness. You give her drugs and she's toast. The DA will never let her testify."

I stepped back from Waters, gaining some space. "What's the other thing?"

"Why do you need her to show you where the EastEnders drop the girls? You know these guys, right? Don't you already know the spots they control?"

He was right. I did know.

I knew where to find the girls, and the boys, run by Barrio Azteca, Sureños, Tango Blast, Mara Salvatrucha, Bloods, and Crips. I knew their turf. I knew their methods. I knew the legit businesses that fronted their operations. I knew their trafficking routes. I knew the EastEnders were rapidly growing, given their backing by a dominant Mexican cartel.

I also knew that no matter how much we learned about all of them, how much actionable intelligence we gained, how many resources or informants we had, we were only scratching the surface. We'd flip on the light, stomp on a cockroach, and fifty more would scramble into the dark corners where we couldn't get them.

It had only gotten worse since Harvey. Unlike Katrina,

which had drained the delta of its undesirables and sent them to Houston, Harvey clogged the city with more homeless than it could handle. Shady contractors descended on the neighborhoods piled high with Sheetrock, subflooring, and kitchen sinks. Instead of rebuilding homes, they'd spend their cash on women and drugs. The gangs, which we'd gotten better at tracking, had scattered. We'd lost our grip on informants. All of them together floated untethered and just out of our grasp. Some days, just when I thought maybe I was making a dent, I realized it was getting harder to leave a scratch.

"It changes," I told Waters. "And it doesn't hurt to check it out, given we have somebody who knows the area."

Waters inhaled. He planted his tongue in his cheek, rolling it around while he seemed to contemplate the idea. "All right," he said. "You head over there with her. I'm gonna drive by White Chapel. Kill two birds with one stone. We meet back here and hopefully the ME gives us a positive ID. Then we get a warrant and hit the place."

"Got it," I said. "I'll meet you back here by sunup."

They say it's always darkest before the dawn. I've got no clue who *they* is, but they're right. I'm guessing they've lived a life like mine, always fighting the glare of the light, seeking the shadowy quiet between midnight and the alarm clock.

I've never been one for daylight. It offers too much promise. I learned a long time ago that hope is nothing but a sexy woman behind the glass. You stuff your credit card into the slot, the curtains peel back, and she smiles at you. But you're not looking at her face. And there's nothing but the promise of a big bill at the end of the month, with an interest rate you can't afford. It's a nasty cycle, the sun coming up every morning. I'd just as soon it stayed sunken low.

It was five fifteen on Friday morning. That's what the clock on my Chrysler said. I couldn't be sure it was accurate. Didn't matter.

The clouds had the streets darker than normal. Third Ward didn't get the attention nicer parts of town got. Powers that be would never let the streetlights go out in Memorial or River Oaks. Hell, if a blade of grass was too long on Inwood Drive, the mayor himself would show up with a pair of scissors. But in the Tre, as local rappers called it, a dead body wouldn't catch much glare, let alone a string of busted streetlights. Gentrification or not, Third Ward was still Third Ward.

I had my window cranked down, enjoying the musty air and fine mist that had settled over the city. Annie tugged on her seat belt, trying to get it to click. "Your car is old," she said, "and I think my belt is broken."

I turned onto Elgin and headed southeast. "I'll drive slowly," I said. "Just focus on where we need to be."

A shirtless man on a bicycle peddled past us, riding the wrong way. His wheels were warped and he had to work the handlebars to keep from tipping over.

"Turn right up here," she said. "Near the train."

I tapped the brake and swung the wheel to turn onto Scott. We were parallel with the light-rail tracks. I started to accelerate, but Annie told me to make a quick right onto Reeves.

"This is one of the spots," she said. "They like us to stay close to the train."

I slowed to a stop, flipped the car into park, and listened to the windshield wipers squeak back and forth, barely cleaning the glass of the water that had collected on it. There was nobody here. We were alone.

I undid my seat belt. "You sure? This is the spot?"

Annie shifted in her seat, inching into the space between the seat and the door. She was facing me. "Yeah. One of them."

She was right. This was one of the spots. Reeves and Scott. Delano and Berry streets. Milby and Tuam.

"When do I get my hit?" she asked.

"You can have it now," I said. "Check the glove box. I've got a couple packets of potpourri in there. Take whatever you want."

Her eyes lit up and she fumbled for the latch at her knee. She plucked it open and leaned toward the opening. She felt around for the drugs, but she pulled her hand back empty.

I rolled up my window.

"There's nothing there," she said.

"Sorry. Check under the seat, maybe I put them there."

Annie reached down between her legs, bending forward as far as she could. I turned on the radio. It was a static-riddled AM station playing jazz. Herb Geller, I think. His saxophone cried through the blown speakers. It was like the sax was drowning.

Annie started to pull back from her search when I reached across the seat and placed my hand firmly on the back of her neck. She struggled, but my fingers slipped through the greasy tendrils of her mouse-brown hair. I wrapped them tightly and applied pressure, forcing her to stay down, while I used my other hand to manage an orange rope from underneath my seat and around her head. I pulled it tight around her throat and yanked her back toward me, where I could watch her.

Her eyes bulged, looking at me in a way that told me she either finally recognized me from the last time we'd been together, or she recognized that her sad, pathetic life was ending. The pain was almost over.

She kicked against the door, reached behind her head to

grab at me with her fingers—the fingers she'd spent much of the night chewing. Annie was stronger than I'd figured. Her legs pushed. Her arms flailed. There was a determination, a desire to live I didn't expect from a drug-addled hooker forced into the sex trade by bad men who kept her under their violent thumbs. For a split-second, I considered letting go, letting her breathe.

It crossed my mind I could give a couple of hundred from my wallet and put her on a Greyhound toward Oklahoma or Kansas. She could start clean.

Who was I kidding? There was no such thing as clean. So I pulled harder on the rope. I closed my eyes and tugged. I gritted my teeth and tightened my grip.

As I watched the life and color drain from her face, I promised her this was for the best. It was the same thing I'd told Mary Ann four nights earlier. And Liz a week before. And Cathy two months before that. And Jane. I couldn't remember how long ago I'd helped Jane. Six months? Nine?

Annie's body shuddered and went limp, her head dropping onto my shoulder as the rattle left her lungs. I sat there for a moment and stroked her forehead. I told her about the things I'd done, the women I'd saved one way or another. I told her she wouldn't be the last. I couldn't let her be the last. There were too many to help, too many to set free.

I told her how, in some ways, it had gotten easier with each of the girls. In some ways, it had gotten harder. I told her about how I'd first understood my calling, as Harvey roiled under the doors and walls of my dank first-floor apartment off the South Loop. I was neck-deep before I escaped, ducking under the water, tasting the gasoline and motor oil, the dog crap, and the grass clippings, as I'd swam through an open window and free of my home.

I'd blown the air from my lungs and surfaced next to a flooded Ford F-150. As I'd risen from the water, the distant calls for help, the sounds of sirens, and the whoosh of cars driving the wrong way on the Loop above filled the muggy air.

The lights were out. It had been dark, the sky almost milky from the storm that would not go. And yet, as I'd wiped the water from my eyes and spit it from my mouth, I could see clearly for the first time in a very long time.

The city needed this flood. It needed a cleansing. And after the waters were gone, it would need me.

I found the task itself less daunting, more automatic. It ushered in less anxiety but produced less of an artificial high. Mary Ann's salvation hadn't sustained me as long as Liz's. Liz's ascension wasn't as satisfying as Cathy's.

Somehow, I'd built up a tolerance.

I inched Annie off my shoulder, gently setting her upright in the passenger seat, and reached into my jacket pocket. It was still damp, but the pill bottle inside it was sealed. I uncapped it, shook the last of my Cilatopram into my mouth, and chewed.

On the radio, Geller's sax screeched through the broken tweeter, sweetly eulogizing the girl next to me. Outside, the clouds grew too heavy and the rain started again.

CITY OF GIRLS

BY LESLIE CONTRERAS SCHWARTZ

Aldine

Sergeant Dan Correal opened the door and heard the delicious hush, the whir of the air-conditioning, and the dog snoring gently on the couch. He locked up his holster in the safe, put in the Glock 22, which he'd secretly named Lady Lisa, after his wife. Just taking off the holster made his shoulders and neck ache as if he'd lifted weights for hours, like he used to, but he had hardly moved much from the seat of his cruiser for his entire shift.

At the end of his shift, he'd had to make a domestic disturbance call on Bissonnet, and he already felt old and grizzled as he climbed the apartment steps to the third floor. His radio and its perpetual buzz, the sun's hot-white glare still strong in the fall, gave him a headache that pulsed into his ears.

He'd knocked on the apartment door, which pushed it open. A young woman, Charlie, stood in a transparent black shift dress. She was a regular, both sad and disturbingly attractive to Dan with her shifty, bottomless gaze, full lips, dark eyes. "He's already gone," she said, pushing back her hair into a sleepy pile, a mound of soft cleavage peeking through the V in her dress. Dan shifted his eyes quickly to the window, the spoons, the collection of flip-flops and heels that had been kicked off by the door. A pair of brown work boots, the laces undone in long snakes.

She'd met his gaze, made a small, teasing smile. "Oh, he

left those, I guess." She'd sighed and walked to the kitchen. He did his check, his to-do, and left.

Now, without the weight of the pistòl and its responsibility, he let himself think about the black lace trimming Charlie's breasts. She looked just like his daughter's friend Chickie, and this thought both plagued and haunted Dan every time he saw her on his calls. Chickie's little doppelgänger, he'd thought as he saw her striding toward him in a spaghetti-strap dress, the weight of her breasts, the curve of her ass.

Dan closed the bathroom door behind him. He hadn't changed out of his uniform, wanted to feel the cold dangle of his handcuffs a little. Chickie, in Charlie's black dress, pulling up the thin hem, pulling down her panties. He remembered the massage parlor, as he did during these moments—that hole-in-the-wall where his father took him for his first time. Those red lips, the mix of humiliation and the sheer pleasure of an orgasm with a live girl, the warm flesh beneath his hands, its softness and its salty taste. Chickie and her wet lips.

"Dad, what the fuck?" The door pushed against him abruptly, the knob jamming into his back as he climaxed.

He looked in the mirror and saw his daughter and Chickie, covering her face. "Oh my god."

He turned quickly, realizing they'd seen enough in the mirror. He shut the door, locked it, pushed his back against it, holding up his pants. Maybe they'd seen only a bit, he reasoned, zipping up and clearing his throat. He heard them rush down the hall to his daughter's room.

She was old enough to understand her father was a man, he figured. He looked in the mirror and washed his hands. They felt dirty and he washed them a second time, scrubbing under his nails the way his mom had taught him. He stayed in the bathroom until he heard the girls leave. He wasn't sure what he did during that time, waiting, except stare at his hands. What broke through his shock was the hard sound his wife made coming home, the thud of her purse on the kitchen counter, all the hurried noise she made after entering the front door. Only then did he dry his hands and go to change his clothes.

The sky was about to crack open and release everything held in its dark clouds, but Chickie Rodriguez didn't care. She kept swimming, ignoring the shade creeping from the clouds, cooling off the water. She'd paid her two dollars—money she'd saved by skipping lunch—and wasn't going to waste it.

She sank again into the water, held her breath, let it blow a big balloon in her chest, beneath her breasts. A hot-air pump, made of anger.

At home, her mother waited to be fed, bathed, comforted like a child. But Chickie would no longer be the one to do it now. Thinking of her mother's stench, Chickie held her breath as she spun upside down, feeling her hair cast wet fingers from her head, floating her legs into a perfect V. She held it as long as she could, picturing her mother's crooked smile that was no longer a smile.

It's not so bad, she thought as she left the pool in her worn bikini bottom and the anti-drug campaign T-shirt she'd had since second grade. For instance, she could be that lady in the studded bathing suit with her little brats, clearly trapped in a life of watching them grow and shit and scream. Diamond ring glinting as she moved to grab one child or another, to keep them from scratching or biting each other. *Golden handcuffs, lady.*

Chickie never cried. She didn't cry at her father's funeral, and she didn't cry when the two police officers showed up at their filthy apartment, full of empty vodka bottles and pills, to take her mother away.

One of the officers was a woman who acted overly compassionate and warm, and to Chickie, it seemed feigned and slightly arrogant. This disgusted her. For some reason, it mixed in her mind with the disgust of finding Renee's dad in the bathroom pleasuring himself the day before.

"It's going to be okay," the officer said, patting her shoulder. The condescension made bile gather in Chickie's throat. *The fuck it is.*

Chickie walked to the room she shared with her mother and packed up her clothes: a cotton shirt with the logo of a Mexican restaurant they'd loved, a pair of faded, too-loose jeans, a busted bra, an extra pair of underwear that used to be gray. She looked at her mother's things, especially the ceramic elephant sitting on the windowsill. Chickie had always admired the figurine, which was probably a gift from one of her mother's boyfriends. It symbolized the precious, hateful, and painfully loving relationship she had with her mother. She would run her fingers over its lines and indentations after putting her mother to sleep beside her. *We'll be okay*, she would say to herself during those times. But she didn't mean it the way the police said it.

They were waiting. She left the elephant on the sill and left the room for the last time.

Farah Peña is always that other woman. She imagines that, on some other planet, she walks around in a nightgown, fresh from a bath, living the life she should've lived. That other Farah leans against the brick of her house, exhaling sweet breath, holding a wineglass to her mouth, tasting something foreign and glistening. Her mouth is not a horrid thing—just a mouth. Her breasts and torso held lightly in a gown for sleeping, and just that—a body. She listens to the crickets' and frogs' music. She goes back into her own house, disappears behind a thick layer of curtains fat with dreams, with hours and hours stitched inside them. Oh, how that other Farah sleeps.

She hasn't heard the sound of frogs and crickets in years. It's annoying and sad—the wrong background noise for a concrete lot with pitiful fists of grass and weeds growing from split cracks. Farah stubs out her cigarette on the bottom of one of the black stilettos—the ones that don't slide against the spa floor, that give off a solid crunch when she walks in them, like she might be safe in them. She likes the gritty sound they make when she walks, the way they're too big for her feet and not two or three sizes too small. She took them from Mary's feet while she slept off the fresh bruises one of the johns had left. It was a repeat guy, a soccer-dad type who spooned his wife at night—the worst kind. Farah's prepared for the same john now, her little stash lined up neatly at least an hour before he's expected to show up: the plastic card with the Pizza Hut logo propped against her can of spray lubricant.

Back inside, Justin tells her to put on the bright pink lingerie—the cotton candy one, he calls it—the one most coveted by all the other girls. Farah used to care about such things, and about Justin's preferences more than anything.

When she first met Justin—her friend Chickie's cousin— he paid attention to Farah like no one else ever had. Called her twice a day, bringing her flowers, food, jewelry, little notepads, and drawings. Soon he was fingering her in her bedroom with the door half open while her parents walked around the house, oblivious. She didn't want to do it, but was willing to endure, to keep his attention on her. Wasn't that what it meant to matter?

Then, he asked her to endure more things—things she didn't mind at first, until she realized she minded very much and had all along. Things like him touching her beneath her clothes when he dropped her off at school, a favor her parents appreciated, once they warmed up to the idea of their fifteen-year-old dating a nineteen-year-old. She endured him pushing her head into his crotch on the freeway, on the road to her house, in parking lots behind factories and chain stores, before and after dinner. She endured this with him and soon with others, and he promised her dinners, clothes, makeup. Suddenly, *no* seemed unavailable. *No* had disappeared. *No* had been swallowed with semen and the salt from sweat and tears. She was sneaking out at night to meet grown men behind her house, by the bayou. Not because she wanted to—because it was something she had to do to see Justin, to win his favor. She didn't know how to stop it.

Months later, Farah packed a backpack with all her money—two hundred dollars accrued from a summer job and six months of skipping lunch—and a notebook in which she'd already written one sentence: *And now I'm pregnant, and he has met his goal of destroying me.* She left her parents' home—her family, Chickie and her other friends, and the rest of her life—with no plan, only the thought that she couldn't live this way anymore.

She had gotten as far as Antoine and Frick Road, near the middle school, before Justin caught up to her in his Chevrolet, as if he knew exactly where she'd end up. Without a word, she got into his car. What else could she have done? She had swallowed that *no*, and that *no* was now her life.

She's over that now. She comes and goes like a ghost, the same way she did in her house with her parents before she ever met Justin. Now she sees the new girls come in with hope in their eyes and takes any opportunity to show them how stupid they are, were. *Welcome home.*

Farah waits for the other girls to finish making their food at the small stove littered with old pots caked with sauces and sticky noodles, surrounded by takeout containers. None of them care to clean, despite the roaches that scurry behind the stove. When Farah first got here, she cleaned all the pots she could, sometimes during her assigned nap times. She'd throw away the containers and scrub the counters hard with a dingy sponge, barely moving the grime and grease. She did this until she learned, truly, where she was. Not just in physical space, but where she was stuck, inside.

Farah imagines herself as the other woman, living the life she was meant to live. At fifteen, Farah is sure she's already fucked that woman's husband. She'll be happy to tell her so, if they ever meet.

Chickie woke up in a strange room. Across from her, a strange girl sighed in her sleep. This could be anywhere, and that girl could be any of the ones Chickie had met—other versions of herself: runaways, caretakers of drunk or high parents, abandoned or otherwise without a family.

Sleep was the only thing that gave Chickie relief. It kept her from hearing the other foster children, the twin toddlers screaming in their cribs. It was the only way to escape the television playing its gaudy reality shows throughout the night, the disembodied voices and music, the sickeningly sweet jingles that frightened her. There were too many sounds, colors, facial expressions, and products to keep track of in that perfect square. It made her believe the world was too overpowering, too complicated, and that she should just give up.

She realized her face was wet, her dark hair damp and

matted. She'd dreamed of the past: Farah warming an eye-liner with a match and letting Chickie rim her eyes with the melted black. Riding in Justin's backseat, sipping whiskey, then watching porn while his parents sat outside the room eating dinner. She'd dreamed of her mother, standing in the kitchen in a white dress, chopping nothing, then crawling to-ward her with the knife, like a baby.

Chickie lay in bed remembering the days before she'd been taken away, and thinking of all the days since. All the foster homes she'd been shuffled to, and the one she was in currently.

Now that she was awake, she felt greedy for that sleep that had come so easily the night before. The way she'd collapsed into her bed like it was a lake and she was sinking to the very bottom. To stop these thoughts, she threw the cover off her body and sat up. She had to leave. She wasn't sure where she'd go or what would change, but she had to stop living this way.

She found Justin—and Farah—on the same road where he'd found Farah months before, right next to Shotwell. It was as if he'd planned this all—had seen this coming from the day the girls were born.

Sergeant Correal kicked open the door to the parlor's back room. It was dark and smoky, but he could see a hall with a row of showers at one end, closed doors at the other. Men were lined up in the shower stalls, looking at the opened door with frantic faces. It was the typical setup Correal had seen in these salons. The men chose a girl and then showered, a sign of the owner's "protecting" the girls from disease, since the johns refused to wear condoms. Steam from the showers pushed through the crowded entrance, carrying the smell of blood and sex and something putrid, like flood rot and bayou.

Past the stalls was a small kitchen with covered-up windows and a filthy counter stacked with pots, knives, and open food containers. As Correal's eyes adjusted to the light, the other officers moved in beside him, and he realized there were two girls immediately to his right. They stood behind glass—a display window that revealed their faces and the upper halves of their torsos, one in garden-pink lingerie and the other in a skimpy black slip. Waiting to be chosen.

He thought of buying lunch for his daughters at a fast-food drive-thru a few days before. The window was the same height, with young women standing behind it. He saw his daughters' faces in their place: his seven-year-old in leggings and a tank top with cartoon characters, his sixteen-year-old in faded jeans and an Astros T-shirt.

Correal looked at the two girls here, both backed against the wall. They didn't seem afraid. Instead, their faces, masked by long fake lashes that fanned out when they blinked, glittery charcoal eyeliner, dark lipstick, were held frozen in an expression that seemed prepared for the worst. A sort of going-away glaze over their eyes. Correal was familiar with this look.

Later, when they'd been removed from display, one of the girls asked him, "How did you know I was here?"

He'd been about to say something like, *Girls, you're okay now. We're here to help*, or some other nonsense that shrunk beneath the weight of this place and its horror, its revolting smell. Then his gaze rested on her face and he recognized her as the girl who had disappeared from his neighborhood last year. His daughter's friend. He searched his memory, past images of other such busts—black lace panties, a skirt lifted, flesh on his hands—and found her name: *Chickie*.

Her broad cheekbones were cut up, one side bruised purple. The lips made full with red lipstick turned hot pink in the neon light from the signs that said, *Massage Alegría*. The same kind of sign had glowed over him thirty years before, in this same kind of place, where his father took him for this eighteenth birthday. With a deep sinking feeling in his chest, as if some bottom had dropped beneath him, he wondered for the first time how old that woman—that sweet, delicious woman—had been. He looked at Chickie. She couldn't have been a girl, could she? He shook his head until he realized what he was doing and stopped.

He answered her question with, "I would've come sooner if I did." He knew better than to reach out or move close.

"How long will I be in jail?" the other girl asked. Her eyes were like ponds: no trace of fear or surprise—just a glassy sort of dreaminess, her dilated pupils reflecting the neon. Despite himself, Correal imagined being a customer to this child, taking her into one of the small rooms, and what would happen, however gentle or violent, and how those pond-like eyes would stay the same throughout. *I'm a bastard for even thinking about this.*

He remembered, now, the last time he saw Chickie. She'd been sitting with his daughter on her bed, laughing, when he opened the bedroom door to tell them to go to sleep. After he'd walked away, he heard them whisper, howl with laughter, and continue murmuring throughout the night. In the morning, he'd watched them from the living room window, looking over the backyard where they jumped on the trampoline. The way they flung themselves into the air had made him ache in his chest, his throat. Their unfiltered joy as their limbs kicked toward the wide sky, their faces in full sun. *When will this end for them?* he'd thought. *Two years? Three?* "Take a look at these girls," he'd said to his wife. He'd watched for several minutes, making sure they didn't fall.

"We're here to help you," he said to these girls now. "Not send you to jail."

This was Farah, he now recalled, another girl from his daughter's school. She looked bored and uninterested, with a sly pinch in her upper lip.

Correal stepped aside as the outreach group and social workers approached the girls. Farah bent awkwardly to take off five-inch black heels, then stood barefoot, barely five feet tall. She looked like a girl playing dress-up. The sliver of sarcasm that aroused and terrified him had disappeared.

Chickie was shaking. She turned to one of the social workers who had led them out the back door. "I'm so sorry. Tell Mama I'm sorry."

Chickie's mother was dead. She'd been dead for months now, as Justin had informed her when he'd started working here. Chickie made that knowledge available to herself only sometimes. For the most part, her mother existed as a being with whom she couldn't communicate, who couldn't hear her. She was there now, walking beside them. Chickie was still caught up in the heroin high and needed this woman to give her mother the message.

But the woman misunderstood. "I'll help you find her. Come with me."

Chickie and her dead mother followed the woman to the car, through the loud noises of the men being arrested and shouted at, feet moving quickly, police, and sirens.

For Chickie and Farah, the sounds were muted. The things still alive within them were kept hidden—almost completely covered.

In the backseat of the car, the girls lay their hands next to each other, not touching.

MILES'S BLUES

BY WANJIKŪ WA NGŨGĨ

Montrose

I t happened one night in Montrose, in the Fielding Café
on Fairview Street. There, love found Jennifer—in the
form of Miles, named after Davis himself.

Fielding Café was actually a bar that featured new psyche-
delic rock and blues bands. Jennifer burst through its doors
because Lola's, her usual dive bar, was closed for renovation.
Struck by the youthful clientele, she sat on the barstool nearest the band, the only one left. She could have joined the
table with an empty seat, but she had never been the social
type. With a tequila firmly in hand, she studied her surround-
ings. In front of her was a small stage with black curtains and
a framed pencil drawing of Obama plastered above. That's
what this place was like: amateurish drawings and pictures
and paintings. Artists clamoring for walls on which to express
themselves. Take, for instance, the silhouette of the woman
standing over a grave in a dark forest; or the man standing in
front of a burned-down house with the rainbow flag blowing
in the wind; or the children standing in front of an old police
truck with fists raised high; or the woman, her blond hair cas-
cading in the air, her arms outstretched in front of her. Pent-up
emotions splattered on the wall.

As the band did their sound check, Jennifer paid for another drink. The bartender handed her the whiskey sour, and
she spotted, above the bar, a picture of Lance Armstrong

holding a little girl. Probably his daughter. She remembered sitting on her father's shoulders during season games. She had often wished, even as a child, that she was someone else. Or that her father would one day show up at her school to watch her perform poetry at the talent shows, even though she never won. Or that her mother would, like her friend's mother, take her to the park for a picnic. Or that the popular boy in school would spend his time with her instead of making fun of her looks. Wasted youth, she thought. It was one of the reasons she had gone into teaching—to be close to the youth she had missed.

Her thoughts were interrupted by the drums. And that's when she saw Miles. She held onto her chair and took a sip of her drink, captivated by his long arms and the way they hit the drums as if they had done him wrong. She could tell he was letting go of something. She watched his face as he hit the red drums, how, in those precise moments, something revealed itself.

This love came as a surprise, like most things in Jennifer's life. Their relationship developed fast that first night. Right there on the corner of Fairview and Grant, in the early hours of the morning, Miles reawakened in her a longing as covetous as the one she first felt at age five, in her family's two-bedroom bungalow on Crocker Street. This bungalow was a couple of miles from Dunlavy Park, long before it was named for Eyran Chew. Before the bulldozers entered Montrose, eliminating bungalows and cottages with wide porches in order to conform to standards Jennifer's family and the other residents had no say about, and displacing them.

Her father was a short man with a penchant for politics and cigarettes; he spent most of his free time exchanging opinions at West Alabama Ice House. So much so that, when he came home, he demanded silence to organize his thoughts for the next day. It had been like this since Jennifer was born, so she'd learned from an early age to temper her tantrums so they only emerged when he wasn't home. One day her father staggered home a couple of hours earlier than usual and caught them by surprise. No one was in their expected positions. Most times, Jennifer's mother would be preparing his food and Jennifer would be in her bed, practicing her nursery rhymes. This was good because when her father came home, her eardrums were acclimated to her voice and not his. His was always a few notches louder than necessary, so it bounced off the walls, creating a raucous sound.

On this day, however, Jennifer and her six-month-old baby brother sat on their mother's lap. It was a small house, so his breath that reeked of ethanol and yeast filled all the rooms as he pounced around the space her mother occupied, pointing out her insufficiency. When he pushed her chair backward, Jennifer's mother had to make a choice. She chose to hold onto the baby because, as she later explained to Jennifer, his skull was not yet fully formed.

Fortunately, except for the bruises in her heart and the shock on her body, Jennifer escaped unhurt. But from then on, she preferred to sit in her room. In that room, she developed the longing, only she did not know what it was she longed for. She carried this yearning everywhere she went. She only ventured outdoors to try to figure it out.

Once, as a child, she walked two miles in her sleep. Then, as a teenager, she walked ten miles away from Montrose in the daytime. Then she traveled twenty-six miles to attend Clear Lake College. Over time, she had come upon three truths about herself. One was that she had developed a distrust for adults. The second was that she harbored undying love for a youth that had passed her by. The third was a realization that the yearning was a part of her.

So she returned and set up house down the street from the Montrose Remembrance Garden on Converse Street, an homage to the neighborhood's violent past. She often sat outside her one-bedroom apartment surrounded by antique stores, redbrick luxury apartments, and townhomes and watched pub crawlers prowl through. She knew how lucky she was to have secured a place she could afford on her meager teacher's salary. The longing, however, remained buried inside her, under the membranes of her skin, until the night she saw Miles play his drums.

After the first set, he asked if she wanted a drink, and she declined. He asked if she wanted to buy him one, and she declined. She wanted to walk away, but he kept talking, saying things about her face and her hair and her body. His shirt clung to his torso and his boyish smile lingered. A wisp of hair fell on his forehead, and she had the urge to push it back. He hung onto her every word. When she indicated she wanted to go home, he would not accept it and asked her to stay for their second set.

She asked why they played so late into the night and he asked why not, tilting his head back and laughing. He said it wasn't like he had a curfew or anything. She laughed uneasily. He told her he liked it when she laughed. He touched her hand as he ordered another shot, and the touch stirred something inside her. His hands were soft, and when his eyes danced on hers, she knew he saw only her. She decided to wait until the band was done.

Later, outside, he put his hand on her waist. She started to protest, but then surprised herself by kissing him.

On that first night together, she sat nervously on the edge

of her bed while he sat beside her, his breathing audible, holding her hand. She stood and went to the kitchen for shots. While there, she decided to take a pill. Then, everything fell into place.

After, he played with her braids, which rested on her shoulders and chest and on the bed. He asked her how her face was the same color as her braids and wondered how she kept that much hair in Houston's heat. He marveled at how she kept her body so youthful. He spoke to her about his dreams. He spoke to her about rules and how he disliked them.

It was uncanny, their meeting. Moments before she saw him at Fielding Café, she had stood still in this house, imagining standing on a wooden chair. Her head tethered closer to the ceiling, contemplating what it would feel like if her feet were suddenly suspended from the chair.

What a difference time makes, she thought. As she lay on her bed, she thought only of Miles—not of her father, not of her students, and not of all the collective moments prior to Miles.

This continued for days and weeks after. Sometimes she stood at the entrance to the High School for the Performing and Visual Arts, where she taught ethics and history, watching the kids trickle in, and thought of how good fortune had escaped her most of her life. But now, like a lottery, she had won it back.

She and Miles saw each other during the daytime, but couldn't let others know about their relationship. Although Miles belonged to her, he lived with another woman. They were cautious. Any attention might delay their plans.

The hours she spent with Miles and the love they had brewed so quickly played and replayed in her head. They relieved the repetitive memories of her father, knocking living and nonliving things out of his way. There were also more recent memories of days spent in Montrose streets and parks, peddling wares.

These memories were stubborn. They sneaked in and transported her to the time before Miles. Sometimes they appeared real in her mind, just as when they'd happened. There was the night she'd sat on her bed, counting her good fortunes, and heard a knock. She slipped on her robe and the knock got louder. A shadowy, tall figure stood at the door. He was not familiar, but his words were clear. A warning. From higher up the supply chain that oversaw the distribution of the pharmaceutical capsules she was given to sell. She tried to close the door. He blocked it with his foot, then pushed it wide open, but made sure to lock it behind him. She ran toward the bed and he followed. He jumped over the bed, narrowly missing her as she made a dash for it. She stumbled, then picked herself up. In the kitchen, she opened the drawer and drew a knife, but he lunged and wrestled it away from her. There was pain. Then the knife plunged too close to her heart, and she became numb as darkness filled the room.

Jennifer had explained to her mother that the attack was because of the cupcakes. Her mother did not believe her, but it was the truth. She'd barely graduated from Lamar High School, but had picked up a few of life's skills, such as baking, and put them to use. In the morning, she would fluff eggs and mix them with vanilla, flour, and cocoa powder. She kept the mixture waiting in the fridge until she acquired the dried, shredded hemp-leaf powder, the most essential ingredient. It made the cupcakes a hit on Saturday nights by Hyde Park or at Lola's Depot, the dive on Fairview Street. The distributors lurked around these places, refilling orders and collecting their loot after the peddling. Soon enough, Jennifer graduated to selling their pills. Along the way, she picked up more tricks of the trade, including keeping some of the pills for herself, so she didn't have to share all the profits.

After her knife wounds healed, she realized she was underqualified for that job and chose the opposite path: enrolling in college. It had been the right choice, because it had changed everything—except the visions.

They were invasive, visiting during the most sacred times. She watched herself step on a chair, next to the rope dangling like a carrot, and saw her feet suspended in the air. She couldn't have been dangling, really, because she was in her bedroom. With Miles. Between his whispers, she saw herself hanging from the ceiling in various corners of her apartment. She was not present, and Miles felt heavy. His whispers became loud. She moved her head, leaving him to whisper to her arms and then her legs and then her feet, so she could not hear the promises he made her. Not even when he clutched her face between his hands, which were cracked and calloused, probably from too many hours of playing drums. His mouth moved to hers as if in amazement at a new wonder. His breath reeked like Joe's Crawfish. He moved to her ears.

She could hear his rapid breathing, not in synch with hers. Her tongue refused to form the words in her head, and the fear pressed on her lungs, interrupting her breathing. He was moving fast, as if his life depended on it. Her eyes became blurry and her body could not distinguish who was who. Her mind did, but she could not get them to work together. He pulled her hair ever so gently. The sharp pains sprang from her memory, moving from her head down her body, piercing her insides, and she became paralyzed. When Miles was done, he took a deep breath, rested his hands behind his head, and smiled. Her tears compelled him to pull her in for a hug. This was the part she longed for, actually. His arms wrapped around her faded the memories to the background, sharpened her affection for him. Their breathing finally fell into synch. She held him as he fell asleep. She had to fight to preserve this feeling.

She watched him for thirty minutes, her body folded into the curves of his, because it was almost eight o'clock—time for him to return to the other who loved him. She did not want him to go, but if there was anything she had learned in the world, it was patience and kindness. Patience for the time they would finally exit Montrose together, and kindness for the other woman who cooked for him.

When he was gone, she jumped into the shower and closed her eyes, listening only to the sound of the water. After, she hugged the pillow, searching for his smell. She tried to make new memories that involved moving away from Montrose with Miles, away from judgmental eyes. Life could be filled with an old pickup, rustic furniture, and a slow life, many towns away from Houston.

The months moved fast. The exhaust pipe of her blue Nissan collapsed, eaten up by the rust as the mechanic had explained, and set them back in their aspirations. Miles talked and Jennifer escaped to her memories. The nice ones, about him. She found a way to interrupt her visions of the chair by simply concentrating on the first time she saw him at the club.

She thought about how, in school, he was no different from the others. It was as if, during their nights together, he was transformed from that person in the classroom.

Meanwhile, she was many things to him—his lover, sister, friend, and mother. When he wanted to be careless, she gave him advice. She knew that for things to go well this time, she had to control everything, including his love for her.

Finally, several months later, he insisted on leaving Montrose. He didn't understand why they couldn't just drive off and be together. She reminded him that money played a role in their lives. However, this no longer made sense to him. He wanted to know why she was so concerned with her job when he was sacrificing everything for her, including those he loved. He threw a glass at a wall, narrowly missing her, and then he left her apartment, banging the door on his way out and making new promises that did not include her.

The longing that kept her alive began to escape, inviting fear in its place. The vision reappeared, causing spasms that felt like they were pushing her heart out of her body. She clutched her chest and reached for her cell phone. In that moment, she realized that it had been her all along. They could have left anytime. She said this to a voice recording on his phone. Then she waited.

Past midnight, the door unlocked and he fell into her arms. She felt her breathing stabilizing and thought about how close she had come to losing everything. Just like the first time, she cupped his face and kissed him, and her entire body was riddled with a blinding happiness. His hands were not as active as hers, she realized. Then the trembles started. At first, they were small tremors, but they grew as the minutes stretched. She lifted her face from his chest and looked at him. His pupils had disappeared.

Jennifer felt terror. She needed to act, and fast. First to save him, then to save their love.

It was better if he was outside. If they found him in her apartment, there would be too many questions, then repercussions that would foil their plans. She took his cell phone and shoved it into her back pocket, then she kissed his mouth, even as it foamed. She pulled him from the couch and toward the door. With his limp arm over her shoulders, she dragged him by the waist, out into the streets in the dead of night. She did this out of love.

At the street corner, she called for help. She kept her breath steady and enunciated her words correctly. Any mistake she made, such as giving the wrong address, could cost him his life.

She felt an urge to cover his shivering body with her own, or with her jacket or a bedspread from her house. But this could be traced back to her, so instead she left him words filled with love and plans to escape when he got back from the hospital.

As she entered her house, she heard the siren and breathed a sigh of relief. For the rest of the night, she thought only of packing as she waited for him to burst through the door. The hours were not many, but they were long.

They stretched into the morning, into her workplace. One hour into her history lesson, the principal appeared at her door and motioned for her to step outside. Jennifer walked in silence next to the principal, whose usual jovial spirits were missing. Jennifer broke the silence, but the principal assured her the matter was better broached in his office.

Had they found out? she wondered. The familiar longing emerged within her. Inside the office, Jennifer stood still, waiting for the principal to say something. She motioned for Jennifer to take a seat on the couch next to her, opposite the mahogany desk. The principal said Miles's heart had stopped in the early hours of the morning, and that the doctors had done everything they could.

For a second, Jennifer felt relief, because it meant the

principal did not know. Then the reality of what she had heard set in, and her mind went blank. She did not hear the principal offering to tell her students that their classmate had succumbed to a drug overdose, or saying how heartbreaking it must be for Miles's single mother, who had sacrificed everything to get her son to college.

Jennifer went straight home from school. Just like in her vision, she stealthily stepped onto the chair. She carefully placed the rope, like a necklace. Then she pushed the chair.

PART IV

UP-AND-COMING AREAS, NEWLY REVITALIZED

HAPPY HUNTING

BY ICESS FERNANDEZ ROJAS
North Shore

> *Hunting is not a sport. In a sport, both sides should know they're in the game.* —Paul Rodriguez

The dark-green Ford F-150 skids across the three lanes of Beltway 8's feeder road, tires smoking like a dying fire. It roars past abandoned gas pumps and overflowing garbage cans, then rumbles to a stop at the convenience store. Its front door is only a few feet away, close enough for Marisol Gomez to see into the brightness inside.

She grunts as she steps out of the truck. Since the killings started, her muscles have forgotten how to relax. Glaring at the cashier through the thick, dirty store windows, she almost smells him—the foulness of what he is.

"Murderer," she whispers.

This Stop & Shop is the only convenience store still open at night in the crumbling, frightened East Side. Inside, he perches on his stool like a fat toad behind the counter. Reading. Hardly paying attention. In plain sight. He's taunting her, she knows. She wishes she'd figured it out sooner. Maybe then, Demetria and all the other women would still be alive. Children would have their mothers and boyfriends, their loves.

The oppressively hard rain has been beating on more than just pavement and buildings. Marisol is damp all over. Her clothes cling in an unbearable hug and her hair is wild with frizz. Her perfectly applied makeup is long gone. Everything she thought made her intimidating has washed away. Everything except the 9mm at the small of her back.

This is her moment. She's done something the puto cops couldn't do—or didn't want to. Her hustler's brain has figured out who the serial killer is, and she's going to bring him to justice. North Shore justice.

This could go one of two ways: a long chain of devastation and sorrow ends, or she becomes a statistic—one more body for the cops to find and put in the unsolved file. Marisol stuffs that thought down inside herself as she walks to the door, opens it, and steps in from the rain.

This one is for her girls.

"You're scary when you get like this."

Yessenia, timid as a newborn cat, tried to cool her fear with frozen yogurt. It was more soup than yogurt, with chunks of mango floating like ice cubes. The more she heard about Marisol's crazy plan, the more the soupy yogurt found its way into her mouth. Her best friend had conjured a plan that terrified Yessenia. Marisol wanted to capture the serial killer hunting brown and black women all over the East Side—North Shore, Channelview, and Sheldon—meaning every woman they knew. The plan would result in either jail time or death, and Yessenia didn't think her friend would look good as a corpse.

"It's gonna work, chica," Marisol practically yelled, her voice ringing through the interior of Menchie's frozen yogurt parlor. She used her siren-red manicured fingers to mimic shooting a gun. "Two pops to the head and it's over!"

The two young women sat in the long, narrow establishment that screamed with hot pinks and lime greens. It echoed with bad pop music, meant to keep up customer spirits. Outside was a sweltering wet heat; inside was comfortable enough for a penguin and his family to enjoy. But the blinding colors and air-conditioning couldn't keep customers' minds from the news: there was a serial killer on the hunt.

So far, eight women had been found in nearby parks or wooded areas, each strangled with a piece of clothing they'd been wearing: shirts, bras, panties, even shoelaces. Not raped. Never touched below the neck. It wasn't about sex. Yessenia said it was about control, winning, or maybe even ending something. She and Marisol knew all the victims—they were all friends, friends of cousins, or former classmates. That was the East Side: more connected than a politician and only half as shady.

"Aren't you tired of this shit?" Marisol asked, hands gesturing to accentuate every word. "It's like the freaking *Hunger Games*. It's to the point that we're not sure if our own friends are out to get us."

"They aren't. Probably aren't." Yessenia tucked a sliver of dirty-brown hair behind her ear, avoiding Marisol's wildly gleaming eyes.

"Come on, Yessenia." Marisol's own hair—curly, wine-red, crunchy with hairspray and gel—shook with her words. "You haven't left your house in three weeks. Every time I call you, you're too scared to answer."

"We have to let the police do their thing, Mari. Just chill."

"Those bunch of good ol' boys? They love brown and black extermination. Since Freddie Gray and Sandra Bland, we're being hunted. And with that dude as president, it's open season. You heard the latest, right? No? Amber in Channelview. Check this out."

Marisol whipped out her cell phone in its glittery pink

case and tapped the screen, bringing up a video of two deputies aiming guns at two men in a bright-blue mustang. Yessenia
recognized the car. She looked away. The gunshots sounded
like firecrackers on the phone's small speakers, reverberating
throughout the shop. Marisol identified the wounded, and
those names sounded familiar too. Everything was too familiar.

"That went down after finding out about Marissa. Them
boys are mad as hell. And after Dejah, the streets are lit. How
many more have to die before this fool gets caught?"

"Why us, though? Like, why can't the homies . . ." Yessenia
trailed off and wrapped herself tighter in her brown cardigan.

"The homies ain't about handling any business but their
own. Amber had kids, man. I met them. She brought them
to the house to pick up a registration sticker. Now they're
orphans—part of the system. It ain't right."

The stickers were an old argument between them. For
Marisol, selling fake car registration and inspection stickers
was a means to an end. Either you hustled, or you got hustled. Sometimes Marisol thought Yessenia considered herself
too good for the East Side, with its taco trucks and discount
grocery stores. Too good for the oil refineries and the upwind
from Pasadena. She couldn't bear to walk on a street with
no sidewalks. Didn't she know, sometimes folks need to make
their own way in the world? That's what Marisol was doing.

Yessenia stirred her orange yogurt soup in disappointment.
Marisol's fake car stickers were bad enough. She also charged
little old ladies to fill out their Lone Star card applications for
food stamps. Twenty-five dollars a pop and no guarantees. But
they kept coming, because they needed someone who knew
how to read and write English. Grandmothers, the disabled,
single mothers—Marisol took advantage of everyone equally.
She even seemed proud of it.

"I wish you'd stop doing that stuff."

Marisol rolled her eyes at her best friend. "Ain't no one worrying about no damn stickers right now, Yessi. We're being killed, pendeja!"

Nearby, an old woman sitting with her young granddaughter glared at Marisol, who responded with an ugly look of her own, daring her to say something, before continuing her train of thought: "I bet you he's a cop. They know about killing us and getting away with it."

"Mari, that's not fair."

Yessenia's phone buzzed. She glanced at its screen, then placed it facedown on the table. "Can we take a break from talking about this?" She pushed away her yogurt and stared out the window, her face flushed as snow.

Marisol leaned over to hug her. "I'm not letting anything happen to you, I promise," she whispered. "Ain't no one messing with my girl. Nobody."

The promise hit Yessenia's ear in a boom. This was how it was with them: the whispers were never quiet, and the secrets never stayed secret. Usually, there wasn't anything Yessenia could keep from Marisol. So it surprised her that Marisol hadn't noticed the new gold bracelet on her wrist or her dangling earrings. She was too caught up in her anger.

"Wet out there, ain't it?" she says.

Behind the counter and the thick glass, the cashier flips through a magazine and doesn't acknowledge Marisol. His name is Roscoe, Yessenia found out. It's obvious he wants nothing to do with his customers. He's almost forgettable in his bright-blue cotton polo and khakis. Roscoe wears his role like camouflage, Marisol thinks, sizing up his prey without her knowing. She's just a woman alone, stopping into the store for a drink. Not paying attention to the cabrón about to crush her windpipe. He's one of those East Side country white boys, cowboy boots and hat like an unwritten uniform. If not the cowboy uniform, then an old trucker hat like every man in his family wore after they went bald. That was years away for Roscoe. He kept his blond hair short on the sides and longer on the top. He wasn't Marisol's type, not by a long shot. She preferred her country boys like white noise, in the background and hardly noticeable. But this one, this one looked like he had something to prove.

Even the hunting ground is incognito—just an average convenience store. This one is about the size of a thumb, with bright fluorescent lights flooding every corner. Not one place to hide. A strong smell of bleach punches Marisol's gut. It's like a hospital, but filled with snacks. She has to admit, it's a logical setup. If she were a killer, she might've thought of it herself.

"Bathroom?"

Roscoe points to the back of the store where a gray door stands open.

Marisol walks slowly past the rows of candy bars and motor oil, casing the area. No one but her and the guy behind the bulletproof glass.

Fuck! How am I gonna get this fool to come out from behind the counter?

If she can't do that, the piece at the small of her back is useless. The restroom door scrapes against the floor with a loud noise as she closes it behind her.

"Where are you going to get a gun?"

"I got a cousin," Marisol said.

"Of course," Yessenia muttered under her breath. She

wrapped herself tighter in her favorite brown cardigan—the one that made her feel safe. She'd put her hair in a messy ponytail, ready for whatever Marisol had planned for the night. Her jeans, however, were new, and had cost enough to fill the truck's gas tank three times over. They were a gift, and she wanted to show them off, even if only to her best friend. But Marisol was once again distracted.

The Hartz Chicken Buffet parking lot was empty as last call at a funeral home. Marisol watched the employees through the stained windows. They buzzed around in dark aprons, cleaning and serving the final customers of the night.

A slow, steady rain made the streets as slick as glass. Cars slithered down Uvalde Road, careful and saint-like. No speeding. No running lights. North Shore had never been this obedient. The most recent murder had been discovered the night before. Bethany Ife, former cheerleader at C.E. King High School in Sheldon. They found her in the wooded area behind a neighborhood off Beltway 8.

The parking lot lights hummed a dull yellow on cars for sale, cracked pavement, and a long-abandoned ATM decorated with weeds. There was once life here, where a haircut, polished nails, and a good meal were possible. Now those options were gone and an uneasy silence filled every crevice in these neighborhoods. There was a collective holding of breath, a closed eye, the frozen-contortion-before-the-doctor's-needle type of pause. The East Side sat motionless in thought, waiting, wondering who was next.

Inside the truck, it had been an hour of off-tune humming and air-conditioned chill. Marisol watched Hartz customers get their fill of the all-you-can-eat chicken and roll themselves into their cars. A scrawny discount rent-a-cop escorted each woman from the restaurant to her car. He looked fresh out of high school and still in puberty. *What's he going to do if real stuff goes down?* Marisol wondered.

"We should add security services," she said, then mentally added that to her business plan for Marisol & Company Investigations. That meant adding extra people. Yessi, with her scared ass, could stay in the office doing spreadsheets or whatever assistants do. This new hustle would be better than the selling all those stickers or filling out those forms. She could be a legit business owner, calling some shots around here. She'd be important. Everyone would know her.

"What are you talking about?" said Yessenia.

"We're gonna start, like, a detective agency. A chick detective agency. In North Shore. Dope, right?"

Yessenia wasn't surprised. Marisol loved money more than herself and she loved attention more than that. Surely she'd name the thing after herself and make Yessenia file papers. *It was my idea!* she'd say, making herself the hero and Yessenia the lame sidekick.

Yessenia flicked the air-conditioning vent closed and changed the subject: "Why are we meeting him here?"

"He likes symbolism, the big pendejo." Marisol flicked the vent back open. When Yessenia didn't respond, she sucked her teeth loudly. "Ay, I have to tell you everything? You don't know about the Channelview cheerleading mom? That white woman who wanted to get her hija on the team, so she sent someone to kill that other girl's mom? They planned that shit right here."

"Mari, you need to reconsider this stupid plan of yours. It's going to get you killed."

"It's not stupid," Marisol snapped. "Look—if you want to go back to your house and the little scraps of life you've made for yourself, dale. But me? I'm gonna catch this son of a bitch, then ride this gravy train to the end."

Yesenia rolled her eyes. "Why does it have to be you?"

"Because no one else is doing it. No one else is gonna be out here making this cheddar. Can you imagine if I off this guy? Word spreads on the street, and folks come running to the door."

"You're not Batman, you know."

"Nah, I'm better. I'm his half sister they don't talk about, from the barrio." Marisol winked.

A female vigilante—why the heck did Marisol think she could be such a thing? Yessenia peered at her friend's face in the pink light from a flickering neon sign and thought she looked more like the Joker. Which, when she really thought about it . . . why was he a villain, anyway? Maybe he was misunderstood and only trying to make the world a better place. Maybe the Joker was the true hero.

Suddenly, Yessenia's phone buzzed in her back pocket, making her jump.

Marisol laughed, a couple of seconds longer than necessary. "Who is it? Your boyfriend?" Her schoolyard tone rubbed Yessenia like sandpaper.

"Stop laughing at me."

"You're scared. Like, little-girl scared. When are you gonna put your big-girl panties on? Damn, no wonder . . ."

"No wonder what?" Yessenia tried to make her words rumble into a growl, but couldn't quite manage it.

"He's here."

A Dodge Ram, so black it nearly disappeared, rolled into the parking space next to them. The driver's-side window opened enough for a pair of glaring eyes to survey the scene. Then a man—a beast—emerged from the truck. Marisol's cousin was six-foot-plus and built like a bull. Short buzzcut. Eyes like the bottoms of bullets. He marched toward the back cab of the truck.

"Stay here." Marisol hopped out of the truck and sauntered over to her cousin. He gave her a knowing nod and she nodded back. The exchange was swift. Marisol pointed, the cousin leaned into the darkness of the back cab. She yelled at her cousin and he yelled back. In the end, he handed over a covered bundle and she kissed him on the cheek.

Yessenia read a text on her phone. She responded, *I'll see you soon*, and stuffed the phone into her pocket as Mari opened the door.

Smiling as if she'd just walked away from an explosion in an action movie, Marisol brandished a gun from the bundle. "Now we ride! And we're gonna get 'em—soon!"

Marisol's heart drums like a death march. Inside the bathroom, she feels claustrophobic, the sand-colored walls closing in on her. She grabs the gun, places it on the sink, and punches the hand drier button. She turns the nozzle up to dry her hair. She leans into the heat and closes her eyes, letting the air play with her long curly locks. This is going to be tougher than she thought.

She can hear Roscoe talking to someone. She cracks the door open, not far enough to repeat its loud squeak, and peeks through. The round-bellied cashier is on his cell phone. Marisol catches shards of conversation.

"Are . . . sure . . . yourself . . . let you know . . . going to be fine . . . smile . . . chula . . . right."

The day after Marisol got the gun, Yessenia hoped the downpour would deter her search for the killer. But Marisol showed up at her door dressed in all black: jeans as tight as yoga pants, and black boots with heels so high they could be considered weapons. She looked like a Latina superhero, but without a cape.

"This is stupid," Yesenia said as Marisol barged through her doorway. "I can't believe you're serious about this."

Marisol looked her up and down. "You look like a librarian with the flu. Go get ready. And hurry—we need to pick up something on the way."

"What if I don't want to go?" Yessenia swatted at a loose strand from her messy ponytail and adjusted her dark-rimmed glasses.

Marisol rolled her eyes and tossed her curls. Hands on her hips, she stared down on Yessenia. "Look, stop being a punk, huh? You act like you didn't even grow up here. What else you got to do tonight? It's not like you have a boyfriend. What are you gonna do—play with your cat and watch Netflix?"

"I was in the middle of—"

"When did you turn like this?" Marisol waved her hand dismissively. The words were gasoline, and Yessenia knew the match would soon follow. "You're so weak."

Yessenia shuffled toward her room, her house shoes scraping the dusty clay of the Saltillo tile with each reluctant step. Marisol flung herself on the couch, a leg over the armrest and her cell phone between her long fingers. She pounded out social media statuses as she waited for Yessenia. She didn't notice the new-furniture smell in the living room or the pair of men's tennis shoes under the couch.

The drive was filled with Marisol's off-key singing to the radio's latest Tejano song and Yessenia's tense silence.

"You know I love you, right?" Marisol always started the apologies with a question. "I'm sorry if you thought I was mean. It's just that, sometimes . . ."

"Sometimes?"

"You need a push toward what's good for you. If it were up

to you, you'd live in that house and never leave. Just work and home. You even get your groceries delivered."

"I don't get my groceries—"

"There's a whole world out there, Yessi. I know North Shore and the East Side ain't much, but damn, girl. Get with it. Get a hobby. Get laid! Something!"

"Actually, I just—"

"This world that you created for yourself ain't right. You're like one of those mole people who never comes out the house."

"But I was out all day today. In fact—"

"You gotta interact, girl. There's a whole world out there for us. Give me a smile? Come on, smile."

The station had started its commercial break with one about a new weight-loss tactic to improve your love life. Marisol watched as a slow smile spread across her friend's face and nodded her approval.

She closes the restroom door again. She can hear her heartbeat in her ears, trying to escape through her throat. Her hands are shaking and she can't stop them, no matter how tight she balls her fists. Closing her eyes, Marisol thinks, *Breathe in, breathe out,* on repeat until she's somewhat still. Still enough. "You got this, Mari," she whispers to herself.

She grabs the 9mm from the edge of the sink, the sound of the metal on porcelain louder than she intended. Returning it to the small of her back, the piece is like a reassuring hand. With a final shake to take out the last nerves, she opens the squeaky gray door into the store.

She steps into darkness. The bright hospital lights are off, as are the lights outside. *Shit.* It will take a minute for her eyes to adjust so she keeps her back on the wall. *Don't call out. He knows I'm not in the bathroom anymore.*

The frosty refrigerators are cold on her back. She remembers there were six coolers along the rear of the store. They end at the coffee machines. In front, the chip aisle is closest to the Cokes. She remembers that from last time.

Marisol steps deliberately to the right, her heel making a loud click. Quickly, she slips off her boots and leaves them on the floor. Steps left. Then right. Her toes feel the polished, unyielding floor. She reaches back and grips the piece like her cousin showed her.

"You're not going to make this easy, are you?" His voice rings through the dark and drips with playfulness.

Marisol's stomach flips. She doesn't speak. She'll let the gunshots be her response.

"Cat got your tongue? This is the first time you've shut up in years."

Marisol sees outlines in the shadows. She's now in front of the chip aisle. To her right is the coffee pot, still hot and full. Next to the pot is a doorway to the back. She aims at that space. Readying herself.

"You should have noticed something by now. But you only see what you think is important, don't you?"

The voice is close, almost close enough to touch. She keeps the gun trained on that space, ready to move fast, to follow his voice.

"Oh, no? She didn't notice? Not at all? This will be delicious."

The first night of patrolling was about as exciting as a trip to the dentist. The duo drove all night, looking for anything suspicious. Yet they didn't know what, exactly. Old cars? Random men walking down the street? A deranged guy running with scissors? They drove past refineries and grazing fields peppered with horses. They drove past darkened strip malls and abandoned easements sheltering the sleeping homeless. Using the freeways as their personal Grand Prix and the Beltway like a drag race course, they drove past Waffle Houses and libraries, into neighborhoods that had seen better days when better days were more plentiful. Even North Shore's Walmart, with its normally towering parking lights, was dim and abandoned. Channelview was worse, and Sheldon looked like no one lived there anymore. That was the worst part of searching for the killer: seeing their neighborhood looking like a ghost town and feeling like a slow death.

On the seventh night of patrolling, with nothing to show for their efforts but sleepless nights and empty gas tanks, Marisol wanted hot Cheetos and a Big Red. The Stop & Shop convenience store called to her like a beacon in a sea of darkness.

"Maybe we should just go home," said Yessenia.

"Don't be a baby," Marisol scoffed.

Inside, the store was bright with whitewashed walls and stung with the strong smell of Clorox.

"It stinks in here, man!" Marisol yelled to the cashier behind the thick plexiglass as she pushed open the door, Yessenia shuffling behind her and smiling apologetically.

"That's the smell of clean," the attendant replied, looking up from his book, *Programming for Dummies*, and winking at Yessenia. The fluorescent light bounced off the plastic badge on his chest, illuminating the name *Roscoe*.

Marisol rolled her eyes, walked to a refrigerator full of sodas, and saw a familiar face: Demetria Jenkins.

"Girl, how you be?" Demetria swooped Marisol in a bear hug, her boxer braids falling into her face.

Yessenia smiled as she watched this scene and prepared for Demetria's crushing embrace. But Demetria kept talking with

Marisol, so Yessenia shuffled to the chip aisle. She peeked at them through the bags of discount Doritos. They giggled and gossiped like they were back in high school, falling into the type of easy banter Yessenia didn't have with anyone—not even her own best friend. She wondered if Roscoe saw what was happening and guessed how embarrassed she felt. Eventually, she got tired of eavesdropping and walked back to the pair.

"Oh, where are my manners?" Marisol said when she finally noticed Yessenia had reappeared. "Demetria, you remember Yessenia Perez, right? She went to school with us."

Demetria cocked her head to the side and made her eyes into slits for a moment before shaking her head. "Sorry, I don't remember."

Marisol and Demetria continued catching up, so Yessenia carried their items to the cash register. Roscoe smiled at her warmly. His grin tickled his earlobes and it made her blush for a second. His too-tight work shirt covered his belly over his belt buckle. As he rang up her purchase, Yessenia noticed the callouses and scrapes on his hands, worker's hands. They knew what it was like to get at life the hard way.

"Is there anything else you need?" he asked in a low voice.

"Let's hope not." She gave him a small smile.

"You know where to come if you do."

Yessenia responded with a shy laugh and left the store. It was another fifteen minutes before Marisol joined her in truck.

"It's been awhile since I've seen Demetria. Isn't she great? We're gonna get together soon, after all this murder stuff dies down."

"She didn't even remember me," Yessenia said. "And she used to cheat off my homework."

"She's getting married next month. Invited me to the wedding." Marisol slid the truck into reverse and then drove into the night.

Yessenia nibbled on a chip. Her phone buzzed. She occupied herself with its screen as they rode home, with Marisol talking about Demetria all the way.

Two days later, when a pair of runners found Demetria's body in Gene Greene Park, Marisol sank into the type of sadness that made her snap at everyone around her. Yessenia received the brunt of it, as she was used to.

"We should have been able to find this asshole. Pero no—you had plans. If we'd been out searching that night, Demetria would still be alive!"

"Are you blaming me?"

"I have to blame someone!"

"Maybe Demetria said or did something she shouldn't have."

"Demetria was amazing. No one who knew her would want her dead!"

"No one's a saint, Marisol."

Yessenia made a hard right and skidded the Ford F-150 across three lands of the Beltway 8 feeder road. She'd always wanted to drive like that—like she owned the road. In her car, she'd been much closer to the street. In this truck, she could see everything. That was why she'd bought it several months before. It'd proven very useful.

Marisol was extremely proud of herself for figuring out who the murderer was. She yelled at Yessenia to drive faster, worried that another woman would be attacked before the night's end. Yessenia did as commanded, as usual.

The truck rumbled into the parking lot. Marisol glared at Roscoe through the window.

Yessenia watched her watching him. "What if it isn't him? I mean, what makes you so sure?" Her phone buzzed in her back pocket, but she ignored it. She wanted to hear Marisol's answer.

"It's totally him. It's the only thing that makes sense. Plus, look at him. He just looks like a crazy loser. God, why does it have to be raining tonight?"

"You don't know anything about him."

"He just looks like he hates black and brown women. Plus, he's, like, forty years old and doesn't even have a car. Look— there's no cars in this parking lot except us."

Yessenia wanted to argue, but there was no point. Marisol saw what she wanted, never what was in front of her. She handed Marisol the gun. "Here—it's a full clip," she said.

"I mean, we'll find out for sure. At the very least, I'll scare the shit out of him and make his ass confess."

Yessenia nodded solemnly.

"Hey, but . . . if this doesn't work . . ."

"You know what? You've got this. I believe it now."

Marisol tried to hide her proud smile and assume a tough look. "After this is done . . . we should take a break. You know, before we start our business?"

"Sure. Anything you want."

Marisol reached over and squeezed her friend's arm. She'd been too hard on Yessenia—too mean. She'd taken her for granted. After this was all done, she'd tell her so. Buy her something nice, like a dinner or something. Marisol smiled again, to let Yessenia know she wasn't scared, and slipped out of the truck.

Yessenia waited until she saw Marisol walk through the store, into the bathroom. She picked up her phone.

"Hey, baby."

"Are you sure you don't want to do this one yourself?" said the voice at the other end.

"No, amor. I'm still tired from Demetria and Bethany."

"All right. I'll call you know when it's done."

Yessenia hung up and put the truck into gear, pulling out of the parking lot, toward the freeway home. Behind her, Roscoe flicked off the store lights.

THE FALLS OF WESTPARK

BY PIA PICO

Westpark Corridor

There must have been an accident. Traffic on Westpark seemed unnaturally thick, even for four thirty p.m. Jules sat idling in her Malibu, studying the view of the Falls of Westpark apartment complex, the Presidium office building, and the brackish ditch that ran between. Today, a Home Depot cart enriched the vista, the telltale orange basket jutting toward the scrubbed aluminum sky. An afternoon breeze kicked up by a hurricane brewing in the gulf whipped a few plastic bags from their sticking places in the weeds. Empty soda bottles littered the tamped-earth trails on either side of the water, which resembled the aguas negras Jules had seen in Mexico as a child. She watched three or four day laborers head toward Windswept Lane, just parallel to Westpark and rife with low-rent apartment buildings, liquor stores, small markets, and casas de belleza that served the Hispanic population in the vicinity around the Houston Flea Market.

A text popped up on her phone: *Glad you wouldn't give me a ride bitch! Nice traffic. Looks like you're fuked.* This was followed by a smiley-face emoji.

It was Kelly, whom she'd left at the Triangle Club, after the 2:30 open-discussion meeting. He'd asked her for a ride home, but she'd begged off. She needed to shower and eat before her eight p.m. shift at Kroger, so he'd hoofed it to the

Shell station, where his sister would pick him up to drive him back to his halfway house.

WTF! Jules texted back. *I've been sitting here for 10 mins. Find out what's going on and text me back.* She eyed the engine temperature gauge on the control panel of her Malibu—the needle edging toward red.

She rolled about .3 miles over the next fifteen minutes before she saw the text from Kelly drop down over the top of her Instagram feed: *Holy shit. Lady's body found in dumpster outside of Westpark recycling center. K9 having a field day.*

??!!!

Turn around and go the other way if I was you, he wrote.

Good idea. Jules did just that.

As she got ready for work that evening, Jules listened to an anchorwoman on the local news: *"Deputies are unable to identify a woman's body that was found in a dumpster at the Westpark Consumer Recycling Center in the 5900 block of Westpark. Crime Stoppers is offering a reward of up to $5,000 for information that leads to an arrest."*

The next day, before the 2:30 meeting, Jules and Kelly sat at the green plastic picnic table on the Triangle Club's cobblestone patio, smoking. The Triangle Club occupied a dingy office flex space in the Westpark Business & Ed Center, an industrial park built in the 1970s. The club served as a space dedicated to the principles of Alcoholics Anonymous. Kelly had almost six years of sobriety; Jules, six months. Kelly's style of dress rarely varied: he wore extra-large T-shirts, khaki or camouflage cargo shorts, Teva sandals. A Houston Astros cap often topped his graying pageboy. Despite his yellow-brown teeth and pocked face, Jules liked fellowshipping with him before the meetings, hearing his stories of what it was like before he got sober. He used to be able to drink three beers, he said, no problem, but somewhere between three beers and eleven, he'd find himself at the dope house. He'd gone nine years without drinking or doing drugs, he said—a dry drunk—before prison. Before prison, he'd had a wife, a full-time job at one of them big oil companies—all the things. When he lost his job during the Houston oil bust, when his wife left him, when one night he ran into his old drug dealer in the corner liquor store, then it was back on.

"I told my old dealer I ain't got no money," Kelly said. "*That's all right*, said the dealer, *I can cover you*. He knew that once I started doing that shit again, I'd be selling for him in no time. It got so bad: I was doing meth, cocaine, *heroween*. I went home to my dad's house and asked him to lock me up in my old bedroom. He did. He cooked my meals and brought them to me. I was selling drugs through my bedroom window, but he found out and had them deep bars put up over them. But I figured I could get the customers to meet me a few houses away, so I would sneak out. I did that about two times, and when I got back to the house he was standing there on the porch, arms folded. *You don't even want to get well!* he said, and kicked me out. Soon after that, I ended up in prison. That's what it took for me to get sober, and not one or two years. It took four or five years for me to get it."

Whenever Kelly acted like he was making some sort of pass at Jules, she reminded him: "Practice the principles. No thirteenth-stepping." Her sponsor said that to her often. Even still, Kelly didn't stop staring at her boobs. She figured it was an honest enough exchange: he'd share his stories; she'd let him stare. As long as his advances stayed visual, she could handle them. She was trusting her higher power to keep her safe.

"I think the killer is Jake," Jules said. Jake was a guy who recently stopped coming to the 2:30. The word was that he'd relapsed. "Remember he works at Home Depot? He probably carted her body to the recycling center in that Home Depot cart I saw dumped in the ditch yesterday. I pass by that ditch every day and always look at it. That cart wasn't there before the body was in the dumpster."

Kelly laughed hard at her theory, accidentally blowing smoke in her face. "Girl, there's Home Depot carts in every ditch and bayou in this city! First off, no perp is gonna take that kinda time. Trust me. I know perps. What you got against Jake, anyway? And Christ on a bike! Why you always looking down a ditch?"

"How do you know he didn't do it?" Jules asked. "You always tell me to watch out for people with clay feet."

"First of all, Jake ain't got no clay feet, because them's that do gotta be uppity types—you know, people that looks high but aims low—and Jake ain't uppity. Second of all, I know Jake; he's good people."

"Well, I don't know. I just have a feeling about him."

"What—he stare at your titties more than the rest of us?"

Dan, the leader of the 2:30 meeting on Wednesdays, arrived in his suit and tie, looking every bit the lawyer. He never said what he did for a living, and neither Jules nor Kelly ever asked. People in AA didn't ask each other that kind of stuff. Everyone was happy to just show up at the club for another day sober. "Keep coming back," they said at the end of each meeting, holding hands. "It works if you work it."

When Jules wondered aloud why Dan always led the 2:30 in a suit, Kelly answered, "He's faking it—faking it to make it."

Dan stopped by the picnic table on his way into the meeting. He smelled good. Jules recognized the Comme des Garçon Wood-something-or-other her ex used to wear.

"What are y'all yakking about?" Dan asked.

Kelly took a drag off his Camel and turned his head to blow the smoke to the side, away from Dan, but he kept his eyes on Jules.

Jules said, "About the girl's body they found in the Westpark Recycling dumpster yesterday."

"God," Dan drawled, "that's a grisly thing, isn't it? I heard about it on the news last night."

"I think the body was dumped outta this Home Depot cart I saw in the ditch yesterday," Jules said. Kelly kicked her under the table.

"What does that cart tell you?" Dan asked. He had a knowing tone in his voice.

"That some homeless dude or some Mexican did it," Kelly cut in. "Those are the sorts always stealing shopping carts."

"Hey," Jules said, "I know you don't know this, cabrón, but I'm Mexican."

"Ho!" Dan laughed. "Don't step on the toes of your fellows; they'll retaliate!"

"You're not Mexican," Kelly said. "What kind of Mexican are *you*?!"

"The Mexican kind," Jules answered. It wasn't worth going into it with him. Like everyone else, he wasn't going to believe her—because of her strawberry-blond hair, her blue eyes, her pale skin. Only Mexicans seemed to know that not all Mexicans looked alike; not all of them had brown or black hair, brown or black eyes, and brown skin.

"Anyways," Jules continued, "those guys walking back and forth along that ditch? They're Salvadorans."

"Now how would you know that?" Kelly said.

"Ricas pupusas," Jules said, referring to the handwritten neon poster she passed every Sunday on her way to the Trian-

gle Club. Families from Windswept ambled along the ditch's dirt trails to the parking lot of St. Michael's Academy, where they lined up to buy these homemade savory stuffed-corn tortillas. Jules stubbed out her cigarette and stood. "Salvadoran comfort food," she said, blowing smoke straight into Kelly's face.

She left him sitting by himself and entered the door held by Dan, who'd pulled it open for another woman. Jules had never seen her before, this girl of maybe twenty-two, wearing a spaghetti-strap camisole, jeans ripped at the knees and studded with rhinestone butterflies.

For the past four months, Dan had been leading the Wednesday 2:30 open-discussion meetings. Daily attendance at 2:30 meetings ranged from four to fifteen people. The hotter it was outside, the more people in the small, windowless room. While other meeting leaders read from *Alcoholics Anonymous: The Big Book*, or from the daily meditations in *Twenty-Four Hours a Day*, on Wednesdays with Dan, the topic was always the same: alcoholism.

Halfway through the meeting, when Dan passed the basket, Jules dropped in her two dollars, then handed it to Kelly, who looked at her, shook his head and grumbled, "You're not Mexican."

"Kelly?" Dan called on him. "You wanna share?"

"Um, uh," he passed the basket without putting money in it, "I'm Kelly, and I'm an alcoholic."

"Hi, Kelly," the group chorused.

"I, uh, I think I'm just gonna listen today." He folded his hands on top of his belly and grimaced at Jules.

After the meeting, while Kelly was in the restroom, Dan approached Jules.

"Grab a coffee with me."

Shocked, Jules hesitated. She and Dan had never exchanged any type of back-and-forth before. "I'm waiting for Kelly," she said.

Dan smirked, laughed. "Oh." She could tell he had the wrong idea.

"We're not together, me and Kelly. I was just gonna say goodbye."

"Okay. Meet me at Starbucks on Hillcroft and 59," he said and walked out the door.

"Come on, come on." Jules banged on her steering wheel as she waited to turn left onto Westpark. Not far north, Hillcroft turned into Voss, and the dilapidated apartment complexes of Woodlake and Briar Meadow gave way to the seventies single-story mansions of Piney Point. But here, amid the thicket of electrical transmission towers and the sooty skein of overpasses and underpasses, a single-family dwelling would likely incinerate under the scalding sky. The only habitable enclaves in the immediate vicinity were one hundred– to three hundred–unit apartment complexes, one of which was the Falls of Westpark, a phlegmy stucco building that Jules passed each day on her way to the club. The Falls' walkways faced the road, open to the air but shrouded in shadows. One whole flank of the building rubbed against the cindery bulk of State Highway 59. Jules suspected most of its inhabitants were the day laborers who loitered in the shade of the 59 underpass, waiting for jobs. Every time she drove past the Falls, she stared at its dim walkways and wondered what the people who lived there felt, what they hoped for, how they dealt with all the noise and exhaust from the freeway. She noted a few children's plastic toys through the grills bordering the walkways. Maybe some of the day laborers had families with them, wives or mothers or sisters who worked as nannies and/or housekeepers for families in Piney Point, Uptown, Hunter's Creek, River Oaks.

Since she'd broken up with her ex, Jules was all alone in Texas, family-wise. She'd moved to Houston seven years prior from Seal Beach, California, to attend Rice University on a diversity scholarship. Her plan had been to graduate with an English degree and return to the West Coast for law school, but she'd ended up getting serious with Larry. They'd met when she started working weekends at the Signature Kroger for extra cash; he was her manager. With only six hours left until graduation, she took a break from school and moved in with him. During this time, her drinking progressed to the point of her blacking out nightly and throwing up each morning. Within the year, Kroger had fired Larry, he had kicked Jules out of their shared apartment, and she had become a full-time cashier to pay her own rent. Going back to college, even though she was nearly finished, seemed beyond her physical and emotional capacities.

While her mom urged her to return to Seal Beach, something about Houston's hardscrabble, unsentimental landscape appealed to her. Despite the superficial prettiness of Southern California (paradise, some people called it), she'd grown up in an infernal household, her alcoholic father constantly yelling at her and putting her down, her mother enabling all of it, her younger brother addicted to surfing and speedballs to cope with the consequent racket in his brain. After this brother died from a heroin overdose, Jules could no longer bear the sight of the Pacific Ocean. The difference between the external beauty of her homeland and the internal bleakness of her heart was too much for her. Houston fit her; she fit Houston.

Traffic would not ease up. Four minutes passed as Jules

waited for a break in the oncoming cars, although she probably missed a couple opportunities, so flustered she was by Dan's invitation. Why would he invite her to coffee? Or command her, more like it. He had (he said) twenty-plus years sober; he wouldn't flirt with a woman in recovery, would he? Especially one as new as Jules? She checked her face in the rearview mirror; the Rum Raisin lipstick feathered out from the smoking lines over her upper lip. She needed to stop smoking, but goddamnit, one thing at a time. She'd given up almost *everything*.

When she looked back at the traffic, she saw just enough of a break to swing out left, then turn immediately right onto the road which ran between the Hillcroft Transit Station and a wooden complex that housed businesses such as Jaycee's Exotic Dancewear, Relief Ambulance Services, Video and Surveillance Equipment Outlet; a church, Iglesia Pentecostes: Camino Al Rey de Gloria; and a Hindu temple, the Sanatan Shiv Shakti Mandir. At the intersection of Harwin and Hillcroft, Jules's pussy started pulsating and thumping against the seam in the crotch of her jeans. Her heart sped up; her breath grew thin and shallow. "Uh, uh-h-h," she groaned, shocked by the sudden flush of lust. Waiting for the light to change, she shook her head no, feeling betrayed by her body. Dan must have something of the governor in him—a personality that, like alcohol and drugs, she was powerless against. Although she hadn't picked up this energy consciously, her body had absorbed it and was making it known now to her mind. But dear god! She was living by the principles now; she needed to place principles above pussy.

When she arrived at Starbucks, her underwear was so wet she could barely catch her breath. She feared that if she went into the Starbucks, then, true to previous form, she'd be back in the parking lot in less than thirty minutes, straddling Dan in the passenger seat of his S-Class, sliding up and down his lawyer cock while he sucked her tits.

She found an empty parking spot next to his Benz. She checked his windows: they were duly tinted. As she headed to the entrance, she said a prayer to her higher power that she'd learned from one of the old guys in the meeting: *Help me, help me, help me. Thank you. Thank you. Thank you.* It was her favorite.

Inside, Dan stood near the front of the line. Jules stopped behind the last person, hoping to calm herself down, but he saw her and waved her toward him.

"What'll you have? My treat." He placed a hand on her back and moved her in front of him.

Behind her, Dan was a force, a magnet attracting her hips toward his. She stopped herself from leaning into the almonds, madeleines, and gift cards, afraid she would just succumb and press her ass against his package. "Dark roast, please," she practically gasped to the barista.

"After two p.m. we only have Pike's Place," the barista replied.

"That's fine," she said. "I need to use the restroom," she murmured to Dan, and sped off before answering the barista's question: "Room for cream?"

When she emerged from the bathroom, Dan was sitting at a counter near the front window.

"Can we sit outside?" Jules asked. She trusted that the gaggle of Bangladeshi men at one of the tables, the roar of the freeway two hundred feet away, and her own hypochondria about breathing in car exhaust would dampen her lust significantly.

"Just to be clear," Dan said, when they'd situated themselves at a free table on the patio, "I'm not trying to thirteenth-step you."

"You're not?" Jules replied, both embarrassed and relieved.

"I mean, good! I hope you're not." She tuned her ears for a moment to the sound of semis trucking north on 59 while Dan removed his suit jacket and tie. Outside, in the afternoon glare, she could see that his eyes were sort of topaz-y, and his cheeks had more color than they did under the fluorescent lights of the Triangle's windowless rooms.

"No. I'm not. I wanted to talk to you about Kelly."

Jules took a sip of her Pike's Place through the slit in the plastic top. She adjusted herself in her chair. Her pussy-pounding had ebbed almost completely.

"I see the two of you together a lot," he said.

"We only see each other at the meetings. My sponsor told me to show up twenty minutes early and stay twenty minutes late, for the fellowship. Kelly's the only one there, usually, until right before the meeting. Sometimes I give him a ride back to his halfway house, but it's so far away that most of the time I don't."

"Definitely don't give him any rides. Frankly, it worries me seeing you two together so much."

"Why?!" Jules set her cup, which was scalding her fingers, onto the table.

"What do you know about him?" Dan asked.

"I know he went to prison for selling drugs. That's where he got sober. He was sober in prison for six years, and he's been sober since he got out around two years ago."

"Selling drugs isn't the only reason he was there," Dan said.

"Why else was he there?"

"Voluntary manslaughter."

"What does that mean?"

"It means he killed someone in the heat of passion."

"Like his girlfriend?"

"Like that."

"*Did* he kill a girlfriend?"

"I can't tell you that, but I *can* tell you that you should beware of getting too close to him."

"Does it seem like we're close?"

"Don't underestimate the power of the program to bring people from completely different walks of life together in the back of a van."

"What? You mean, like, in the back of a van—having sex?"

"If it's rocking," Dan shrugged. He handed her a business card. "Feel free to give me a call if he starts to freak you out."

Jules looked at the card. It was heavy white card stock with the name *Dan P.* printed on it. The only other information was his phone number centered underneath.

"Is this your AA card?"

"That's right. Put my number in your phone now," he instructed her, "and call me right here. That way, I'll have your number and I'll know it's you when you call, and I'll pick up. You can call for other reasons too, but I want you to have it in case of emergencies. Neither I nor my wife mind me getting calls at all hours of the day, and believe me, I've been called at ALL hours of the day."

Jules finished plugging his digits into her phone. She paused before pressing the red button. "Your wife?" she said.

"Thirty years. That woman has been with me through it all, as they say. She's a champ. We have six kids."

"*Six* kids?" She pressed the button, sending her number. "How is that even possible?"

"Surely you know," Dan said.

Before work that evening, she plugged Kelly's first name—that's all she knew—into the Google search bar on her desktop, along with the years *2007* to *2014*, which she figured allowed for a margin of error in the amount of time he served, and the words *voluntary manslaughter*.

Nada. No surprise. Maybe his name wasn't Kelly.

The next day, in the corner of the Half-Measures room of the Triangle Club, Jules sat at a table with a black rotary phone and a fake plant. Because of her young sobriety, her sponsor constantly texted her with opportunities for service work, and today she was answering Intergroup phones for three hours. Being present to answer the central AA number on a phone that may or may not ring, that may or may not have a desperate person on the other end—a person hoping at that moment to get sober, or just someone without a computer looking for the closest meeting—seemed like low-hanging-enough service work for her to manage. It was a step above emptying ashtrays and making coffee. "Service is the third estate of recovery," her sponsor kept telling her. "You do it or you'll drink." Jules didn't want to drink or drug anymore. Her bottom had been when she almost said yes to heroin—*heroween*—after her brother's overdose, knowing full well it wouldn't make anything any better. Now she sat next to the rotary phone, holding her own cell phone in her hand, scrolling through Instagram and Facebook and Twitter to pass the time. A noon meeting of around fifty people—a more professional crowd—was taking place in one of the club's larger rooms. The folks at the noon meeting intimidated her.

The phone rang. She picked it up. "Intergroup Houston," she said. "Can I help you?"

"Jules!" It was Kelly.

"How did you know it was me?"

"I know your voice," he said. "Nah! I'm just shitting you.

I saw you were gonna be answering phones 'cause your name was on the board, so I thought I'd give you a call."

Before Dan warned her about Kelly, she might have found this phone call funny, but now it seemed sort of strange. "Wait, did you call because you need to talk to someone at Intergroup?" she asked him.

"Nah, girl. I just wanted to talk to you over an actual phone instead of over text."

"I gotta go," she said. "What if someone who really needs to talk is trying to call?" She hung up.

Her volunteer shift ended at two. Even though she attended the 2:30 every day, today she wanted to leave as soon as possible because she didn't want to see Kelly. She needed to find a new meeting to attend. *He must not be outside at the picnic table yet*, she thought. *Otherwise he'd have come in and found me by now.* But then, in he walked with his Astros cap, camo shorts, *Ride or Die* T-shirt, Tevas.

"There she is!" he sang, and it suddenly seemed to Jules from the warmth in his voice that he had been living for these afternoons. "Wanna go into the meeting, or wanna go out and have a smoke first?"

She smiled at him wanly. "You go smoke. I'll meet you in the room."

"K, save me a seat," Kelly said.

The leader of the Thursday 2:30 meeting was a guy named TJ. He called on her to share. The topic was about the fellowship, about unity, about how being in the program allowed things buried inside to start to come out. She liked that line, *things buried inside coming out*, and she shared how that was truer and truer for her in sobriety. Before, she had tried to reach that buried mystery with drugs and alcohol. And at first, these had worked: she'd had a mystical experience. But then, they stopped working, the drugs and the alcohol. She felt every head in the room nodding at this. Now, when she practiced the principles—even when no one was looking—she felt . . . How did she feel? She felt like that church song "Nearer My God to Thee." TJ nodded and smiled. "I'm grateful," she said. "It's like every day I'm closer to understanding that heaven is on earth."

After the meeting, she told Kelly she needed to feed a friend's dog—a lie that came to her when he scootched over to make room for her at the picnic table. She stayed standing.

"Well, be careful," Kelly said. "They found another body last night—this time in the ditch. You hear about it?"

"They did?" She hadn't heard.

"Young girl. Butterfly jeans, rhinestones." He looked at her, waiting.

"That girl who was at the meeting yesterday?"

"The same. Hey, Johnny," he said, turning to the big black dude sitting across from him at the table, "you see Jake here yesterday?"

"Nah," Johnny said. "I ain't seen Jake in a couple weeks."

"I want to ask you about some other good meetings," she said, leaving a message on Dan's voice mail. "Call me back when you get a chance, please." She sat in her Malibu, the afternoon sun beating through her windshield, the heat rising vigorously from the concrete parking lot where the group members parked. Large summer thunderheads rose into fantastical castles in the sky. Staring at the bumper sticker on the truck parked in front of her car (*Legalize Freedom*, with a marijuana motif), she felt her iPhone vibrate in her hand. The text on the screen said *Dan P.* She hit *Accept*.

"Hey," she said.

"Is this an emergency?" Dan asked, sounding genuinely worried.

"No. Well, it sorta is. I just found out that girl who was at the meeting yesterday, the one you held the door open for, was pulled out of the ditch last night. Did you know that?"

"I did not."

"I'm sorta freaking out. I think that you telling me about Kelly has me freaked out."

"Good," Dan said. "I meant it to freak you out. Hey, you know what? I'm waiting on a delivery and need my phone free. Why don't you meet me at my office, and you can look on the computer at Intergroup, and I'll direct you to some good alternatives."

"Um, okay? Where's your office?"

"The Falls of Westpark."

"The Falls of Westpark?"

"I own the building."

"You're kidding."

"Surprise."

When she entered the grimy three-story complex, she pulled out her phone to text Dan that she was downstairs. Tejano music wavered from behind a closed door somewhere to her left. The sharp smell of something—lardy tortillas being cooked on a hot comal, maybe—caught her nose.

Just as she was typing her message, she heard her name called and looked up to see Dan in his dress shirt and suit pants, leaning over the railing of the third-story walkway. "There's a staircase to your right. Come on up."

Inside Dan's "office," there was a desktop computer sitting on a white folding table cluttered with papers and receipts and a couple of Styrofoam cups. Several legal-looking books stacked upright on a few shelves occupied the lone bookcase against the wall. A framed law certificate hung next to the bookcase, cockeyed. There was a nubby couch under the window near the door, and there were two leather desk chairs on either side of the folding table. The kitchen looked bare. Through a doorway into a back room, she could see a bed, neatly made, and through the bedroom window, the large red-and-white sign for Pare de Sufrir, a mini–mega church on the 59 freeway feeder.

"Did you know that girl?" Jules asked him. She sat in the leather chair in front of the desk. He sat in the other desk chair, across from her.

"Did *you*?" He flipped through a couple receipts, avoided meeting her eyes.

"I'd never seen her before yesterday," Jules answered. She could feel her body getting nervous. What in the world made her think it was okay to be here? With Dan P., who before this afternoon she would not have imagined in this place, not in a million years. "So you own this building?"

"Actually, my wife does. Her family."

"Ah." He'd lied to her. Must have been easy to do. Here she was, and who would ever find her here? She hadn't told anyone where she was going. She thought about texting Kelly now, but what would he do? Because, suddenly, she felt doomed, and not the kind of doom she'd felt yesterday in the parking lot of Starbucks. This was darker, heavier . . . fatal.

"I think I'm gonna go," she said, standing up.

Dan leaped up and cut her off from the door to the apartment. "You haven't found another meeting. I'm gonna help you. Let me get you some water."

"It's okay, I really need to go. I forgot that I have to feed a friend's cat. I actually haven't been there in days. Could you text me about the meeting?"

She knew she wouldn't be getting out. The front window's blinds were drawn. She thought of screaming, but her voice was suddenly gone. It really was like in her nightmares, when she tried to scream and nothing came out.

"Sit down," Dan said.

"Please let me out," she croaked.

"Sit down."

"I'll scream."

"Lots of screaming here all the time. It's a perfect place for screamers to scream all they want. Nobody's going to do anything. They're all afraid of the law here."

He approached her slowly, and she felt like she would faint. Just then, she heard a raucous banging against the apartment door.

"Open up!" a voice yelled. "Police! We've got you surrounded!"

Dan bolted toward the back of the apartment, and the door busted open. It seemed like twenty cops stormed into room, but it was probably only five. They had Dan down on the bed, a knee grinding into his back, before Jules could find her legs and turn toward the door.

One of the cops had her in cuffs within moments. "Don't think you're going anywhere," he barked. "Some help!" she heard him call before the room turned to static, and she passed out.

"I never liked that guy," Kelly said. "What'd I tell you? A total faker."

Jules had stayed away from the club for two weeks, but now she was back. She hadn't drank or used, but she hadn't been able to stomach a meeting, nor could she go back to work. Her sponsor stayed with her for the first week, until her seventy-three-year-old mom could fly in from California to help her for an undetermined amount of time—until Jules could manage being alone again, whenever that may be. Her mom had driven her to the meeting in the Malibu, and she would be back twenty minutes after it was over to pick her up and drive her home, then cook enchiladas for her and sit next to her on the couch watching Netflix for hours. Knowing that the rooms of AA were filled with sociopaths and criminals made it hard for Jules to return, but she was aware that staying away for too long meant she would probably drink, and to drink again meant she would probably die. The meetings had helped her stop suffering—*pare de sufrir*, indeed. She knew she needed to continue to make them. *Meeting makers make it*, one of the sayings went.

Plus, Kelly was here.

"Now you know what feet of clay are," he said. "You really know, and like the Promises promise, *No matter how far down the scale we have gone, we will see how our experience can benefit others!* You're facing your fears, girl. Not fucking everything and running."

She and Kelly were sitting on one of the picnic benches after the noon meeting. A whole gang of fellows surrounded them, some leaning against the wall of the courtyard, some spilling out into the parking lot under the blinding, relentless sunshine. Most of them chatting, laughing. They knew what had happened to her. She'd shared it in the meeting. She'd had to do it. "We're only as sick as our secrets," her sponsor had said. She was seeing a counselor now, too, who agreed that going back to the meetings was a good idea—just not to the 2:30.

"You gotta stay in the middle, girl," Kelly was saying. "Don't let the fuckers out on the edges get you. You survived.

Your experience is gonna help some other person. Now you got one fucking hell of a story! Believe me." He smiled at her through his yellow-brown teeth.

By some act of grace, he'd been at the Shell station, waiting for his sister to pick him up, and had looked up to see Jules on the third-floor walkway at the Falls of Westpark. He'd seen Dan lead her through the apartment door, the blinds drawn.

"You're sorta hard to miss," he said. "Even though that place is full of Mexicans, just like you, you stood out like a sore thumb." He smiled broader. "I just knew that some seriously bad shit was going down. I called that 1-800-TIPS number—you know, that Crime Stoppers number? Told them I had information on the perp who dumped those gals in the bin and ditch, and that I was pretty sure another dumping was about to take place pronto. I'm amazed how fast they showed up."

"You gonna get the $5,000?" Johnny asked.

"I'm not telling you if I do!" Kelly laughed.

Jules looked at her watch: 1:20 p.m. A few seconds later, she heard her mom honk the horn of the Malibu. She stubbed out her cigarette and stood. "I gotta go."

"You gonna be here tomorrow?" Kelly asked.

"Probably." She was taking it one day at a time, for reals.

"Keep coming back," Johnny said.

Jules smiled at him.

"You gonna be all right?" Kelly asked.

When she turned to look at him, he was staring at her boobs. She slung her purse over her shoulder, reached her hands behind her waist, and thrust out her chest, as if to crack her back. "I think so," she said. She waited for Kelly to look her in her eyes again before she dropped her arms. Then she turned and headed into the merciless glare of the parking lot.

RAILWAY TRACK

BY SEHBA SARWAR

Lawndale

Holding my ping-pong paddle—or table tennis, as I referred to the game—I served the ball and tossed a question to Sanjay: "Want to help me track the Raincoat Hombre?"

Sanjay missed the serve. "Sure," he said. "Let's follow the hombre!"

I slammed another serve that Sanjay missed. Our fingertips touched as we stooped to pick up the orange ball. Electricity rippled through my body. Leaning forward, I placed my lips on his. Sanjay responded by thrusting his tongue into my mouth. Two men playing a few tables away stopped their game to watch us. We broke apart.

Collecting our belongings, we drove away from the university rec center. Sanjay followed me to my house, where I uncorked a bottle of wine. After a few moments of watching the news, which showed protests against the upcoming presidential inauguration, I turned off the TV and used my phone to play Bollywood music from a wireless speaker. Sitting close to each other, we hummed tunes until the freight train's whistle cut through the music. I turned off the sound.

On cue, the man I had dubbed Raincoat Hombre appeared in my window, walking down Jefferson Street. Once he dropped out of sight, Sanjay and I slipped out of the back door and into my car.

I drove half a block to the stop sign, where we glimpsed the man below another streetlight. He disappeared into the dark, and I rolled my car forward.

The road curved, and the Raincoat Hombre turned and looked directly toward us, his face a flash of white. Sanjay gasped.

I swung my car onto Hackney Street. Three minutes later, we were back in my living room. I poured more wine.

"It's hard to hide in a neighborhood where no one walks," I commented.

We clinked our glasses and found ourselves six inches apart. Sex on my handwoven carpet from Karachi was more satisfying than on my luxury king mattress.

Sanjay and I had met through mutual friends at the University of Houston and bonded over weekly table tennis games, which were followed by drinks, and often more. With my braids and jeans, I could pass as a college undergrad. Sanjay looked older, even though he wore track pants and a baseball cap. His narrow frame stretched a few inches taller than mine, but arm muscles bulged beneath his shirt. He was as zealous about working out as I was about reposing on my sofa.

Though Sanjay's background was different from mine—he had been five when his family moved from New Delhi to Houston, and he considered the Bayou City his home—we spoke the same language. I was not yet familiar with the city and its enclaves. My family was in Karachi, and I had landed in Houston to pursue a doctorate in social work. Sanjay helped me find my two-bedroom rental down the street from campus, in a quiet East End neighborhood called Houston Country Club Place. Sanjay deemed the house safe for a single woman, but drawled, "You'll be the only Pakistani around here!"

For the most part, when I worked on my papers at night, I was accompanied by croaking frogs, chirping crickets, and the passing cargo trains. No neighbors ever appeared, until one winter Thursday night, the Raincoat Hombre—as I later referred to him because the Spanish spoken in my new neighborhood had begun to seep into my system—appeared as if he had been teleported to the spot beneath the streetlight closest to my house. His khaki coat swung around him as he strode past Mr. Rodriguez's crepe myrtle tree, and his hoodie cast a shadow on his face. The first time I saw him, I nearly fell out of my chair. But over the course of the month, I adopted a Thursday-night ritual: the freight train's eleven p.m. whistle became my cue to set aside my seminar report, watch for the hombre, and ponder over where he was headed.

The murder was reported on the morning after Sanjay and I had attempted to track the Raincoat Hombre. That afternoon, after a day of listening to stories—a woman having an affair, a teenage boy struggling to inform his parents he liked boys, an older man trying to cope with his wife's death—I took a moment to check my phone. An alert from my neighborhood association popped up on my screen:

> Last night at 10:30 p.m., the body of Lawndale Street resident Mrs. Alicia Hernandez was found inside her car parked near Fiesta. An autopsy is being conducted. If you have information, please contact the police or the neighborhood association.

Registering that Alicia Hernandez's body had been discovered just a few blocks from my house, I forwarded the e-mail to Sanjay. I also shot off a description of Raincoat Hombre to Mrs. Alfaro, the neighborhood association secretary, who I had briefly met.

Within minutes, she called me. "Would you like to come over for coffee tomorrow? You can tell me more about this mysterious man." Curious to learn more about the murder, I agreed.

The following morning, Saturday, I walked to her house, one block from mine. Along the way, cars and trucks basked in the sun and oak branches fluttered in the breeze. Doves cooed. A police siren wailed on the other side of the railway track.

Clad in my adopted uniform—jeans and hoodie—I knocked on Mrs. Alfaro's door. I had stopped wearing shalwar-kameezes and saris after the election.

Mrs. Alfaro served me iced tea, then settled in her rocking chair. "Tell me—you've seen someone mysterious wander our streets at night?" Her voice was squeaky. "No point talking to the police—yet. But I'll alert the association. They can follow this man, to ask some questions."

"I'd like to talk to him as well." I sucked on a piece of ice.

Mrs. Alfaro pressed a hairpin into her gray hair and used her little finger to push up her glasses. "I don't see why not. According to your story, though, we have till Thursday, yes?" She refilled my glass. "You know that the Hernandezes just moved here. Alicia was from Guatemala, and Luis is from South Texas. He's a security officer in the medical center."

I nodded. "I met them last month, at the Christmas concert at the convent. She seemed like a gentle woman."

"That night, she was going downtown to meet a girlfriend, but she never left the East End." Mrs. Alfaro's words spilled like a soup pot bubbling over. "We didn't want to frighten anyone, so we didn't say more in the newsletter. They found Alicia in the backseat, wearing just her shirt and . . . panties. The murderer used her skirt to strangle her. She had bruises on her face—it was blue with punches. They say Luis was crying so much, he could hardly identify her."

At ten thirty the following Thursday night, two men knocked on my front door, introducing themselves as part of the neighborhood watch team. I invited them to the backyard, where my landlord had left sagging chairs and a wooden table on the cement patio.

The older neighbor, David, said, "Our community is small, so we take responsibility to patrol blocks." A stout man with a twirling mustache, he looked as if he was visiting from the eighteenth century. "We've caught burglars. But this is the first murder since I moved here thirty years ago."

Juan, a tall man with wrinkles ironed into his forehead, nodded. He leaned against the wall. In the dim light, I glimpsed a flash of steel—a pistol tucked beneath his jean jacket.

"Where are you from?" asked David.

I tried not to flinch. "Pakistan."

Neither man responded, but I knew the questions they didn't ask: *Isn't that where terrorists come from?* Followed by: *Are you Muslim?*

The cargo train sounded its whistle, drowning out the cicadas' whirs. We peered around the wall. The streetlights cast shadows, but no one was in sight. David and Juan waited another hour, but the street remained empty.

Luis Hernandez's front door opened onto Lawndale Street, overlooking the steel gates of the Villa de Mittal convent. Hands shaking, Luis offered me iced tea. Several weeks had passed since his wife's murder, and the police were no closer to solving the crime than they had been when it occurred. I had seen Luis at the nearby Fiesta Mart. When I greeted him, he responded with teary eyes and asked if I could help him. Without hesitation, I had agreed.

Now, leaning forward on his sofa, Luis tried to smile, but his lips trembled. "Perhaps you can look through her things and see if you want anything? Or you could give things away?"

I sorted through boxes of clothes in their bedroom while he watched from the doorway.

"I'm sure you're tired of questions," I commented.

"I've told the police everything I know. After she drove away to meet her friend, I went to my buddy's house to watch a basketball game. The police called me around ten thirty that night." Tears trickled from his eyes.

I replayed the time line in my mind. Luis had seen Alicia around six p.m., after the winter sun had dipped into the horizon. There was a four-hour window during which the murder occurred.

"I still have nightmares about how she must have suffered," said Luis. "I want to go back to the Valley to be with my family, but it's not so easy to get a job."

Being a mental health counselor is like being a detective: both professions require listening skills. Growing up in Karachi, I heard our housekeeper share stories about her abusive husband. When my mother helped our housekeeper file for divorce, I served as babysitter for her daughter and listened to the little girl's stories about hiding in the closet while her father struck her mother.

My mother and her friends had infused women's rights into my blood. "I lived through General Zia's times," my mother told me. "We marched when I was sixteen. And we saw women's rights being wiped like grease from a table. No one could produce enough witnesses to a rape or win a case contesting an honor killing."

Religious extremism had fomented over the decades, especially as war escalated in Pakistan's northern regions. Though my personal life remained unaffected—I was raised in a progressive home, attended a coed school, and experimented with drinking and sex in Karachi as well as in the United States—I saw many of my Karachi classmates embrace an extremist version of Islam.

In California, at the women's college I attended, my listening skills attracted new friends who told me about dates and sometimes date rapes. Wanting to help, I decided to study human behavior. That was what had led me to Houston and its university's doctoral program. All the stories.

Assuring Luis I would return with more boxes to finish packing his wife's clothes, I left his house and walked to my own. A police car sailed past me on Lawndale and parked under a crepe myrtle. One officer leaned against the car while the other remained in the driver's seat, his face shadowed.

"Any progress on the murder?" I called out.

The officer shook his head and introduced himself as Javier Garcia. "We hear you've seen strange activity."

"Just a man wearing a raincoat," I responded. "He walks at night. But I haven't seen him since the murder."

"Aren't you from the Middle East?" Cop Garcia asked.

"Pakistan. It's part of South Asia."

His face remained blank. "There aren't many immigrants from your country in this neighborhood. If you feel any threat, or if you see anything suspicious, just call us." He handed me his card before they drove away.

The second murder was reported on a Friday afternoon. My friend Sylvia called with the news: "A girl was killed last night."

I jotted down notes: A twenty-two-year-old Filipina, Maria Lee, who lived a few streets from Sylvia's house, had been murdered. If a neighbor walking his dog had not seen her body on the train track, Maria Lee would've been crushed by the eleven p.m. freight train.

Within an hour, I was at Sylvia's house. She lived in her family home, across the tracks from mine, and had once told me the railway line was a border dividing the prosperous and the working class. "You've moved into a war zone," she had said.

Squeezing a lemon wedge into the Corona Sylvia offered, I listened to her fill in the story. "Maria and her mother are from the Philippines. Her mom's been in Houston for several years, but Maria arrived last month. She worked at a nearby taquería."

I asked, "Was Maria in a relationship?"

Sylvia shook her head. She walked to her front door to double-check that it was locked. "Maria had an evening shift—her mother expected her after nine that night." Sylvia shivered. "Her face was bruised and blue when they found her. And she was wearing a tank top and jeans. The murderer used her sweatshirt to strangle her."

I sucked a lemon wedge. "Sounds familiar."

"Makes me scared about living alone. But I don't have a choice."

Back at my house, I scanned the neighborhood association's latest update, but there was no mention of Maria Lee. My telephone buzzed. My brother Hasan was calling from Karachi.

I gave him a rundown of my news.

"Are you safe?" he asked. After I reassured him that I was fine, he shared Karachi updates. "There was a bombing—this time at Sehwan, at the Lal Shahbaz shrine. More than eighty people dead. Women and children also."

Closing my eyes, I remembered the shrine of the Sufi saint, Lal Shahbaz Qalandar. Throughout Pakistan, guards armed with machine guns stood outside shopping malls, cinemas, and even shrines. I wondered why this bombing by extremist forces had not been stopped. Violence was increasing in Pakistan.

When I met Sanjay for a drink at Bohemeos, an East End café/bar, and told him about Maria's murder, he exclaimed. "You shouldn't stay there alone! When does your lease expire?"

"Six months." I sucked a lemon wedge. "Weren't you the one who told me the neighborhood was safe?"

Sanjay's brows pushed together, making him look like a vulture. "I didn't know these murders would happen!"

The television above him streamed images of men and women protesting. One banner read, *Collapse the Walls*.

"I can't sit back and watch these girls die. The police aren't getting answers. One of my Karachi friends—he's a detective in New York—has been giving me a crash course on finding clues and checking alibis."

"So what's he telling you? *Don't get into risky situations?*"

I shrugged. "I've also talked to the police here." I had been enjoying our open relationship, but Sanjay's new protective comments made me flinch. Trying not to sound terse, I said, "I keep my doors locked and alarm on. I'm from a city filled with six times as many people as Houston—in Karachi, people are murdered every day. Their deaths don't even make national news."

"This isn't Karachi!" Sanjay said. He flexed his muscles. "Want me to move in? You need protection. You're the foreigner in this neighborhood."

"*We're* the foreigners in this country," I responded. "And

we always will be, even if we're born here. Did you hear about the Indian man killed in Kansas?"

"I suppose they've always hated us," Sanjay conceded. He sat in silence for a moment. "The murders here have one thing in common: both were women, and both were new to this country. And the killing style was the same. I'm surprised there was no . . . sexual assault."

I leaned back, continued sucking on my lemon. "Good observations, Dr. Watson. People in my neighborhood haven't connected the murders, because the second victim lived south of the railway track. If these are anti-immigrant hate crimes, I'll surely be next." I downed my beer and stood. "I have to go. I'm going to visit Maria's mother." I leaned over and kissed him. "Come over tomorrow and I'll fill you in."

I walked away, aware of Sanjay's eyes pinned on my back.

In her apartment, among faded paisley sofas and framed photographs, Norma Gomez twisted her hands together. "As soon as they release Maria's body, I'm returning to Manila."

"This must be so difficult for you."

Norma shook her head. "I didn't tell the police, but one time someone sprayed on our door, *Go back to where you came from.* I wiped away the writing before Maria saw. I didn't want her to be afraid. I've been in this country for five years. No one's done that before. Things are scarier now that Trump is president."

"Tell me what happened," I said, aware I sounded more like a detective than a social worker. But Norma was so ready to talk, and I wanted to help her.

"After her shift, Maria called to say she was going to dinner. I didn't ask questions. I just wanted her to be happy, so I was glad that she had met a boy." I nodded, and she continued: "I'd made her favorite stew that night. I kept the food hot, in case she was hungry when she returned. She loved to talk and never ate when she was being social. But . . ." Norma mopped her tears with a tissue.

I gave her a moment, then said, "Tell me more about Maria."

"She was my daughter from my first marriage. I met my second husband in Manila—he served in the US Navy. We got married, and I flew to Houston, but Maria stayed with my mother. I sponsored her after I got my citizenship."

I didn't drive home until late that night, just as the freight train sounded its whistle. The gate was down once I reached the tracks. I stepped on my brakes, made sure my doors were locked, and turned off my engine, knowing that I would have to wait at least twenty minutes for the train to pass. The street was still, with no sign of Raincoat Hombre or anyone else.

The night's excitement didn't end when I got home. During the evening news, Mrs. Alfaro and the two neighborhood association men, David and Juan, knocked on my door.

Mrs. Alfaro spoke first, pushing up her glasses: "We heard you talked to Mr. Hernandez. And that you're helping the mother of the other girl who was murdered. Have you talked to the cops?"

David interrupted before I could respond, his voice sharp: "Why're you getting involved? We're increasing neighborhood patrolling, so you'll see more men walking around at night."

"We go to Stephanie's Ice House afterward," Juan added. "Join us sometime. When you take time off from visiting families." His voice was almost a snarl.

"We were, um, wondering," Mrs. Alfaro pushed up her glasses again, "who's the gentleman that visits you. One of your relatives?"

Before I could respond, my telephone vibrated. I stepped inside.

Luis Hernandez was on the line. "Can you meet me at a bar next week? I need to talk. I can't live here anymore, without my wife . . ."

When I got off the phone, Mrs. Alfaro and her team were still on the steps. Her voice pitched higher: "Stop trying to fix things, okay? The cops will solve these murders. Just keep your house locked and stop spreading stories—people will be afraid to come here!"

I ushered them to the street, slammed my door, and dropped onto my sofa. Unhooking my bra, I pulled it off through the sleeve of my shirt. Just then, another knock sounded, this time at the back door.

Sanjay stood outside, satchel flung over his shoulder. I invited him in and twisted open two beer bottles. Sanjay's eyes strayed from the drinks to my unbuttoned shirt and bra-free breasts.

One eyebrow raised, I said, "Everything okay, Dr. Watson? Want to tell me on the rug?" Pressing close to him, I continued, "I've had many visitors today. And now Luis is creeping me out—he keeps calling me for help . . ."

Sanjay tilted his head. "I want to hear more, but first, read this!" He held out his phone, which displayed a message from the university's Indian student association.

I skimmed and absorbed that the body of an undergraduate Indian student, Nadia Masood, had been found in a freight train boxcar near the university. She had been strangled with her scarf, and her face was punched up. Nadia had been living in southwest Houston with extended family, and her parents were on their way from Ahmedabad, India, to collect her body.

Twisting away from Sanjay, I headed to my bedroom, re-appearing in my uniform of form-fitting T-shirt, hoodie, and jeans.

"Wait! I thought we had other plans." Sanjay followed me to his car.

As we approached campus, we saw six police cars with flashing lights parked alongside the railway line. Orange cones closed off one lane, and yellow emergency tape wound around the train. Sanjay dropped me off next to the railroad track and I walked toward the train, melding into the crowd of students.

Past the graffiti-covered railcars, I glimpsed an older fe-male officer with silver hair shaved to her skull. I recognized her as HPD's homicide supervisor, Henrietta Jones. Her photo had been shared in the neighborhood association newsletter as the officer in charge of the murders.

I attempted to approach her, but a police officer stepped in front of me.

"Could I talk to her?" I gestured toward Ms. Jones.

"Do you have information?" The officer's voice was terse.

"Questions."

"Call the station for an appointment." The officer handed me a business card and turned to speak to a student who had tears trickling down her cheeks.

My night was haunted by dreams of an army of raincoat-clad men and women, marching along the railroad track, stepping in and out of boxcars. I woke up tired, no closer to answers than I had been when I fell asleep.

Two days later, Sanjay and I drove to southwest Houston. We knocked on a dark-brown door, and a tall woman named Aliya answered. She led us to her living room, dark with burgundy curtains drawn across the windows. Incense smoke made my eyes water. A couple, Rana and Ahmed Masood, sat on a cream-colored sofa, each clutching a mug of tea.

Their daughter Nadia had not lived at the university. Instead, she stayed with Aliya, her mother's cousin. Each morning, Aliya dropped Nadia downtown, where she caught the Metro Rail to campus.

"She didn't have many friends," explained Aliya. "Being a Muslim from India, she didn't fit in with the other Indians or Pakistanis. So she studied. She was doing well—she was searching for jobs and looking to change her visa status. She might even have met someone . . . Sometimes she came back late. She was a quiet girl and never told me who was giving her rides."

Rana Masood adjusted her dupatta scarf and dabbed her tears. "We didn't want her to go to America. Everyone warned us. But she wanted to study computer science. She got a scholarship from our community association, and she got a visa."

Ahmed Masood hunched his shoulders. Sweat broke out on his forehead and his lips trembled. "Our community raised money for our tickets. We just want to bury our daughter and return home. But the police won't release her body. The time to bury her in accordance with Muslim practice has slipped away. She remains in the morgue . . ."

Rana Masood tugged my hand. Her palm was sweaty. "I don't trust the police here. But I found Nadia's diary." Reaching into her purse, she drew out a notebook. "She didn't write much."

A few pages were filled with handwriting belonging to a person who spent more time on a machine than with a pen. I scanned the text, gleaning that Nadia had met a man who sometimes drove her home from campus. *He takes me to dinner in a hotel—some neighborhood called the Galleria. We hold hands. He listens to me and understands.*

I flicked to the last page: *I promised him I wouldn't write more, but one day I'll share the story of the man I love.*

Thirty minutes before I was to meet Luis at the bar, my phone rang.

"Can you meet me by the cemetery instead?" Luis stammered. "There's graffiti on my wife's grave." He said the cemetery closed at sunset, and an iron bar blocked the entrance. "You can park across the street and enter from the side. I'll wait for you."

Making sure my phone was charged, I drove up Lawndale. Darkness had fallen, and there was no moon. As I pulled up across from the cemetery, I saw Luis waiting for me. I parked my car and crossed the street to join him.

Luis and I walked across wet grass to the curling cemetery road, a labyrinth with which he seemed familiar. I had been to Forest Park Cemetery just twice: once to attend Alicia's funeral, and the second time for the smaller service for Maria Lee, who was buried in the mortuary since her mother could not afford a grave. Those burials were my first encounter with any US cemeteries. Forest Park's grassy landscape stretched over hundreds of acres—the opposite of what I knew in Karachi, where bodies were buried on top of each other.

"Thanks for meeting me here," Luis mumbled. "I don't trust cops." His eyes were teary and his hair disheveled.

I glanced around at the winding road, lined by pink and white azaleas. Far away, police sirens competed with the hum of the nearby freeway. Occasionally, a roar erupted from airplanes landing or taking off at Hobby Airport.

Finally, Luis stopped in front of a grave. The tombstone had been knocked flat.

I aimed my telephone's flashlight at the flat stone. "This

is not your wife's grave! Who's Joanna Martinez?" I turned to face him.

Luis's face was shadowed. His eyebrows seemed thicker and his arms were long as he lunged for me. "Don't move," he whispered.

Though Luis's frame was not much larger than mine, his arms felt like an iron belt. I clamped my teeth on his shoulder. He winced, loosening his hold. Squirming away, I folded one leg to knee his groin, but he thrust me onto the wet grass. I landed on my back, feeling scratchy stalks push against my shirt and jeans. The scent of jasmine from a nearby tomb clung to my nostrils, contrasting with the danger.

"What're you doing?" My heart pounded so loudly, I could feel palpitations through my chest. "We're not near your wife's grave!"

"Shut up, bitch," he muttered. He closed his fist and punched my right cheek.

My face tingled, but despite the pain, I registered that Luis's hands were covered with latex gloves. I called out with as loud a voice as I could muster, "We're close to the children's grave site! Why'd you bring me here?"

He grabbed my shoulders and shook me, causing my teeth to chatter.

"You should've gone back to where you came from! Too late now, bitch." His voice was a hiss. Pressing his knees into my stomach, he wrenched my body to pull off my sweatshirt.

I thrashed my legs and tried to call for help, but Luis pushed his knees harder into my gut and slapped my cheek. I fell back, and he returned to twisting my hoodie to make a rope.

Just as he leaned forward to wind the fabric around my throat, I saw Luis shiver. Cold metal touched the back of his neck. He turned to see six plainclothes police officers surrounding us, one pressing a .45 caliber pistol into his back.

"Why didn't you tell me you suspected Luis, and that you were talking to the police? You could be dead!" Sanjay's lower lip protruded, making him look ten years old.

I leaned back on my sofa and pressed an ice pack against my cheek, now padded with a bandage. "You were out of town. Remember I told you that Luis was being creepy? I had to do something."

"I don't understand why he went after you." Sanjay removed his baseball hat and ran his fingers through his hair.

"Maybe Luis thought I was talking too much? I had a weird feeling when he asked me to meet at a bar. So I went to HPD's homicide department and talked to Henrietta Jones. Remember, I saw her at the railway track? Even though I had no evidence—just a gut feeling—she listened to me. Maybe because she's a woman too. Or maybe because we're each working in terrains where we're outsiders. Anyway, she said the story was going cold. No one wanted to talk to cops, especially not Asian immigrants. My fear made sense to her, so she agreed to have me shadowed.

"Her team set up a wire on my phone so they could tap into my conversation with Luis, both live and on the phone, while also tracking our movement." I sucked the lemon wedge in my glass of water. "We were supposed to meet at Stephanie's Ice House, but he changed the plan at the last moment. When they heard him mention his wife's grave, the cops went to her tomb. I kept talking, trying to give them clues. Still, it took them time to find us. If they'd arrived a few minutes later, I wouldn't be here!"

There was a knock on my front door, and I paused. Sanjay answered, returning with Henrietta Jones.

"Thank you, Mona Naeem! You led us to a mass murderer," she said, perching at the edge of an armchair. Henrietta frowned, which made her look older than her fifty years. "Luis wasn't on our list because he had an alibi for each murder. But now we know his alibis were army veterans like him. They covered for him."

Sanjay and I listened, keeping our eyes fixed on her.

Henrietta continued: "His real name is Charles Wilson, a veteran from upstate New York. He used stolen identities. If he's who we suspect him to be, he might have killed more than six women in different cities. He's a bragger. Hates immigrants, especially women. *They shouldn't procreate*, he told us. He married Alicia so he could maintain a front, but he always intended to kill her and leave Houston. Maybe he killed her sooner than planned because she found out about a girlfriend . . . He had four flip phones on him. Different numbers. All messages deleted, and a different name for each phone." She paused. "He'd studied Spanish. Liked to pretend to be an immigrant himself. Helped him gain trust with the women he victimized."

I took a gulp of water while digesting her news.

"And you? Maybe he thought you were getting too close. We'll find out." Henrietta stood up, her shoulders sloping. "Thank you for leading us to Charles. This will be a long night."

After letting Henrietta out, Sanjay crept close to me. We fell asleep curled against each other's bodies.

I poured myself a glass of ice water and stepped into the steamy night to sit on my front steps. Inside, my belongings were packed in boxes. The semester had ended without me completing even one class. I was going to move into Sylvia's house for a month, finish my papers, and then spend the rest of the summer in Karachi.

As always, Jefferson Street was quiet. Rivulets streamed from my walkway to the street, reminders of the afternoon rain, and the warm air felt like a clammy towel wrapped around my body. Grackles croaked from a nearby tree, and when Raincoat Hombre appeared below the silver streetlight, I nearly choked on the lemon in my mouth.

"Howdy," he called.

"Howdy," I responded, using a word I had never before dared.

He moved closer. I saw that he had a furrowed forehead, shaggy white eyebrows, and long silver hair.

"I've seen you before," he said.

"I've seen you too."

"You shouldn't be out alone," he said.

"The killer was caught." My black eyes met his brown.

"I know—I saw your photo in the news."

I blushed. Over the last month, I had been featured in more television interviews than I would be for the rest of my life.

"Why'd you stop walking?" I had more questions I didn't ask: why Thursday nights, why after the train went by, why the raincoat even when temperatures soared? But I decided to swig water instead. After all, I had solved the bigger mystery.

Everyone in Houston now knew Luis's—aka Charles's—story. He had served two terms in Iraq and Afghanistan and been diagnosed with PTSD. Upon completing his Afghanistan assignment, he returned to New York, where he inherited family money. He was an only child. After his mother passed away, he moved across the country without leaving a trail. The Lawndale house—like previous homes in which he had lived—was owned by a fellow veteran who vouched for him whenever needed. When Charles applied for jobs, he used fake identities and never registered at veteran centers. Before Houston, he had lived in Miami, Mobile, and New Orleans, where he dated and killed at least eight women from countries including Mexico, India, Panama, Indonesia, and Guatemala.

"I don't discriminate," he had bragged in court, choosing to defend himself without a lawyer. "I hate *all* immigrants—especially women, 'cause they breed like rats. Sex I had to have, but I cut my juices off. Couldn't mix with those women."

Raincoat Hombre stood a few feet away from me. "I live in Montrose, but I explore at night. That's what insomniacs do. I walk different neighborhoods: East End, Second Ward, Fifth Ward, Third Ward, Freedmen's Town. I stopped coming here when I noticed a car following me." He looked at me, one eyebrow raised. "And after the murders, I decided to give the East End a break." He turned to glance at the curve of the new moon. "See you next week?"

I nodded, not bothering to tell him that the following week I would be in a different East End house, on the other side of the railroad track. If he walked as much as he said he did, I would encounter him again. Probably while sitting on Sylvia's steps, brooding over whether to proceed with my doctorate, accept the job offer from the Houston police, or return to Pakistan for good.

Coat swirling around him, Raincoat Hombre navigated my walkway, turned right, and headed toward the railway track.

JAMIE'S MOTHER

BY STEPHANIE JAYE EVANS

Sunset Heights

She was walking through the streets at midnight because she had a man to meet, she was carrying a gun because she was going to kill him, and she was wearing high heels because she hadn't thought it through.

For the first two hours, she sat by Jamie's sleeping, dreaming body and ignored the pings his phone made. He lay on her couch, curled to fit his frame in its embrace.

She got a stack of clean white washcloths. Held them under the faucet and wrung them out, restacked and covered them with plastic wrap. Put them in the refrigerator. Then, one by one, she took them out and used them to bathe his face, as if he had the kind of fever that could be relieved with cool cloths. The kind that could be relieved by a mother.

He murmured in his sleep. Smiled, lifted his brows, sank more deeply in. She pushed his hair from his face. Her hand stopped at his temple, at the tiny dimple of a measles scar. Oh.

She remembered him in her arms. Solid and muscular even at four, bigger than the other children. The way his heavy head felt against her breast as she rocked him.

His phone pinged, facedown on the coffee table. A quick pool of light, then draining away.

In his jacket pocket, she found a pack of cigarettes. She went to the front door, disarmed the alarm, unlocked the door, and realized she didn't have a lighter. She took a box of matches from the utility drawer and carried them with the cigarettes to the front porch.

They'd bought this town house, close to Downtown, in this still-iffy but gentrifying Heights neighborhood, when Jamie had graduated from high school and left for college. They didn't need the big house anymore or the good schools and they didn't want the commute. They were happy here for two years.

She struck the match against the side of the box, sniffed the sharp bite, watched the pure flame spring up. Lit the cigarette and drew on it hard. She hadn't smoked since college, but you don't forget how. She tilted her head back and let the smoke spiral from her mouth. She used to look sexy when she smoked—men told her so. She leaned on the railing and peered down into the flower boxes. The cyclamen she'd put out for Christmas had taken a beating and were spattered with mud from yesterday's rain. She rubbed at them with her thumb; the petals were stained.

This new white town house was three blocks off 610. Closer than they'd wanted to be—you could hear the freeway traffic. That meant it cost less. Jamie was going to a private university. They were being careful.

She sat on the glider, moored to the front porch by a chain thick as her wrist—the sort you'd imagine holding the *Queen Mary* fast. Her husband bought it the morning they woke to find all the new townhomes on their block, a block dotted with crumbling shotgun houses and an auto-body store, had their porch furniture stolen. Only theirs was left, which was so funny. Kenneth went to C&D Hardware on 11th Street and came home with this absurd chain, and that made her laugh even more. First he'd been cross with her, then he laughed too, and they went upstairs and made love on the new bed they'd bought to match this new house and new way of living. They pretended the traffic noise was a river.

She got up and poked a hole in the soil of the flower box, dropped in the finished cigarette butt, covered it, and patted it down. She wiped her hand on her suit and went back in, locked the door, set the alarm.

Her son slept on. Happy. A faint smile on his face, the kind of smile a full and content baby makes when his mouth falls away from your nipple, eyes closed and lips wet with your milk.

He was still beautiful. Not the way he was when he played football. He'd been huge then—she and Kenneth could hardly believe they'd made this massive golden man. It had been so sweet to go to Jamie's games and hear his name called, the crowd roaring for him. The golden muscled mass of him racing down the field.

He was beautiful. Not the way he was then. Not like a giant. A god.

He was beautiful like a tubercular. Like a Spanish martyr. Like a heroin addict.

The first time, he'd gone into rehab straight from school. His coach put him on the plane, so they didn't get to say goodbye. Only a phone call. When the phone call was over, Kenneth turned to her and said, "Was that him? I don't think that was him. It didn't sound like him."

She remembered when they sent his clothes home. Boxes and boxes. This was, oh, a year ago. Her husband was gone by then. They blamed each other. They blamed themselves. She couldn't bear his face—his eyebrows just like Jamie's. Bird-wing eyebrows.

That day, the FedEx man piled the boxes on the front porch. She came out and dragged one into the dining room, and the FedEx man brought the rest into the house. She'd tried to give him money, fumbling in her purse, then upending it on the floor and scrabbling for dollars, holding out a fistful.

She'd locked the door, set the alarm, and gone into the kitchen for a glass of ice, a bottle of bourbon, and a paring knife. Kneeling on the hardwood floor, she filled the glass with bourbon, took a drink, and sliced open the first box. Jamie's smell, faint, rose from the box. She put her face to the crack in the cardboard box and breathed in. Over and over. Great breaths of him. The way she'd put her face against his new-born skin and breathed in the sweet hay smell of this living, perfect child God had given her, after all the doctors told her it couldn't happen.

That day, sitting among the boxes, she poured another drink, then fitted her hand into the slot and felt softness. She pulled out his shirts, one after the other, sky blue and pink and lilac and butter yellow—all the colors Lauren made polo shirts in. Sixteen of them. Made of really soft cotton, like baby clothes.

She pulled out his clothes and school books and the note-books filled with his tiny, cramped handwriting and bordered with doodles—monster bodies with human faces and trees with cereal boxes hanging like fruit. The invitations and the dried-up boutonniere still pinned to the jacket lapel. Every-thing she pulled from the box, she laid on top of her heart. A business communication textbook that cost more than three hundred dollars: she put the six-pound book on her heart. Seven pairs of Levi's 501s: seven pounds on her heart. A T-shirt: six ounces. That made an ounce too much. Her heart was crushed under the weight and she crumpled, resting her face on the smooth, cool wood. She held Jamie's T-shirt to her face and smelled him. Then she lost herself, screaming, Jamie, Jamie, Jamie, baby, and she screamed at her God, who had not protected her son although, God knew, she was on her knees every night praying for his deliverance. Promising God anything, anything, anything, only please God, please. Please.

That was a long time ago. Now she looked down at her sleeping son, his cheekbones like a model's. The skin under his eyes deep purple.

His phone pinged on the table again.

Months before she knew, really knew, what this was—what had him—she'd picked up his ringing phone once, while he was in the bathroom.

Before she could speak to the caller, Jamie flew from the bathroom, holding his pants closed with one hand. He snatched the phone, hurting her, crushing her fingers. He raged, screamed down at her. She edged around him, her hands held up, apologizing again and again. Fled upstairs to her room, shut the door and locked it.

Told herself she wasn't afraid of him. She slid down and sat with her back pressed against the eight-foot solid-wood door and tried to stop the shaking. Because she wasn't afraid of her boy.

Ping.

His blond lashes rested on his cheeks. His cheeks were covered in red-gold hair. His huge hands lay open on his thighs, his whole body loose and easy and at peace. He was happy. This was happiness.

The doctor told her, "He needs it like air. You're trying to keep him from air. So be careful."

Ping.

She picked up his phone.

Jamie had an appointment.

When Kenneth moved out, he gave her a gun. He said the

neighborhood was rough; he wanted her to be okay. He showed her how to load it and sent her a link to a video about how to use it. She stuffed it in a Tampax box, but also watched the video.

Now, she went upstairs and got the gun. Put it in the zipper pocket of her purse. Then took it out of the pocket and put it in the loose bucket of the purse, with her loose change and loose bills and the lipstick she used every day and a package of Kleenex. She came downstairs with her purse and a quilt made of stitched-together biplanes. When Jamie was ten, she'd bought two of these quilts at the Neiman Marcus Last Call. For his bunk bed, back when he could fit into a bunk. Back when sleepovers happened every weekend. Now she laid the quilt over her son, drawing it up to his chin and tucking it around his feet.

Here's something she remembered—something she'd pull out every now and then: Her boy at two years old. She would put on a CD and turn up the volume, and they'd dance. Holding him on her hip, her left hand clasping his right. They'd spin and dip and twirl across the family room floor. He would throw back his head and that bright splash of golden hair would flare as they spun and he would laugh and laugh and laugh.

She was careful with that memory. That memory could kill her—crack her open so everything inside would slide out, and she would not ever be able to keep things together again.

Once she knew what she was up against, she did her research. She called in sick to work, which God knows was the truth because the night before she'd stood frozen in Kroger, in the canned vegetable aisle, dialing his number over and over, crying without shame. Her hands shaking, praying, *Please, God. Please, God. Please, God.* Barely aware of the small woman next to her, patting her arm and murmuring consolation in Spanish. She'd walked away from the kind woman, walked away from her full cart. Drove home and poured a bourbon. Put in her earbuds and played Adele's heartbreak as loud as the iPhone would go. She'd danced by herself, bourbon in hand.

Philip Seymour Hoffman was a heroin addict. He overdosed, he died. His mom had twenty-three good years when he was sober. She would take that. Twenty-three years? Yes. She'd take that deal.

There were people who'd gone down that road and found their way back, she learned. But if the numbers told the truth, she would bury Jamie. Jamie wouldn't bury her. This was the truth. She did numbers for a living and believed in them. They hadn't given her false hopes and, God knows, God had.

Months ago, they pulled into a gas station to fuel up, and Jamie said, "Mom! What the fuck? You can't stop here!"

She ignored him. She usually ignored what Jamie said by then because, like her husband, she wasn't sure it was Jamie saying it.

She slid her card through the slot and turned, and three men glommed onto her, touching her, pressing in. One needed bus fare. His mom was sick. If she could only . . . *Ten dollars, lady. Ten dollars.*

Jamie's face was turned away from her, stony. He'd told her. What the fuck.

She pulled out of the station, stopped at the red, and a zombie peered in her window and said something she was sure she had misunderstood. She drove through the red. "Jamie, did that woman proposition you?"

He smiled a smile that was a lot like Jamie's. "She propositioned *us*, Mom."

* * *

When her friends asked about Jamie, she lied. When they pressed, she dropped her friends. Ignored their calls. Stopped going to church. It was easier.

Here was a piece of good advice: she needed to go to Al-Anon. At least three meetings.

She went to one and sat there for an hour and a half, listening to the terror and desperation of strangers. She didn't go back.

The text said he had what Jamie wanted. *Gooood shit. Truth. Meet the same place as last time.*

She scrolled through the text messages and found the last time.

A couple of months back, maybe three, she got a call from her bank. There was a young man. The signature—they weren't sure.

She heard herself say, "That's not my signature." Then she walked into her boss's office, said she was sick and had to go home. She looked sick. He walked her to her car; she didn't want him to.

At home, she pulled up her account and did the math. Seven thousand dollars, give or take.

She went to her grandmother's dresser, opened the top drawer, and took out the navy velvet box where she stored her wedding ring and the pearls her father gave her on her wedding day. The ring had been her husband's grandmother's. She was saving it for Jamie's bride. For when he got better.

She didn't shake the box. She carried it downstairs, poured a bourbon, and sat at the dining room table. Drank the bourbon. Waited until her heart was still. Opened the box.

The ring was there.

Covering her face with her hands, she wept with gratitude. It was such a gift, such generosity that Jamie hadn't taken the ring. Oh, he did love her. He hadn't taken the ring.

He had taken the pearls. Could have been both, but it was just the pearls. And seven thousand dollars. Give or take.

She used the phone's map app to find where to meet the man. When she saw how close it was, she pressed the walking-man icon and got directions.

Here are some of the lies she told herself . . .

No. She was done telling herself lies.

She wiped Jamie's face with a fresh cloth. Put a glass of ice water on the coffee table and pulled the table within his reach. Turned off the sound on his phone.

She blew out the spruce-scented candle. Dimmed the lights. Turned the television on to the Pandora channel and let Zoe Keating pour comfort and healing on her child.

She got on her knees and put her arms around his shoulders and held him close and breathed him in. He was still beautiful, you know? He was warm and bony and her Jamie, deep inside. She was sure.

She didn't want to be late. She dropped Jamie's cigarettes into her purse, filled a paper cup with ice and bourbon, set the alarm, and locked the door behind her.

Oh, that cool air. The breeze lifted her hair at her temples. It felt good. See, that was something else she'd learned: to take her pleasures where she could. It felt good to click the wrought-iron gate behind her. To be walking these happy streets by herself at night and not feel afraid. Because she wasn't afraid. She was doing something for Jamie.

Her heels made a nice *click click* on the street. This block didn't have sidewalks. She felt great. Healthy and strong, not too cold, not too warm, and the bourbon was good. She'd poured just the right amount: not too much, not too little.

Here was the house that had been on the market for three years—it went for seven hundred–plus and now there was a baby swing on the porch. Right next to it, Juan's house. When she first moved to the Heights, she thought Juan was a slum-lord. He had a four-unit garage apartment in back—she knew from the garbage cans out front on Thursday. He sat in a plastic chair in his front yard with a Chihuahua named Tiny on his lap. Neither Juan's house nor his garage apartment had seen upkeep.

She and Juan were friends now. Long ago, Juan was a profes-sional baseball player in St. Louis. He'd brought his whole family over from the Dominican Republic. He wasn't a slumlord—he was a family man.

She passed under the massive oak tree some builder had the sense to save. The Heights had these lovely old oaks—more than a hundred years old and as big around as a row-boat. She walked up to the tree and pressed her cheek against the bark. See? She could enjoy this. This tree and the bark and the weather being good and her feet not hurting even though she hadn't thought to change her shoes.

There was a jumble of flotsam on the lawn ahead. A closer look showed it to be a pair of red sneakers, a plaid flannel shirt with tag still attached, a pair of black pants. Two feet from the clothes was a blue loose-leaf notebook—*GET AN EXPERT PERSPECTIVE ON AN HIV TREATMENT* printed on the cover. As if the occupant of those clothes had been raptured away right before she walked by.

She loved neighborhood mysteries.

Her friends from the suburbs thought she and Kenneth had lost their minds, moving to this ghetto corner of the Heights.

The Rose Garden parking lot was full, and light and laughter streamed through the cracks in the blinds. Another night, she would go in and sit at the bar and nurse a Shiner Bock. Visit with Rose, who owned the Rose Garden but hadn't named it or been named for it.

See, her friends couldn't get this—how cool it was, this old beer garden in the middle of a residential neighborhood.

A block from the Rose Garden, the Tiki House was hosting a klatch of young men, some straddling bicycles, all with their heads shaved, all wearing white wifebeaters and baggy low-slung jeans. They were raucous as grackles, but went quiet when they saw her, leaving just the *click click* of her heels. She tapped one of Jamie's cigarettes out of the package and walked over to them, smiling at the way they pulled themselves up and leaned back without giving way.

She held out her cigarette. The boys exchanged unspoken words and then one stepped forward, eyes on hers. Took the cigarette, put it in his mouth, lit it, took a puff, and handed it back to her. She didn't look away. She put the cigarette between her own lips, drew on it, and slowly blew out a stream. Sucked in, gave a puff. A perfect O of smoke drifted away.

The boys exploded in laughter and applause. As she walked away, she added sway to her hips, listening to the catcalls her high school Spanish couldn't translate.

See, she wasn't afraid, walking into the night. This felt good, and the cigarette . . . She inhaled deeply. Why had she ever given this up? This was all kinds of good—the taste, the feel, the nicotine rush, the rising feathered plumes of smoke.

Okay, so now the shoes were hurting.

A pit mix pressed his ugly face against the nearest fence. This part of the Heights, there were those who wouldn't dream of leaving their dogs out all night, and there were those who had bought dogs to be left out all night. The pit watched until she reached his property line, then sighed gustily and returned to his porch.

She should get a dog. A big one from the SPCA. A rescue dog, in case someone needed rescuing.

There was a rescue injection. NPR did a story on it. You had to be the police or an EMT to get one—she'd checked. She couldn't get this magic EpiPen that could draw your child back to life when he slipped into his dreams, deeply, deeply, and loosed his hold on the tether that bound him to the world, where you waited for him, sending out your love and your longing and your terror and your fury like hounds that could sniff him out and find him, find him and drag him back to your arms before he was . . .

Jamie was very far away. She couldn't find him anymore when she looked in his eyes.

Or maybe he was still there. She couldn't see him, but maybe he was still inside.

She used to plan his funeral. Couldn't stop her mind going there. All his friends would come. Walker and Taylor and Nick. They don't come now, but they would come for the funeral and hug her, and the girls would cry and even some of the boys. They don't come now, because he's already dead, as good as.

She turned the corner onto Airline Drive and the roar of the nearby freeway rose to greet her. Airline was lined with Houston's produce suppliers. Avocados and onions and bananas and pecans. The sidewalk was littered with peels and the golden tissue of onion skin floating like shed skin cells. This superfluity of a wealthy, vulgar, living, striving city that could give you life or give you death, and it was all yours, you choose—this road or that one?

Or maybe God chose. Maybe the city chose.

Probably it wasn't that simple.

Oh, here's something she loved: Before it got this bad, every Friday she would take off early and treat her boy to lunch at Liberty Kitchen. He would start with a dozen raw oysters. Gulf oysters, big as a baby's fist. She taught him to pick up the shell and drink the sweet, salty brine. It was something she'd read about. She couldn't eat raw oysters. She'd sit across from him and watch him eat, fill himself, anything he wanted. That was just . . . good.

After, they'd go to Mam's House of Snowballs and he'd get two or three flavors of syrup with a ball of vanilla ice cream under the ice.

That was good.

Off Airline, the freeway was a roar of blare and flare and it bothered her not at all. She was part of this night. She belonged, and she belonged here.

The appointment was behind the Airline Service Station and Grocery. Where she'd stopped for gas that time they'd been propositioned. Tonight, *she* had a proposition.

It was late. Grizzled and gaunt, a man slept open-mouthed as a baby on the sidewalk in front of the store, bathed in the light of a *Texas Lottery* sign promising that you, too, could be a winner. His life was nested in shopping bags around and under him, spilling out. He stank.

She took a last draw on the cigarette and crushed it with the toe of her shoe. She didn't pick it up.

Behind the station was the man who was killing her son.

No point in being mad at him. You don't get mad at tornadoes or cancer or lightning strikes. It's not personal—it's business.

She closed her eyes for a moment, pulled up her chin, balancing the sea in her eyes. This was good. And this was right. She stepped into the dark.

Her heeled pumps with their black glove leather were no protection on the closely mown stubble and concrete rubble and shed condoms and Pepsi bottles and dog shit and fire ants. But she didn't turn back. She made her way to Jamie's appointment under the watery light of the twenty-foot neon sign.

The man had his back to her. He was small and his head moved rhythmically.

She said, "Hey."

The man spun around, popping black earbuds out of his ears.

He was a boy. Black-haired, black-eyed in the dark. Not fifteen. Maybe fifteen, but not older.

He said, "Fuck." He looked past her like he was expecting someone else.

His cheeks were smooth. That boy's mother put her hand against that cheek when he was sick. If he had a mother. Probably he didn't, if he was out here so late.

This wasn't the man who was killing Jamie. This was a boy, and he looked hungry. He needed someone to sit across from him and put good food in front of him. Cold milk. Good bread with soft butter. Some soup.

She smiled at the boy like he was a shy woodland creature and she wanted to show him he didn't need to be afraid. She reached into her purse for some money to give him for food and milk. She dropped her purse and fives and tens and twenties spilled out. Her gun spilled out. It was a mean thing, small and threatening. She looked up to reassure the boy.

He wasn't looking for reassurance. Fear bloomed in his face.

His arm, loose and jointless, swung to the back of his oversized jeans. It snapped back, now rigid and straight, with a black-and-silver gun that was bigger than her own.

The air went dead—there wasn't enough to breathe. She couldn't hear the traffic. Couldn't hear her own voice. She held up her hand, unfolded her fingers to say stop. Wait. I won't hurt you. I was going to, but that was when I thought you were someone else. When I thought I was someone else. Before I knew you.

He didn't hear any of those things her raised hand was trying to tell him. He did what his big brother taught him to do in such situations. He aimed at her chest and shot her.

He'd never shot anyone before. It was dark and he was scared, so the shot was low. His arm circled back and tucked the gun into the waistband of his jeans. He pivoted like a dancer and ran.

The blow knocked her against the back wall of the service station convenience store. She stepped back and out of one fine leather high heel, her foot landing on the gravel and the loam of garbage. She clasped her belly as the fiery pain and the warm rush spilled down her legs. The pain and the blood a surprise all over again. She sank down to the damp weeds and plastic bags and pooling blood, back against the brick wall, knees splayed.

I won't bury Jamie, she thought. *I won't bury Jamie*.

She cried this time too. This was so good. She was so grateful.

Thank you, she thought. To God, probably.

ABOUT THE CONTRIBUTORS

Canterbury Photography

TOM ABRAHAMS is an award-winning television journalist and a member of the International Thriller Writers. He is a hybrid author (traditionally and self-published) who writes postapocalyptic thrillers, action adventure, and political conspiracies. Abrahams lives in the Houston suburbs with his wife Courtney and their two children. Read more about his work and join his Preferred Readers Club at tomabrahamsbooks.com.

Dana Kroos

ROBERT BOSWELL has published seven novels, three story collections, and two books of nonfiction. His play *The Long Shrift* was produced off-Broadway. He has earned NEA fellowships, a Guggenheim Fellowship, the PEN West Award, and the John Gassner Memorial Playwriting Award. His stories have appeared in the *New Yorker, Harpers,* the *Atlantic,* and *Best American Short Stories.* He holds the Cullen Endowed Chair in Creative Writing at the University of Houston.

Phillippe Diederich

SARAH CORTEZ, councillor of the Texas Institute of Letters, has had poems, essays, book reviews, and short stories anthologized and published in *Texas Monthly*, *Rattle*, the *Sun*, *Texas Review*, *Louisiana Literature*, *Arcadia*, *Midwest Quarterly*, and *Southwestern American Literature*. She has won the PEN Texas Literary Award and the Southwest Book Award. Her most recent book is *Vanishing Points: Poems and Photographs of Texas Roadside Memorials.*

Nina Subin

ANTON DISCLAFANI is the *New York Times* best-selling author of two novels, *The Yonahlossee Riding Camp for Girls* and *The After Party*. Both were Amazon Books of the Month and Indie Next picks; her work is being translated into thirteen languages. She lives in Alabama with her husband and son and teaches creative writing at Auburn University.

STEPHANIE JAYE EVANS is a fifth-generation Texan. Her first book, *Faithful Unto Death,* was a *Library Journal* Debut of the Month, and a *Houston Chronicle* Ultimate Summer Book List pick. *Kirkus Reviews* writes of *Safe from Harm,* second in the series, "As charming and wry as Evans's bright debut, filled with reasons to own dogs, love your children and your wife, and have faith." She is currently working on a Southern gothic set in the Houston Heights.

DEBORAH D.E.E.P. MOUTON is an internationally renowned performance poet, a three-time Slam Champ formerly ranked the #2 Best Female Poet in the World. She was named Houston's poet laureate in 2017. Her work has been compiled on two albums and has been featured on BBC, NPR, Upworthy, Blavity.com, in *Black Girl Magic*, and was featured in the opening video of the Houston Rockets 2017 season. For more information visit LiveLifeDeep.com.

Sami Sallinen

WANJIKŨ WA NGŨGĨ is the author of *The Fall of Saints* and former director of the Helsinki African Film Festival. She has been a columnist for the Finnish development magazine *Maailman Kuvalehti*, and her essays and short stories have appeared in *St. Petersburg Review*, *Wasafiri Magazine*, *Auburn Avenue*, the *Daily Nation*, *Pambazuka News*, and *Chimurenga*, among others.

Britt Thomas

ADRIENNE PERRY grew up in Wyoming. She earned her MFA from Warren Wilson in 2013 and her PhD from the University of Houston in 2018. From 2014 to 2016, she served as the editor of *Gulf Coast*. She is a Hedgebrook alumna, a Kimbilio Fellow, and a member of the Rabble Collective. Perry's work has appeared in *Copper Nickel*, *Black Warrior Review*, and elsewhere. She is at work on a novel and an essay collection.

Diego Brown

PIA PICO resides in Houston, Texas, where she teaches high school. Born and raised in Los Angeles, she spent the nineties touring the Australian outback and east coast with her punk band Killy. She earned her MFA in creative writing from New York University, and her writing was included in the anthology *Gynomite: Fearless Feminist Porn*.

REYES RAMIREZ is a Houstonian. In addition to earning an MFA in fiction, he won the 2017 *Blue Mesa Review* Nonfiction Contest and the 2014 riverSedge Poetry Prize, and has poems, stories, essays, and reviews in or forthcoming in: *Southwestern American Literature*, *Gulf Coast Journal*, *Glass Poetry Press*, *Origins Journal*, *the Acentos Review*, *Cimarron Review*, the anthology *pariahs: writing from outside the margins*, and elsewhere. You can read more of his work at reyesvramirez.com.

RJ Eldridge

ICESS FERNANDEZ ROJAS is an educator, writer, and former journalist who lives in Houston and is a longtime North Shore resident. Her work has been published in *Rabble Lit*, *Minerva Rising Literary Journal*, and the Feminine Collective's anthology *Notes from Humanity*. Her nonfiction has appeared in *Dear Hope*, NBCNews.com, the *Huffington Post*, and the *Guardian*. She is a recipient of the Owl of Minerva Award and is a Voices of Our Nation Arts Foundation alum.

Paul Hester

SEHBA SARWAR'S essays and poems have appeared in the *New York Times Sunday Magazine*, *Callaloo*, *South Asian Review*, and elsewhere, while her short stories have appeared in anthologies published by Feminist Press and HarperCollins India. Her novel *Black Wings* was published by Alhamra Press in Pakistan. Born and raised in Karachi, Pakistan, Sarwar lived in Houston for several decades and is currently based in Southern California.

The Shelby Studio

LESLIE CONTRERAS SCHWARTZ is a fourth-generation Houstonian of Mexican heritage. Her essays and poetry have recently appeared in *Catapult*, the *Collagist*, *Tinderbox*, and *Luna Luna Magazine*. Her book *Fuego* was published by Saint Julian Press and her second book of poems, *Nightbloom & Cenote*, was published by the same press in 2018.

LARRY WATTS has published six novels and a book of short stories during his twenty-one-year career in law enforcement. His latest book, *Dishonored and Forgotten,* written with his wife Carolyn, is a historical novel about Houston's first police narcotics scandal.

Dat V. Lam

GWENDOLYN ZEPEDA has published three novels, one short story collection, two poetry collections, and five children's books. She served as Houston's first poet laureate from 2013 to 2015.